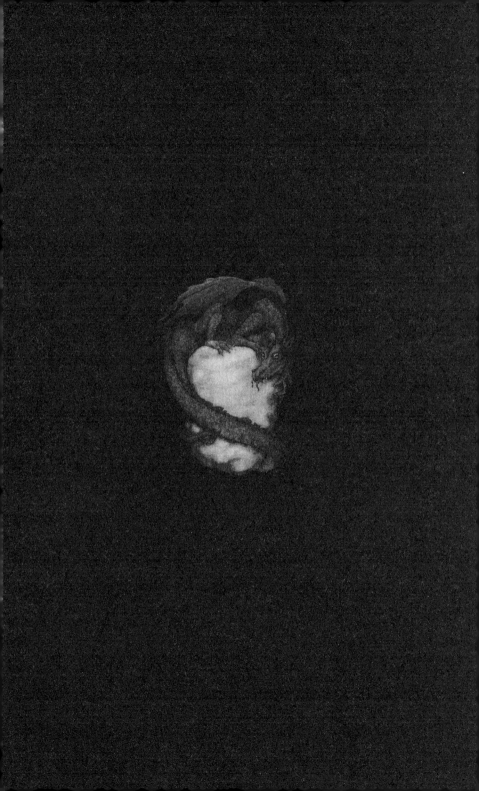

AMULET BOOKS
NEW YORK

THE DRAGON OF CRIPPLE CREEK

A NOVEL BY
TROY HOWELL

Library of Congress Cataloging-in-Publication Data

Howell, Troy.
The dragon of Cripple Creek / by Troy Howell.
p. cm.
Summary: When Kat, her father, and brother visit an old gold mine that has been turned into an amusement park, she falls down a shaft where she meets an ancient dragon, the last of his kind, and inadvertently triggers a twenty-first century gold rush.
ISBN 978-0-8109-9713-4 (alk. paper)
[1. Dragons—Fiction. 2. Gold—Fiction. 3. Greed—Fiction. 4. Colorado—Fiction.] I. Title.
PZ7.H83844Dr 2011
[Fic]—dc22
2010034362

The text in this book is set in 12-point Horley Old Style. The display typefaces are Halcyon, Rough Riders, and Roulette Caps. The ornaments are from the Adobe Woodtype family.

Printed and bound in U.S.A.
10 9 8 7 6 5 4 3 2 1

Amulet Books are available at special discounts when purchased in quantity for premiums and promotions as well as fundraising or educational use. Special editions can also be created to specification. For details, contact specialmarkets@abramsbooks.com or the address below.

ABRAMS
THE ART OF BOOKS SINCE 1949

115 West 18th Street
New York, NY 10011
www.abramsbooks.com

To my angel mom, in memory of Dad
And to the girl with the pearl

CONTENTS

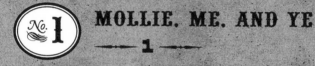
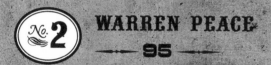
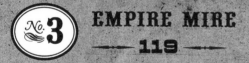
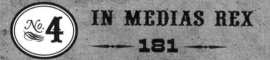

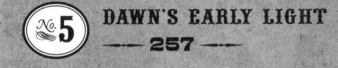

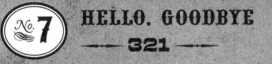

I dreamed about Ye last night.

The dream was light-filled, as if the sun trickled down from 1000 ft of earth to bathe the gold that lay heaped on his cavern floor. With shimmering scales & autumn-moon eyes he chatted with me in his calm smoky voice. He said all he wanted was to smoke & reminisce. We talked awhile about nothing in particular & I saw in his eye my reflection. My face was clean, my hair was combed, my gold-capped tooth was now white. I was happy at last he saw me this way, not the eyesore I had been.

The dream was good—until his eyes closed.

The moment they did, I was wandering in the dark, calling out his name. Wandering in the place he called home. Right here in "God Bless America," land of the free. Underground, where he'd always been safe. Out of trouble, out of sight.

Until I showed up.

CALL ME CALAMITY CAT.

That's what the news media called me. My name's actually spelled with a K, and Kat is for Katlin.

Calamity is for calamity. *An event causing great damage or distress.* If you look it up in the dictionary, which is something I often do—look up words—you'll notice it's a noun.

I've made it a verb.

Kat's *calamiting* again.

I suppose I was calamitous before I ever showed up in a little sky-high town in the Colorado Rockies—but that's when my calamiting reached world status.

• • •

Friday night in Cripple Creek is a two-step back in time, with honky-tonk and colored lights and mobscenities— as my brother, Dillon, puts it—spilling into the streets. It's the Wild West all lit up.

That's when we checked in. The Empire Hotel had vacancies, though you wouldn't know it by the human logjam in the lobby. We'd been on the road since glory knows what inglorious hour, after slouching in the car (as opposed to sleeping) at a restless stop (as opposed to rest), right in the middle of truckers' night out.

While Dillon and Dad were waiting in line, I was crouched behind a couch in the lounge, shaking a pair of dice. They were my own dice and came in handy at times like these.

Handy, as in small cash gain.

"C'mon, c'mon, c'mon!" I said. I said it seriously enough for it to sound real, as if the roll would be strictly chance. "Seven! Seven . . . c'mon . . ." I tossed the dice across the red-and-gold carpet . . . they hit the base trim of the wall . . .

One was a six. I expected that. The other—

Yes! A one.

I grinned at the kid next to me, who was down on his knees by my side. And down on his luck. So far, I'd collected three dollars from him—two ones, two quarters, four dimes, and six pennies—OK, he was four cents short, but I had let it slide.

I stuck out my hand, palm up.

"I only have a five," he said. "I'm not giving you that."

"You will."

It was his turn to roll. But first, he popped up to peer over the couch he'd been sitting on, moments before, fidgety and bored. Not one to miss an opportunity, I had approached him and grinned, flashing my gold-capped tooth. "Got any money?"

"What's it to you?" he'd said, his eyes round as nickels.

I showed him my dice and explained the rules. "I call and roll—if I call it right, you pay me a dollar. You call and roll—if you call it wrong, you pay me a dollar."

"So, whatever it is," he said, protruding his lower lip, "I pay you a dollar."

"Let me finish. If I call it wrong, you keep your dollar. If you call it right—"

"You give me a dollar!"

I shrugged. "Fair enough."

The game was going well.

"All clear," he said, dropping back behind the couch. He cupped the dice. "C'mon! Twelve . . . twelve . . ." He rolled . . . there was the six—

There was another six.

"Twelve!" he said

Was he catching on? I reluctantly pulled out the coins he'd given me and let them fall through my fingers.

"Hey," he whined, scrambling to pick them up.

"This is what you gave me for a dollar," I said. "Ninety-six cents."

He blinked at me.

"I'm being generous," I went on. "You still owe me a dollar. A *whole* dollar."

He surrendered with a grunt.

My turn. So far, it was working better than I'd thought. I could always, or nearly always, count on one die coming up six. All I had to do was guess on the other one. More often than not, I got it right. How long it took my opponent to suspect was the only risk involved.

That and Dad catching me.

"Nine," I said, and rolled.

Eight. A six and a two.

"Ha!" said the kid, and stuck out his hand.

"Nope. You keep your dollar, remember?"

He frowned, tilting his head.

"Hurry," I said. "We don't have all night."

He snatched up the dice, pretended to spit on them, and said, "Four!"

I smiled to myself: So he wasn't catching on after all.

He rolled. Four it was: two twos. Leaning over, I adjusted my glasses and inspected the dice.

"It was a four!" he challenged. "Like I said!"

"I know." I spun one die around—the black spot was still intact. I fingered the other one . . .

"Hand it over," he said, his nostrils flaring.

"Now we're even," I explained. "You owed me one."

His frown returned. Doubt was ticking away in his head. Maybe I'd underestimated him. Maybe it was time to quit. I picked up the dice and plunged them into my pocket. I felt the money there. I'd never make godzillions at this game, but two dollars were better than nothing.

And I knew what nothing was.

The kid finally said, "*How* do the rules go?"

As luck would have it, Dad called out my name.

"Katlin!"

I jumped up. He and Dillon were standing beyond a spittoon and some potted ferns. Dad hadn't seen me yet, but Dillon, good brother, had. He doesn't miss a thing.

"Kat," he said. "Let's go."

The kid said to me, "Wait!"

"Here, Dad!" I said, crawling over the couch.

"Wait! It's not fair!" The kid started pulling my shoe, the one with the floppy sole.

Dad looked in our direction. Hotel guests looked in our direction. A walrus of a woman draped in fur and holding a little dog looked in our direction.

"Lucas!" she bellowed.

Lucas—no wonder he hadn't told me his name—let go

of my shoe. I tumbled off the couch, got to my feet, and, with Lucas trotting behind, went to Dillon and Dad.

Lucas went to the woman, who apparently was his mom, and said, "I gave her some money to fix her old shoe."

"What!" I blurted.

The woman patted his head. "Good boy!" To us she said proudly, "He'll make a great philanthropist."

"He'll make a great liar," I muttered, tugging Dad's arm for us to go.

The woman blinked at me from behind her tortoiseshell glasses, while her silky little dog, who wore a gold-and-jeweled collar that read duchess, yip-yipped.

"Katlin," said Dad, as he headed us toward the stairs, "what were you doing behind that couch?"

"I know what she was doing," said Dillon.

I glared arrows and other projectiles at him.

"Did he give you money?" asked Dad.

"Um . . . not exactly."

"Kat, we're not beggars. We're not subject to charity—"

"*Somebody's* got to make money in this family, haven't they?" I said it loud enough to put Dad on the spot, which wasn't difficult, considering he'd been developing this guilt fret for a long time, and considering several ears were aimed our direction.

"Hush!" he said.

Up the stairs we went.

—◦)|(◦—

I'M REALLY NOT THAT KIND OF PERSON, TO embarrass my dad in public. But I didn't want to give the money back, or part with my dice, and I could see it was coming to that.

We hadn't always been poor.

We used to have two cars that were nice and new.

We used to live in a nice big house. I called it my castle.

I used to go to a private school, where I had the best teachers, best books, computers, programs, even the best schoolmates. Anyway, they acted as if they were the best.

I used to have a horse. He wasn't a purebred, but that didn't matter to me, as long as he had a pure heart. He did, and I named him Angel. All my friends liked to ride him.

I used to have friends.

I used to invite one along when we went on vacations.

Now it was Dillon and Dad and me. But this wasn't a vacation—I was just trying to make it one.

We were outside Colorado Springs when Dillon fanned his fingers in front of my face, saying, "Don't look, Kat."

But I'd already seen the sign.

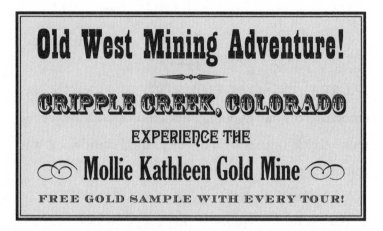

Old West Mining Adventure!
————◆————
CRIPPLE CREEK, COLORADO
EXPERIENCE THE
∞ Mollie Kathleen Gold Mine ∞
FREE GOLD SAMPLE WITH EVERY TOUR!

No apologies, I had this craze for gold.

As a kid, once I figured that gold wasn't just the color of my hair, I wanted everything gold. Gold bed, gold walls, gold shoes. Gold-rimmed glasses, gold jewelry. I got a golden-haired pony on my golden birthday—I had turned four on the fourth of April—and named her Goldie.

In the fifth grade, I saw the Tutankhamen exhibit, and it sent me soaring. All that molten wealth, formed into bugs and beasts and figures and faces. While we studied economics, I tracked the price of gold, and if you don't think reading tiny numbers is exciting to a twelve-year-old, you haven't done it yourself. When those numbers inch up, inch up, almost double, then sink like a stone, it does something to your pulse.

There was only one exception to my total gold thing: Mom's pearl ring. I'd worn it night and day from the moment she pressed it into my hands. Some things mean the world to you, no matter what.

· · ·

So there we were rolling west—south actually, because Dad had got sleepy and taken the wrong interstate—and here was a real gold mine. I wouldn't miss it for a year's worth of fine-free weeks at the library.

I begged Dad to go.

He said his new employer wouldn't pay for frivolities. That had become a pet word with him, "frivolities," ever since we'd turned poor. It kept us from asking for too much.

"I'll pay with my lawn-mowing cash," I said. The very last of my savings, but—

"We don't have the time," he said. "We just lost half an hour."

"Don't we have one extra day?" I said. We had to be in San Francisco by Wednesday, but—

"That's pushing it," he said.

"Can't we do one fun thing?"

"No!"

Dillon groaned. He knew as well as I that when Dad

yelled "No," "Yes" soon followed. That was a habit of his, which had only got worse after Mom's accident. He'd become uncertain of everything, and guilty as a thief he didn't do more for us.

Slumping in the front seat, Dillon said, "One fun thing. *Cripple* says it all."

"*Gold* says it all," I declared.

"The tour will be a detour," squawked Dad, and he took the next exit.

—➤ ⦅—

THE EMPIRE HOTEL WAS BUILT AROUND THE time of the *first* gold rush, and whoever owned it now was doing a good job keeping it shiny and warm, like gold itself. As we scurried up the stairs, I looked back down at Lucas, who was looking back up at me, tongue fully extended.

When we came to our rooms—mine at the dead end of a hall, Dillon and Dad's to the right—Dad said, "Trade." He held up my room key. It wasn't a plastic card you slide into a slot, but an honest-to-badness brass one that went into a keyhole, a keyhole you can peek through.

"For what?" I said. "The kid's money?"

"The dice. You were throwing your dice, weren't you?"

"Dad—"

"Gambling." He said it as if I had robbed a bank.

"But it's legal in Colorado."

"Legal isn't always ethical, Kat, or moral."

"Dad, we're straight down-the-hole broke."

He looked at me wearily. "Let me deal with that."

"I have to deal with it, too."

He looked at the carpet.

It was too true. The calamities that had fallen on us, one after another like dominoes—boulders, rather—troubled us all. But it's also true that after you've shuffled around for a time in your dire straits, as you do in an old pair of shoes, you almost get used to it.

The cracks don't pinch until you try to run.

"I can have a little fun," I reasoned, "*and* make a little money."

He was looking at me again. "We didn't come here to gamble."

"*You* ought to try it. You might get us out of the hole." Playing on his guilt—I was doing it again. "Since *I'll* be the one paying for the gold mine tour—"

"Gambling's illegal for children, Katlin, even in Colorado."

He had me there.

He was still holding up the key.

I was tired. We all were. The night before the rest stop, we'd parked along the road. The night before that, it was a Mega Mart lot. This was the first time we'd got a hotel, the first night we'd get to have beds. Dad figured his new boss wouldn't mind if *one* hotel charge showed up on the bill. I was ready to cozy between covers and jot in my journal and get more than a few winks' sleep, and be fresh for the tour tomorrow.

Reluctantly, I pulled out the dice. I tossed them back and forth in my palms. One came up a six. That was the trick die, the one I had drilled a hole into, in the single black dot, and filled with one of Dillon's small fishing leads, and plugged with putty and painted black again.

I gave him the normal one.

"Both," he said.

I stared innocently at him, while he stared knowingly back. I shrugged, and handed it over. What good was the trick die all by itself?

—⟩ ⟨—

IN THE CARE HOME WHERE MOM LIES IS AN elevator the size of a small closet. Really small, as in five feet by five. Make that a cage and you have the flimsy contraption they use in the Mollie Kathleen. It's called a skip. Add nine passengers, one of whom is the guide, and you have instant phobia, if not hysteria.

For me, anyway.

Above ground, the cage dangles in kind of an oil rig structure—the hoist house. You stand in line and wait your turn; they pack you in and down you go—*clink, rattle, whoosh!*—like that.

There we were, Saturday morning, right where I'd begged for us to be, waiting to take the plunge. I fingered the dice in my pocket, which I'd talked Dad into returning with a promise to keep strictly as lucky charms.

I was tempted to turn my mom's ring, a habit of mine when I'm in deep thought.

Watching group after group squeeze into that cage—innocent, trusting humans, grandmothers, even—I was having my doubts. Why was it called a skip? Was that a subtle hint? Did smart people skip the whole thing, stay in the sunshine, breathe the sweet mountain air, keep their feet on solid ground? Maybe Dillon was right: There'd be nothing fun about this. I could let him and Dad tell me about it later. . . .

If they made it back up alive.

Then it was our turn.

. . .

"I feel like we're in a shark basket they let down in the deep," I told Dillon, who stood with his back against me. "You stick out your arm and you lose it."

"I wouldn't stick out a finger," said the man to my left—*on* my left, literally, his bulk boring into me like a bull against a post.

I didn't look at him; you don't look at strangers who are so close you can inhale their exhale. On my right, the metal mesh pressed into my side, and beyond that . . .

I couldn't stick out my arm—the mesh prevented that—so I poked out a finger. I pulled it back sharp, my fingertip tingling from the force in the shaft we dropped through.

Five hundred feet. Straight down.

"It's insane," I whispered.

"Kat?"

I gripped Dillon's waist.

"You OK?" He actually didn't say, You asked for this, you got it. He must have been getting interested.

"I'm OK," I said.

The skip slowed, rattled through turbulence, and I breathed the gust into my lungs.

"The first level," announced the guide.

We plunged again, another five hundred.

I hiccupped. It *was* insane. How many people get to plummet a thousand feet inside a cage crammed with strangers? The guy on my left could be some serial psycho who was sweating from the possibilities. The woman behind me, huffing down my neck whenever the skip shuddered, could be claustrophobic and break out in wild panic, screaming and clawing us to shreds. Or some mechanism could go wrong, and we'd hang like a spider in limbo.

The gold sample had better be good.

At last we slowed. Here was the lower level, and here came another gust—cold, damp, archaeological.

"Watch your step," said the guide. "No hurry. Wait your turn getting out." He had a bushy mustache, the type you'd expect in a place called Cripple Creek, and his eyes were clear as diamonds, shining beneath his hard hat. We all wore hard hats—plus jackets for those who wanted them—given to us at ground entrance. My hat was at least a size too big, and I had to look down my nose to see anything above sea level.

"Stay together," the guide cautioned. "Stay on the path. The ropes are for your safety. Do not wander off."

Good advice—do not wander off.

—◦}{◦—

I LIKE TO GET TO THE (PUN ALERT) BOTTOM of things. The truth of a matter, or of a place. Things that people think but don't ever say. Things that lie buried.

It's not always easy. You have to watch. You have to ask questions. Sometimes you get answers, sometimes you don't.

The important thing is that you get it right. It helps to jot it down, to put it in black and white. Things that you see and hear, besides what you feel and thoughts you have. That's why I keep journals.

Do journalists keep journals? Do they really check things out, or just dip their pens into some muddy rumor pool? I'd really like to know. Because most of the reports on this thing have been far from the truth.

deliriums of disoriented girl
girl's desperate dad breaks into mine
children scheme to claim ownership of gold
dragon, a chinese kite
dragon, a stuffed galÁpagos iguana

Then there's the fanciful approach. Like *US Online* calling it a New American Tall Tale. It is not a tall tale, such as Pecos Bill or Paul Bunyan. They grew out of yarn spinning that passed from jaw to jaw in barrooms or around campfires.

My story's all true—I swear it on Ye's golden snout.

The BBC News dubbed it a Western Fairy Tale. Western it is, but it's part Eastern, too, and has no fairies. There's no happily ever after.

Only a few reports have come close.

bizarre falsehood rocks wall street

What happened wasn't a "falsehood," but Wall Street did go haywire.

One headline got it right.

calamity cat meets reluctant dragon

But I'm galloping ahead of myself.

• • •

We filed into a murky cavern that glistened under strings of lights. Rough-sawn timbers supported the ceiling and, along the floor, iron rails ran from a dump cart and disappeared down a dark, descending tunnel.

"The Mollie Kathleen was one of the world's greatest

gold-producing mines in the eighteen nineties," began our guide, and I wiped an unexpected yawn from my mouth.

The thing about tour guides—you have to prod them a little. I think they know more than the parts they tell, the parts that are hits with the crowds. So between tour stops, as we walked farther in, I pelted him with questions. He paid me no mind. I kept it up until he acknowledged this babbling girl tagalong.

I learned a few things about Mollie Kathleen, how she'd loaded the family wagon to visit Cripple Creek, and how she discovered gold where men had been searching for years. In fact, they had named it Poverty Gulch because no gold had ever turned up.

So this was *her* mine, not just a mine named after her.

I think the guide thought his answers would hush me, but they only spurred more questions.

"How deep is the mine?"

"How many tunnels?"

"Have they all been explored?"

It was probably more prodding than he cared to hear.

"Where does this one go?" I asked, before he gave me the slip. I had stopped to peer into a closed-off place, lit by one dim bulb.

From the side of his mustache he said, "There are

several closed chutes on this level. They're closed off for a reason. This way!" It's what Dillon calls a nonswer—an answer that tells you nothing.

It was the last one he would give me.

"Why'd they close it off? What could be the reason? Do you mean a single reason for all of them, or does each one have its own reason?"

"Are they dangerous?"

"Are they dead ends?"

"Are they drop-offs?"

Then I mumbled to emptiness—for the guide was gone and so was the group—"Do they have more gold?"

—⟩⟨—

GOLD IS MONEY.

After Mom's accident, we kept hoping she'd recover. We visited her every day. We took turns. Dad rambled to her about the past, the present, and their future together. I read to her and sang sometimes. I read *Alice's Adventures in Wonderland*, one of her childhood favorites. When I read to her, I pictured her in her very own Wonderland, wondering and dreaming. I refused to picture her in some kind of hell.

Hours turned to days, days to weeks, weeks to months.

Our hopes fell. She was diagnosed with PVS—persistent vegetative state. She stared and stared, but those glossy eyes were not my mom's; they were some strange dreamer's.

When the insurance company rejected the case, things went from terrible to unbearable. We were sued. So on top of medical costs, there were attorney fees. They cashed out our savings. Dad took a second mortgage. He took a loan. Several loans. He accepted personal loans from the few friends we had left. He cleaned the retirement funds, completely. We had nothing left but hope, and not much of that.

Dad wouldn't talk about it, but I figured he functioned at work as he had at home, which was more sleepwalking than living, and they dropped him.

When he lost his job, we lost all hope.

Money was everything.

I'd never thought like that before, but there it was, under the surface, running like a crosscut tunnel to what I believed. What I believed came mostly from Mom.

"The things that really count in life, Kat," she'd say, her arms open wide for a hug, "are the things that can't be counted. They have so much value no one can afford them—so they're free."

I still believe those things.

But your head gets bent when you eat Ramen noodles all week. You shop with your friends and say, "No thanks, not hungry," while they gobble up frozen yogurt. You say, "What's wrong with these shoes I'm wearing?" and one of the heels pops off.

The grass is high and the mower won't start. You need a decent pair of glasses and develop a silly squint. The goodbye gift you give your best teacher is a book from off your shelf. You're pulled from private school and put into public, where you hardly know up from down.

Your beautiful horse is sold.

Your beautiful house is sold. To people who don't know its secrets, its good times and its bad, who don't love it like you do. Like the place on the stairs that always felt warm, or the hoofprint Angel put on the porch.

Or the smell of Mom's soap in the bath.

Now she lies unconscious, needing better care, in a place that is hardly equipped. And hardly affordable.

And I'd just spent the last of my savings.

—⊰ ⊱—

A FLIRTY WINK—THAT'S ALL IT TOOK. A sparkle in the gloom. Was that *gold*, just a pebble's toss away? *Real gold?*

You could duck right through the barrier. Or squeeze, anyway.

Which is what I did.

In the Luray Caverns in Virginia, they turn out the lights to show you how dark is the dark. "Put your hand in front of your face," they say. "Watch—"

The lights go out.

You can feel the dark and taste the dark and hear the dark. And I'll tell you, it feels thick, tastes oily, and sounds like a morgue. Not that I've ever been in one.

Then the lights come on and everything's cool.

I figured that's what happened. The tour group had gathered in the next cramped space, the guide probably said to put their hands in front of their faces, and . . .

The moment I stepped beyond the barrier, two things went wrong:

I saw too late the planks beneath my feet.

The lights went out.

My foot broke through the planks, then my leg, then all of me. Fortunately, the chute was not straight down like the elevator shaft, but it sloped enough that I tumbled without stopping.

Rocks, gravel, debris, and me.

Rolling, sliding, clutching, flailing in the dark.

Down, down, down.

Like Alice.

"Umph!"

Only there were no marmalade jars, bookshelves, or maps.

"Umph!"

There was no light.

"Umph!"

Were there bats?

Do bats eat Kats?

Thump! The fall was over.

At least for now.

—⇥⇤—

DILLON SAYS, "CURIOSITY KILLED THE CAT." I should have known that someday curiosity would kill me, or make an attempt on my life.

"Well, Katlin Graham," I said out loud. "You can forget your free gold sample."

I said it to be sure I could speak and hear and know I was alive. My eyes were wide open, trying to stare a hole in the dark. A dark that beat on my eardrums.

Or was that my heart?

I thought of the dawn, clear and clean, that I had woke

to a few hours before. I'd raised the tall window in my room at the Empire Hotel to breathe in the day, and the mountains had lit up like gems as morning washed over the town.

If I had just a sliver of that light! I'd see how banged up I was, and if I could return the way I'd come, or how deep was the drop. I'd see the seriousness of this nightmare, how *mis* this adventure would be.

I dared not move. When I moved—

More rocks tumbled into the blackness below.

So much for my lucky-charm dice.

I turned Mom's ring, realizing my luck not to have lost it. *Mom*, I said, *here I am, precariously perched between the roots of the Rockies and the Great Wall of China. What should I do?*

My glasses were gone, but they'd be no use now. Something poked my right knee, which I reached out to touch. Rough-hewn timber: a brace, most likely. That's what had halted my hair-raising, tumbleweed roll. My left knee was torn and bleeding; I pulled the denim back where it stuck to the blood. My right arm from shoulder to elbow was buzzing with pain. I found two lumps on my head—one above my right ear, the other on my left cheekbone—and a dozen squishy spots up and down my limbs. Gravel was embedded in my palms.

Fortunately, no broken bones. At least I didn't feel any.

Well, Kat, it could have been worse. Much worse. You could have—

———✦———

MY MOTHER HAD FALLEN.

Only it wasn't from curiosity, and it didn't happen in the dark. It happened in broad daylight on an autumn afternoon.

When everything was normal. *Uncalamitous.*

Dad had got a promotion, a raise, a big bonus; we were moving up in the world. I think it went straight to our heads. Except Mom's. While we each wanted things extravagant, Mom remained her simple self. She hung wind chimes along the front porch, put lattice between the windows to grow her roses on, bought birdhouses.

I wanted to upgrade the stable, add heat and AC, put paving stones down.

That's why it happened.

It happened five miles from home, at a rock quarry that had gone out of business. Mom said, "Why get what they have at Whole House when we can get *real* paving stones there?" She just drove around the barrier. It took three trips using our Volvo station wagon, which Dillon calls the workhorse—we'd used it for everything from hauling straw bales to storing books while we painted the living room.

We never completed the paving stone project.

While Mom was lifting the heaviest one of all, which was big as a gravestone, I ran to give her a hand. My foot caught on a half-buried pry bar, and I stumbled against her. She pulled back to keep the rock from crushing me, fell sideways, and rammed her head hard into a jutting boulder.

I'll never forget that sight. How I wish I could just hit delete.

While we waited for the ambulance—Dillon had dialed 911—I sang to her. I sat in the dirt with her head in my lap and sang "You Are My Sunshine." It was the song she sang to me every night when I was little. I sat real still and sang it over and over.

You are my sunshine, my only sunshine.
You make me happy, when skies are gray.
You'll never know, dear, how much I love you.
Please don't take my sunshine away.

It was silly, I guess, but I thought it might wake her up.

It did. Her eyelids fluttered, opened, and that's when she gave me her ring. Her hands had been fumbling with it, and I didn't realize what she'd done until I felt it in my palm. During that brief window of consciousness, she must have sensed her trouble. She tried to speak—her lips trembled—but she said nothing.

Her eyes said everything. *To remember me by. I'm going.*

Gripping the ring in one hand and stroking her hair with the other, I nodded, blinking in total shock. Then she spoke the ghost of a word, and I leaned in close.

"*Promise*—"

"Promise what, Mom? Don't go! Promise what?"

She was gone again, cocoonlike with invisible wraps, before the ambulance came.

⟐

"MOVE," I SAID. "I'VE GOT TO MOVE. I CAN'T stay here forever."

Well, I *could*, but I'd rot.

Facing the slope, with my feet on the brace that had stopped me, I slowly stood. I reached up high, stretched to the limit, and put my hand on a ledgelike rock. I tested it, tugged it.

It broke off and went flying past my face. It struck the tunnel walls—*wham, bang,* farther, fainter . . .

Silence.

I shivered. Had it fallen down a wider, deeper hole? A bottomless pit?

I tried again, feeling for a handhold, something solid, stable, or a crack to wedge my fingers into. The layers were loose, their surfaces pitched downward. More rocks rolled past, adding another lump to my head and a greater sense of doom.

I tried again and again, reaching this way and that, high into the blackness, and found nothing to depend on.

So. Returning the way I had come was out of the question. Even if I did make progress, one wrong move, one loose stone, and the outcome could be worse, far worse.

Deadly.

My fingers went back to Mom's ring. I turned it around.

Her ring is like a portrait—a double portrait, even triple. The design is simple: a silver band with a mounted pearl. The pearl is big, bigger than most pearls I've seen. Sometimes when the child inside me has wanted to curl in Mom's lap, I've gazed into the pearl and seen the smallness of myself, outlined in the haze. When I've gazed long enough, sometimes I've seen Mom's face, gazing back, saying, *I love you, Kat. Be still.*

Sometimes, after staring myself into a mist, I've seen Grandma Chance, Mom's mom, staring back at me through layers of years.

Grandma Chance traded a mule for the pearl when she was a teen, and though the deal was not in her favor—since the mule was useful and the pearl was not—she had no regrets. She kept the pearl as a prized possession, a seal of her independence, her take on life. She kept it through courtship and marriage, three miscarriages and a multitude of trials, including a fire, a flood, and a chain of complications resulting from a copperhead bite.

Then when Mom was born right out of the blue, Grandpa Chance had the pearl set in silver, put the ring on Grandma's hand, and said, "There she is. The pearl we've been waiting for."

That's how Mom got her name.

When Grandma Chance died, Mom inherited the ring.

Now it's mine.

Promise.

Ever since that dreadful day, I've asked myself, *Promise what?*

Whatever the answer, the ring connects me to Mom. I wear it with a hope that someday I'll put it back on her hand, look into her eyes, and know she really sees me, with no darkness in between.

. . .

I stroked the silky pearl, wondering what to do.

"Down?" I asked.

Darkness plays tricks with your sight. You can't see a thing, yet patterns appear, black on black. Shapes move like jellyfish or shadows. Stars float by on the edge of nothing. In my mind, I saw Grandma Chance nodding. Just a nod on a faraway face, but a nod it was. I saw my mother's eyes. They seemed to be hiding a smile.

"All right," I breathed. "Down I go."

I inched over the brace and extended my right leg, testing the darkness beyond. More rubble, more rock. Reluctantly, I eased myself down as you would on a slide.

Slide it was and slide I did. Postrear, as Dillon would say. But it was better than tumbling heels over head, limbs like lunatics. I controlled my slide by braking now and then with my feet. But getting used to the motion, I went a little too casual, a little too fast.

I tried to stop a little too late . . .

And flew into space.

Determined to land feetfirst, even if I were about to die, I arched my back, tried to right myself, and—

"*Umph!*"

—grunted for the *umph*-teenth time.

I had landed in muck.

—➤⦁◄—

I STOOD UP, STUNNED TO BE ON LEVEL, though slippery, ground.

Mom, which way now?

Straight ahead, I felt an earthen wall, so it was right or left. Again I thought of Alice. *That way lives the Hatter,* said the cat with a grin, *that way lives the Hare. Visit either you like—they're both mad.*

I thought of Dillon and Dad. I thought of the mess I'd made. Tomorrow we had to move on. *Had* to, as in do or die.

San Francisco, eight a.m. this coming Wednesday.

It had nothing to do with wanderlust. It was a matter of life or impending doom.

For months, Dad had plodded the résumé trail with no luck. He was overqualified or too old, the wrong gender, or they just weren't hiring. When nothing panned out, he finally heard from a firm in San Francisco. Invisible, Inc., having to do with communications development. The job was his. All he had to do was get there.

Wednesday.

We hated to leave Mom behind. But what else could we do? The plan was to make the move, find a place to live, and come back to get her. How that would be done I didn't have a clue. Dad was hoping to get his new employer to fund it, or at least advance him the money.

When the bank had foreclosed on our house, Dad begged the new owners to let us stay in the stable until we could relocate, and we sold all we had but a few essentials and keepsakes. I made sure Mom's wind chimes were among them, and Grandma Chance's quilt. When they finally said, *get out*, the only good thing was the timing, because that was the day Dad got the call. We packed what was left in a U-Haul trailer and headed west. Clear across country from Richmond, Virginia, to San Francisco, California.

At least we had some place to go.

Not exactly a place to stay, but a place to go.

• • •

Eight a.m. sharp, this Wednesday. Four days away. Our stake in the future depended on it.

Had I put all that in jeopardy? Most definitely,

absolutely, no-brainer. I ached with the thought, and sat back down. Then I saw the mess I'd made for the Mollie Kathleen. The police would be called, a search party organized, all tours canceled. Thanks to my nosy, get-to-the-bottom, kill-the-cat curiosity!

My calamiting.

Kat! *Kat!*

Keep cool. Snap to. Listen for sounds of rescue.

Why hadn't I heard any?

How much time had passed?

I bolted upright. When your body's been battered and your mind's reacting to one thing alone—survival—you have little sense of time. I figured it had not been ten minutes. Not enough time for anyone to miss me. Or if they did, to take it seriously or send for help. Dillon— he would have noticed. But he'd also be expecting me to show up with a tidbit to tell. Dad—he'd be shuffling along with his mind somewhere else.

Yeah, the tour could still be in progress, going from one stop to the next, the guide droning on.

Farther and farther from where I stood.

"Hey!" I yelled. *Why hadn't I yelled before?* "Hey! Help! HELP!"

I listened.

Nothing.

I filled my lungs to capacity, tipped up my head in the direction of the chute, and screamed with every ounce of my being, *"Diiil-luuuuuun!"*

Some screamer I was. There was hardly an echo, and my scream ended in a pathetic squeak and a burning throat, which was dry from the dust I'd stirred up. Despite my doubts, I pictured Dillon scrambling back to the place, leaning over the opening. Any second he would be shouting my name, any second. I held my breath and counted: One-thousand-one . . . one-thousand-two . . . one-thousand-three . . .

Nothing.

"Dillon!" I gasped. *"Dillon!* Down HERE!"

Silence.

"You were right—*it isn't fun!"*

I started to moan, whimper, shake.

Kat! Stop! Get hold of yourself. You'll be OK. Things will turn out in the end. If you have nine lives, which you've always claimed you have, you've only used up two.

Make that three.

I pulled on a finger. One. You survived suffocation when you were an infant. You choked on a pretty penny and Mommy whacked you on the back. You went from blue to gray to white to red; when you went red, you cried. You cried again the next day when the penny came out in your diaper.

I pulled the next finger. Two. You survived a deadly bee sting. The bee was a common mountain bee, the hike was not strenuous, but you had an allergic response. Your arm swelled like a balloon, your temperature hit fireball hot, you tossed and turned so violently in the grass you struck your mouth on a tent stake and broke your front tooth. Second one from the middle, on your left. You slumped into delirium. It was the Apis that saved you. Apis Mel, a homeopathic remedy made from a minute amount of crushed bees. An old hippie hiker who camped nearby carried some in her backpack.

I ran my tongue across the gold cap. Nobody liked it but me. I was into pirates at the time and insisted on a gold one, against my parents' wishes. And Dillon's. And the dentist's. Dad had declared I'd taken this gold thing too far. He'd blurted, "No!"

Of course, he gave in after that.

The next finger I pulled wore Mom's ring.

Would I survive?

—⇥ ⇤—

I TURNED HER RING AROUND.

Mom, what should I do? Curl up and wait? Keep yelling? Whistle? You know, as in whistle in the dark, like you taught me to do so I wouldn't be afraid? Should I wander a ways and return in a while?

If I did, I might eventually see light, find a way out.

OK, I'll wander, just a little. One toe at a time—I was not going to take another plunge down another chute.

But first, I must make a mark of some kind, to tell myself where I had begun. Groping along the floor for a sizable rock, I found something smooth. Lightweight. Plastic. My hard hat! It must have flown off when I fell. No doubt it had given me some protection. I placed it in the middle of the path. If I returned, as long as I kept to the middle, I'd hit it and know I was back.

Right then, or left?

I slowly turned around, which, being in the dark, was not a smart thing to do. I turned around until I got dizzy, until I saw stars. Funny, seeing stars underground. I stopped, steadied myself, and yelled one more time at the top of my lungs—or from the bottom of them—just in case. It only brought more stars.

I headed down the tunnel. Which direction I went—

right or left—I didn't even know. What did it matter? I stretched my arms wide to touch the walls on each side. Not only did this help steady me, I'd be able to sense any opening I might pass.

Then, reminding myself I could fall into another chute if I wasn't careful, I slowed way down, taking one step at a time.

OK, I said, *I'll walk fifty steps, return to my hat, and walk fifty steps the other way.*

Of course, had I known what wonder lay in the great deep beyond, glorious and golden, and how it would change my life forever, I would have hurried ahead.

—⟫ ⟪—

I COUNTED EACH STEP.

Once, the walls veered away from my reach, and I had to feel for them. Once, a sharp rock lay in the path, which I nearly stumbled over. Once, I tramped through water and realized how thirsty I was. I stopped to test it on my tongue—*bleck!*—and spat it out. I prefer water without mud, baking soda, and all the essential and nonessential minerals, thank you very much.

Fifty steps. If something along the way changed dramatically, I'd decide what to do next.

. . .

What to do next hit me abruptly.

I had counted forty-nine steps and was about to turn back when I thought I heard a sound far ahead. Ever so slight. A muffled sound, but a sound.

Something.

What would have made it? It wasn't a falling rock. It wasn't a splash. It wasn't a voice. I don't *think* it was a voice. It was like . . . like . . .

It was like a snuffle a creature might make.

Like a horse, for instance.

I was kidding myself. A horse wouldn't be way down here.

So, what kind of creatures live in caves? All I could think of were bears. But in a cave this deep underground?

I listened, not moving from my forty-ninth step, not moving a nerve.

The snuffle did not snuffle again.

Were my ears playing tricks? Just as my eyes were? Because of the sound I heard, or thought I'd heard, I pictured a bear approaching. A big black bear. I shivered. I felt its presence, coming closer, closer, grinning at such luck, such supper. Grinning and licking its chops. I cringed.

Wait—it wasn't a bear.

It was a bloodthirsty ghoul, all mangy and dripping foam . . .

I scre-e-e-e-eamed. A good, tunnel-length, tension-burning, uvula-waggling, rock-penetrating scream, with no squeak at the end.

I sighed, exhausted. OK, *that* should scare it off! I knew full well, of course, the ghoul-bear had been in my fears. Not real.

I hoped.

But hey, with a scream like that, it's possible somebody heard me. Somebody human, I mean. I turned to go back, and—

Heard the sound again. Definitely. Identical to the first. My impression of it did not change: a snuffly sort of creature. What could it possibly be?

Should I continue?

True to my nature, curiosity said, *Yes. Find what made the sound, Kat.*

After feeling around for more rocks to pile up as a marker, and finding none, I groped my way forward.

—➤ ꘡—

AT FIRST, IT DIDN'T REGISTER.

I'd been wandering in blindness so spongy, the

pictures in my mind leaked into it from time to time. The tunnel had taken a sharp turn that narrowed into a passage the width of my shoulders. I felt ripples along the walls and an occasional formation at my feet, stubby enough to step over. But the curious thing was, I had begun to see textures, ever so faint, and didn't realize it. I was so used to the dark, I thought I saw it in my mind, subconsciously.

But the farther I went, I noticed I *was* seeing something. A softening in the black. Midnight turning to slate, slate to pewter, pewter to dreamy gray.

And the walls were closing in. If it had not been for the growing light, I would have backed out, afraid of becoming wedged till I could move no more. Horrors! I did become wedged, one arm reaching for the light, one reaching behind me in the dark: a frozen pose of despair. Determined to follow the passage to the end, even as it determined to clamp me in its jaws, I pushed and squirmed and weaseled my way through.

The walls widened and the light increased.

Something glinted near my feet, reminding me of the sparkle that had lured me at first. I bent down to see a small metal box, and picked it up. I shook it; something rattled inside. I tried the lid; it wouldn't budge. Squinting with my spectacle-less sight, I saw a circular design, like a bull's-eye, and made out these words:

lucky strike
genuine roll cut tobacco

Never had I thought a tobacco tin would excite me!

Then I did a double take. The tin was as old as the hills, yet here was a scratch in it, bright enough to catch my eye. The scratch looked new.

Had I scraped the tin with my foot before picking it up? No, I was sure I had not.

Either someone had been here recently . . .

Or some *thing*. Some thing with claws or teeth. Or both.

I was back to my bear-ghoul beast.

But now, I could see.

And that might be worse.

With tin in hand, hoping its here-ness meant I was closer to civilization, I quickened my pace toward the growing light. My heart raced.

Deliverance!

But even as I thought so I knew it couldn't be. The

glow did not seem right. It shone like tarnished gold, not daylight. It wavered. And the air wasn't clear mountain air; it had a sulfurous, smoky smell.

I rounded a curve, stumbled through a hazy opening, and instantly forgot the tin for a treasure worth grabbing.

—⊷⊶—

GRAB IT I DID. JUST LIKE MOLLIE KATHLEEN.

When she struck gold in Poverty Gulch in 1891, Mollie Kathleen Gortner did something no woman in Cripple Creek had ever done. She staked a claim in her own name.

Well, pardon me—ahem! That was a man's business. It was fine to name a dog or donkey or saloon after a woman—like Mattie May or Stubborn Sue or Lucky Lola's. But a gold claim? Never!

Too late: Mollie signed on the bottom line before the claims manager could stop her. She knew that Bob Wolmack had been searching the gulch for a dozen years and had come up empty-handed. She sure-as-shootin' wasn't going to let this one get away from her, for *him* to take. In fact, she slipped some of the gold she'd found into her clothes right under Bob's gold-sniffing nose.

. . .

Here I stood, just like her, holding a chunk of gold. Glittering, buttery-as-breakfast, beautiful-as-sunset, buy-the-world gold. Big as my fist!

I weighed it in my hand, pondering its worth. It must weigh a few pounds, which, for gold, is twelve ounces, not sixteen. How much is gold going for an ounce? Once I got out, I'd check the current prices.

Slipping the gold into my jacket pocket, I took a step forward. I was in a cavern of sorts—it was hard to tell, for steam or smoke drifted around me, filtering the light beyond. A trickle of turquoise snaked by my feet.

And here again—Lucky Strike was right!—bigger and brighter than the first, lay another chunk of gold.

I snatched it up. Oh, Mollie—you and me! I wanted to dance. I'd call it the Mollie Kathleen. It would be all the rage. Kids would do it all over the country.

I flung out my arm and stuck out a foot. Dance step number one . . .

"Drop it," said a voice.

It was not a human voice.

Neither was it a bloodthirsty bear-ghoul voice.

It was the voice of a dragon with a smoker's cough.

—⇥)(⇤—

SOME THINGS IN LIFE ARE HARD TO BELIEVE, like monster hurricanes and tidal waves and terrorism and winning the lottery and cameras on Mars. Unless you're one of the few who lives in a backwoods shack and denies we ever set foot on the moon, you stare in disbelief, or shock, dread, or astonishment, trying to accept the unacceptable. After taking it all in, you finally say, OK, this kind of thing happens after all.

When I first saw the dragon, I stood in stone-cold fear, expecting him to lunge at me, tail lashing, to tear me to bits. Then I thought I must be dreaming. I'd fallen into my own version of Wonderland and met my personal Jabberwocky. The "drop it" was just somebody outside the dream. I'd wake up, rise out of my darkness, and all would be plain.

But the dream never burst. It kept going.

The haze had cleared.

In a glance, I saw a scene as unbelievable as the gold. And there was lots more gold—nuggets lay everywhere, ranging in size from bracelet beads to rocks as big as my head.

The cave was large, but not vast—cozy for a dragon. The ceiling drifted in and out of an auburn mist, which

I later learned was called dragonlight. Studded stones winked like constellations. Rows of stalactites jutting like giant teeth met stalagmites from below in a staggered bite. Flowstones as rich as crystallized syrup ran along the floor among various man-made items: a miner's pick, an Orange Crush bottle, a metal flask, a theater bill, an old black boot, a jam jar, a wooden crate with explosives stamped on its side and a chessboard set on its top. On the board were a pawn and two kings, one of which had fallen.

And beyond that, smoldering like a thundercloud at dusk, lay the dragon. He was as tarnished and mythological as ancient history itself. Two gold-leafed wings with silver veins were folded along his back; a scarlet ruffle ran ridgelike between them, into the shadows, where his tail was curled; two silver strands hung from his chin; two filaments of smoke rose from his nostrils; two glowing eyes glared into mine.

Fire-and-cinnamon eyes.

They say that dragons can cast a spell with one look— and I believe it. I was stuck in that stare. If I stepped up and peered into it, I'd see myself trapped like an insect in amber.

I couldn't run—I was paralyzed.

I couldn't faint, for fear of him gobbling me down while I dozed.

I did the one thing there was to do, under the circumstances. He had told me to drop the gold, so I dropped it.

It landed on my toe.

"Ow," I said.

Not exactly the best way to start a conversation with a dragon.

Or with anyone.

————— ⊰⊱ —————

FROM THAT DAY UNTIL NOW, I HAVE PLAYED back our talk in my head, convinced it came out all wrong. It was the most ordinary, run-of-the-mill talk you've ever heard. If not muddled.

Seems to me your usual conversation has a beginning, a middle, and an end. The beginning is for welcomes and greetings, light and cheery. Glad to see you, been a long time—that sort of thing. The middle heads toward serious stuff, more meaningful: How's the after-school job, your class assignment, your mom. If the conversation is going to get sticky—say, disagreeable or philosophical or painful—it usually occurs toward the end of the middle.

Then the end lightens up again, so everyone can be sure they still like one another. No problem, good to see you, we're cool.

Of course, conversation with a treasure-hoarding dragon would be an exception. You'd think it would go something like this:

dragon (*spitting flames*): How dare you finger my gold! I'll burn you at the stake for this! I'll roast your gizzard and gnaw your bones! I'll—
you: I'm sorry, dear dragon. I didn't see you. I—
dragon: Didn't see me? What, are you blind? Behold! (*rising, spreading his wings*) I'm bigger than a boxcar! Big as a mountain! See my shining scales! Feel my fire! Hear me roar! (*Spits more flames, singeing your hair.*)
you: Nice dragon. Nice boy. (*Running like fire and brimstone outta there.*)

Anyway. That's not how it went. Not the usual way, not the dragon way. It was more like taking the bottom end of a down escalator when you're thinking it's the up.

But truth is stranger than fiction.

• • •

Maybe it was the "ow" that did it.

"Did you say 'how'?" he asked in a rusty, crack-of-dawn voice, a voice that sounded like he'd just pulled it out and dusted it off.

"No, I said—" I faltered, trying to figure this out. Logic was kicking in, part of the process of going from shock to acceptance. Was it the fall? The lack of air? The mineral water? Here be a dragon. Here be a talking dragon. It wasn't a crocodile. It wasn't a horned toad on steroids. He was staring at me at the bottom of a mine.

That part was undeniable—the bottom of a mine—but the rest?

I began again. "Did you say: Did you say 'how'?"

"That is what I thought you said. 'How' as in 'howdy,' short for 'how d'ye do.'"

Still numb, my mind shifted to auto-answer. I said, "Thanks for the English lesson. But the 'ye' is outdated. The 'ye' should be *you*."

He frowned—a scrunch-eyed, droopy-eared (or were they horns?), smoky-snouted frown. Less mythological. "*Who* should be me?"

I shook my head. "*Ye*. For *you*."

With a note of suspicion, he said, "I knew you were eavesdropping."

I was emerging from my dullness. "What do you mean?"

"You heard me addressing myself. I heard your scream, feeble as it was. I knew you were close. You were eavesdropping. You had to have been: You know my name."

See what I mean? Muddled.

"I know your name?" I asked. "I heard you cough—"

"You heard my name. Ye. That is me. Or *I*, Miss English-Lesson."

"You are *Ye*?"

The dragon nodded, which sent his chin pendants swaying and smoke signals ceilingward. "I am."

"I'm Kat," I said, strangely relieved this was getting somewhere. "Short for Katlin."

"Come here, Kat," he said. There was no doubt his voice was warming up. "Here, Kitty."

I came here, and I didn't do the Mollie Kathleen. I did the snuffle 'n' shake. If I'd been a dog, my tail would have been whimpering between my legs.

But I wasn't a dog. I was Kat.

And I hate being called Kitty.

I stopped. I had come here far enough.

Ye leaned forward, which brought his head into better focus. Not that it helped my sanity. I was afraid he was going to shake my hand, the one I had buried in my pocket. I saw that his pointed ears were ears, not horns, which he could pivot, like a horse's, his eyes were honey-deep, and his snout had a smudge of soot under it, like a Charlie Chaplin mustache. I tried not to look at his teeth. I glanced at them once, and though they weren't as sharp as they could have been, still, they were big.

"*How* is stereotypical," he snorted. "I never heard an Indian say *how*."

"It was *ow*," I corrected. "And I'm not an Indian."

"I did not say you were. But in the—what do you call them?—the talkies, those moving pictures, the *movies*, Indians say *how*."

I shook my head at the absurdity. "How do you know that?" I asked. "And how do you know words like *stereotypical*?"

"So Long."

"What?" I asked, surprised at his bluntness. Did he want me to go?

"So Long told me," he said matter-of-factly. He nodded again, sending up more puffs. "I have an abundance of words in my vocabulary, an exorbitant amount. In different tongues, too. *Vel caeco appareat*. 'It is obvious.'"

"Really."

"Exorbitant means—"

"I know," I said. "I've looked it up."

"Ah," he said.

"I like big words. I collect them."

"You collect them?"

"You know, like some people collect spoons or seashells or—"

"Or *gold?*" he suggested, making it sound both innocent and condemning.

"S-sure," I said, responding to the innocent part and ignoring the other. "I collect big words and store them in my mind."

"Hmm," he said. "Sesquipedality. *That's* a big word."

"Ses . . . what?"

"—quipedality." He looked pleased with himself. "Know what that means?"

I shook my head.

"It means to use big words, *long* words."

"Ses-quipe-*dal*-ity," I said slowly, filing it away. "Thank you. I'll remember that."

"If you live long—*xué wú zhǐ jìng*, which is Mandarin for 'learning is eternal'—you can collect a copious, prodigious, an incalculable, inter"—he coughed midword, swallowed, and continued—"minable amount of words! And I have lived longer than you can imagine."

"How long?"

"How Long is a Chinaman." He gave me a sideways glance.

"That's a joke," I said, raising my eyebrows along with my voice. "Dragons tell jokes?"

"Truly, it is not a joke." He became solemn. "How, or Hou, actually—spelled with a *u*—Hou Long was So Long's grandfather. Hou was the local tobacconist a . . . ah, a few blinks ago, after Cripple Creek's boom-town days. We would sit and smoke together. He was one of the small handful of humans who would speak with me. The others either ran, fainted, or died." Ye motioned toward a trench along the floor in which a complete skeleton lay.

I was glad I had overlooked it, or I think I would have run, fainted, or died.

"It had to do with Hou's culture," he continued. "Dragons, you see, bring good fortune to the Chinese." A glaze came over his eyes and I thought his lower lip quivered, but it might have been the light. "I miss Hou Long. So Long, too."

Gosh, I didn't know what to say.

"Back to your question," Ye said, snapping out of his mood. "How long have I been here. I do not count time by minutes or hours or days; I hardly count time at all. There was a fire recently. By your reckoning, about a hundred years ago. In the pool—that direction"—he blew an arrow of smoke that slowly wandered off, took a right turn, and dissolved—"nine stalagmites joined their descendants"—he chuckled to himself—"and many others have sprung up." He chuckled again and coughed. "I have seen Halley's Comet numerous times, before Halley attached his name to it. *That*"—he raised a clawed digit—"is how I count time." He coughed again.

I was quiet. Due to a wavering state of unbelief, panic, pain, weariness, and exhilaration, my mind was sitting this one out.

"How long have I been here . . ." he mused. "It was after Huang Ti's reign . . . before Babylon was in full bloom . . . no, before that. Thutmose. Yes, before Thutmose died, I frequented this continent. I flew in on the northeast tradewinds, rode the westerlies up the eastern coast—"

"Virginia?" I couldn't help but ask.

He pulled on a silver chin-wattle. "Is that where you are from?"

I nodded eagerly.

"By then," he continued, "there was hardly any gold

that man had not snatched." He stopped to scrutinize the nugget I had dropped as if to be sure not a speck of it was missing, while I tried not to fidget with my pocket-bound hand. Apparently satisfied, he went on. "I roamed the Far North and holed up around the Great Lakes for a half century. Eventually, I settled in these warmer climes." He coughed yet again.

Was coughing, I wondered, part of his act, like a pet phrase or mannerism? Or did he really *have* to cough? Did the smoke have something to do with it?

"This talk about indigenous people," he said, "who was here first, is pointless."

"Indigenous people?"

"Native Americans. We were here long before any biped walked this land."

"You mean dragons?"

"Dragons. We were the first, the o-r-r-r-iginal" (he rolled the *r*) "Native Americans." He began to inhale, expanding his belly like a bellows.

I stepped back.

His chest began to brighten from burnished bronze to molten chrome, as if embers inside it were waking, fanned to life. He huffed until it glowed stove-hot, his face turning brick red, his eyes flickering in their sockets.

I stepped back again, expecting him to burst from the effort, before he could blow it all out.

Blow it all out he did.

I sat down hard, not from being overwhelmed, but to avoid extreme smoke inhalation.

Smoke flew from his nostrils and billowed out his gullet, forming a cloud that swallowed the stalactites. He blew and blew, and as I gazed in growing wonder, the cloud took the shape of America, unfurling like a flag. He added details, including patches of blue for the Great Lakes, a streak of olive green for the Mississippi, and a chain of cragged puffs for the Rocky Mountains, chugging from north to south like the Glory Train Express. He ended by puckering his mouth and shooting out a jet of tan for the down-turned horn of Texas.

I *was* overwhelmed. "Wow," I whispered, and started to clap.

But then the cloud broke apart and fell in ashes, and it gave me a chill.

"How do you like—" the dragon began, then had a fit of coughing. "How—" he began again, and coughed again. Whenever he tried to speak, he coughed.

I waited.

At last, he said, "Well." His eyes brimmed with

golden tears. He held up a hand, hacked, sighed, and said, "I could have saved"—*cough, cough*—"the cartographers"—*cough*—"a lot of time. Advantage of"—*gulp*—"aerial views"—pause, blink, wipe an eye—"Lewis and Clark and so on . . . you see."

"I see."

His nostrils flared, his chest swelled, and I was afraid he was going to do the up-in-smoke thing all over again.

Instead he said, "I know this land—how does it go?" And in a trembling childlike voice, with a touch of Chinese, he sang, "From sea to shi-ning sea."

I was charmed, picturing Hou, the Chinese man, sitting before him, teaching him the song.

"Do you know who wrote that?" he asked. "'America—"

"—the Beautiful'?" I said. "Um . . . Elvis?"

"Elvis? Is that anything like *elves*?"

"I don't think so. But he had sparkly pants."

"Hmm. You know elves are not real."

"I know. But not so long ago I thought dragons weren't, either."

He settled back down, whether to get comfy or from sheer exhaustion, I couldn't tell. His head was back to its normal burnished bronze, and his body looked considerably cooler.

I was about to ask who *did* write "America the Beautiful" when he said, "Absurd, how a vast geographical paradise can slumber in the sun and rain and snow for millennia on millennia, until someone comes and plants a name on it and declares ownership and writes songs about it"—his voice was past warming up now and into well done, with a spicy edge—"and cuts it up like a cow and says this is yours and this is yours and this and this—"

He glared at whatever scene he saw in his mind, and I began to understand him. This was one lonely dragon, a dragon who'd had no one to talk to for a long, long time.

"They have stacked cities and bureaucracies and mediocrities across this land like it is a game board, and linked them all with wires and rails and roads, like a child's dot-to-dot. But the land will take it back. It always does." He sighed and murmured, "We were the first."

I felt I had to say something, to keep the conversation alive. I said, "But you weren't born here." It came out rude and bold, though it wasn't meant to, so I added, "If you came from the East, across the ocean."

That stirred him again. "Neither were the so-called early Americans, who also migrated from the East and arctic regions. When the Adena people saw me—my first personal encounter with immigrants—they built me a

monument. Though I am no *snake"*—he spat the word—
"as it suggested. Curvy and curled it was. Insulting." His
voice dropped to a murmur, and smoke strayed from his
lips. "I have wondered whether it is still there."

I made a quick connection in my mind. A snake
monument . . . early Americans . . . It sounded like something I'd learned in history. "Do you mean the Serpent
Mound in Ohio? It's still there!"

"I suppose they never saw all of me, it being dusk. But
they got the legend right." He halted and blinked at me
quizzically.

"Legend?" I asked.

He looked away and mumbled something. Something
like, *No . . . no . . . not a chance.*

"Legend?" I persisted.

"It is of no significance," he said with a wave of his
hand. Then he picked at one of his claws the way you'd
inspect a broken nail. He seemed distracted, so I gave him
a little space and distracted myself.

It was easy, with all of this gold. I could hardly
comprehend it. It was as hard to comprehend as Ye
himself. It was hard to ignore. The more I stared at it, the
more golden it became.

What would I do with all this gold? Or even a wheelbarrow full?

My eyes started dreamily wandering. I could see us back in our house . . . wait—in a bigger house, big as a castle . . . it *was* a castle, with a turret for my bedroom . . . I'd peer down and see Angel, my beautiful white horse, galloping freely over the hills . . . a servant would bring iced tea on a platter, and french fries, and cranberry sauce . . . my hair would blow in a breeze . . . I'd invite one good friend, maybe two . . . we'd swim in our indoor pool, surrounded by glass walls and a glass roof and palm trees . . . afterward, we'd watch a movie, or play a game . . .

A game. That was an interesting thought, if not a little berserk. Should I try it?

Would Ye play toss the dice?

I had the two dollars I'd won last night. That may be enough for starters—if I lost a round or two.

Yes, it could put gold in my pocket. *More* gold in my pocket. Because I realized one nugget would not make us rich. It might get us out of debt, but not rich.

Surely, Ye would part with some of this gold. For the thrill of the game, won fair and square. I'd have to play

fair—I mean fair *rules*, since he'd be too clever to fool—
but still I'd have a good chance with my trick die.

Would he catch on? He knew lots of things, and lots of
big words, but was that the same as being smart?

I cut my eyes over to him—he was doing the same to
me. His eye showed a glint I hadn't noticed before. *Hmm.*
I fingered the dice in one pocket, turned the ring with my
thumb in the other.

Well—*gulp*—here was to luck . . .

"Ye?" I said, trying to keep my voice steady. "Before I
go, how about a little game?"

"You are going?"

"I think I should. My family—"

"A little game," he said.

"OK," I said agreeably, pulling out the dice. I gave
him my best grin. "See—"

He frowned. A dire dragon frown, the kind I had
dreaded might come. His eyes narrowed to golden slits,
and the golden turned dark as his pupils filled them; his
ears lay back, and an exclamation point shot out from his
tongue.

Uh-oh. Was gambling a sin to him, too? Was he as
much *dad* as he was *dragon*? Now would come the threats,
roars, flames.

But his voice remained calm. An insurance-salesman calm. And that was worse. "Do that again," he said.

"Do . . . do what?" I stammered. "The . . . the dice?"

"Your teeth. Show them. Smile."

Though the corners of my mouth quivered, I was too afraid not to show my—

"Ah, now," he said. "A gold tooth."

THE DICE WERE BACK IN MY POCKET, MY mouth was sealed shut, my golden dream had burst.

Ye was giving me the look again—the honey-deep, insect-in-amber look. Back to being a dragon.

"You like words," he said slyly. "You like games. Here is a word game for you."

"Um . . . all right."

"Tell me this. What is wrong with the world?"

Some questions are like lariats circling your head, waiting to catch you. I had heard some; I had asked some.

"One word," he said.

The lariat was spinning and so was my mind. I was dragon-weary, cavern-weary. I ached. I was thirsty. I really did want to go home.

I wanted to climb onto my mother's lap.

I put my hands behind my back and fingered her ring. I pictured her face. She was saying something.

Think, Kat, think!

Think. What is wrong with the world? One word.

Hate? Race? Politics? Injustice?

Simple. One word. Right. There were lots of one words.

Hunger? Famine? Disease?

Would it be a small word or a big word? A word I might not even know? A word like . . . *sesquipedality.*

"Is it a long word?" I asked.

"It is ever so short," he said briskly. "But the problem is ever so long."

Gosh, now it was a riddle. I put my hands in my pockets and fingered the not-so-lucky dice.

Think, Kat!

I fingered the gold nugget.

Think!

Wait. Gold nugget. Gold tooth. He asked me the question after seeing my gold tooth.

Poverty . . . economics . . . money . . .

Money. That was a short word. Was it a long problem? You bet it was. What was that saying about money? *Money is the root of all evil.*

That was it, surely.

I licked my lips with a dry tongue, ready to say money, when I saw Mom shaking her head. "It's not *money* that's evil, Kat," she told me one day after some self-righteous classmate called me a snobby rich girl. "There's nothing wrong with *money*. It's the *love* of money . . ."

That was it! I opened my gold-toothed mouth and said the one word.

"Greed!"

I could tell by his eyes I had passed the test. The lariat was tucked away.

"Now," he said, as if my answer had taken no effort at all. "Do you know why they call it a mine?"

There he went again. Yet I felt it was not a game this time, but a lesson.

"Uh," I said. "Not really."

"They call it a mine, child, because the first people who found gold, or gems, or whatever they thought was precious enough to grab, shouted 'Mine!'" He blew out a stream of steam.

The gold in my pocket suddenly grew heavier. I swallowed, not that I had anything to swallow. Then I made my defense. Just as the lawyer did at our trial.

"Well," I said, throwing caution to the smoke, "look at you. Look at all this gold you hoard."

He slinked toward me.

I stepped back.

The gravel had left his voice some time ago. Now it was brandy-smooth.

He said, "I am a dragon. This is dragon gold. I am entitled to it. *All* of it."

It made me want to run, but it also made me bold. Entitled, *really*. I would have laughed, like the trial lawyer had done, but I didn't want to show him my tooth again. I didn't want him ripping it from my mouth.

I said, "And no one else is?"

"Why should they be?" he snapped. "They have everything else, thanks to Greed. All their bright, noisy inventions they scoot down their roads or their rails. They have the world in their hands."

I swept my arm across the golden heaps. "But they have all that because of this!"

He studied me for a while. "This is not your gold," he said. A flatness crept into his voice. "No more than bones in cemeteries are mine."

I scrunched up my face. "What's that supposed to mean? Why would you want peoples' bones?"

"Are they not valuable?"

"That's a *different* kind of value."

"Ah!" He nodded his head in mockery. Only I didn't know what he was mocking. "Are there not laws against grave robbing, body snatching?"

"Of course, there are," I said, perplexed. Where in the world, or under it, was this going?

"There should be laws against gold snatching."

"And why is that?" I demanded, folding my arms.

"Smile again."

"No." I tightened my lips, thinking, *Burn me up. Go ahead, charbroil me. All that's left will be my gold-capped tooth, if that's what you want.*

Then I thought, *And the gold in my pocket.*

I wished I'd put my hands in my pockets instead. It'd be a dead giveaway now. I swallowed, trying to get my heart back down.

Ye was as calm as an October moonrise. He said slowly, knowingly, "Tell me the truth."

"T-truth?" I stuttered. "About . . . what?"

"That gold."

Had he waited this whole time to torture me? To watch me squirm? Had he seen through the smoke, seen me pocketing the gold? But I noticed he didn't say, "The gold in your pocket"; rather, "that gold."

If this was a bluff, I could bluff right back.

"Oh . . ." I shrugged. I gave him the grin he wanted, minus any mirth. "They put that in when I was a kid. Fell down and broke my tooth. No biggie." Now my hands went into my pockets, though the sweat on my face itched to be wiped.

"Ah," he said again, nodding. And it wasn't the kind of "ah" you say at the dentist's. "Here you are, a mere catty of a girl, sliding from the twenty-first century into what is left of my crumpled little world, and you have gold in your mouth."

"My dad paid for it!"

"With what? More gold? They have beat gold into dogs, frogs, birds, cows, bugs, masks, cups, frames, coins, coins, more coins, *more* coins, MORE coins, *MORE* coins—" He took a breath, gave a harsh cough, and went on. "Earrings, finger rings, toe rings, necklaces, bracelets, bangles, medallions, trophies, icons . . ."

"But thith ithn't gleed," I said, pressing my tongue to my tooth.

That stopped him. "What?"

"Gleed!" I removed my tongue. "This. Isn't. Greed. I needed a tooth."

"You chose gold."

"Gold is pretty. I like gold. You like gold. *Obviously.*
Lots of people—"

"Gold—girl, kitty cat, thief, whoever you are—"

His head was closer to mine than it had been before, eyes
all cinnamon and sparks now, nostrils flared and glowing,
like a fevered horse. His breath smelled feverish, too.

"—gold is what dragons become when they die."

——⟩⟨——

I WAS SPEECHLESS. MY MOUTH SPRANG OPEN,
gold tooth and all.

Dragon gold.

"You'll turn to dust," Ye said quietly. "Bones, then
dust. When dragons die, they turn to gold. That is what
I am waiting for."

Dragon gold.

Just like that, it all made sense. Everything. His talk
about cemeteries and laws and grave robbing and Babylon
and Thutmose and greed and value and entitlement. All
the gold in the world, from ancient Egypt to Fort Knox,
was the remains of dragons.

Dragon gold!

It removed my stand-your-ground attitude. It removed

my pride. It removed a lot of things. Not only was I speechless, I was breathless.

It wasn't greed at all. Gold was rightfully his.

Then Ye said something I found even harder to comprehend. I had just got used to the fact that dragons were truly real, and then, that dragons turned to gold, and now—

He said, "I am the last. The last of all the dragons."

He said it as if he stood on a cliff, staring the unknown in the face, waiting to be pushed. I stared into his golden eye for a long, long time. His eye was so mysterious, so deep, yet so gentle. I wanted to sing to him, soothe him, ask him a thousand questions. But I could hardly think of one.

"You're . . ." I fumbled. "You're the . . . There aren't any more? Not anywhere?"

The lid closed across his golden eye but did not close out the light, which glowed seashell pink.

"You've looked?" I asked.

"The whole world over."

—⟩⟨—

AFTER MOM'S ACCIDENT, WE EACH DEALT with it differently.

Dad dug into medical research, looking for any clue that might lead to freeing Mom from her darkness. When he wasn't at work or sitting with her, he sat chained to his laptop, searching and searching. He was up all night, often till dawn. I don't know when he slept, unless it was at the table after he'd eaten something I'd fixed, or in the driver's seat as I pumped gas or got groceries. He wandered in his own subterranean places. You could see it in his face, in the vertical line that deepened between his eyebrows.

Dillon became animated, a clever comic. He was headed that way before the accident, careening from craziness to seriousness and back again. Mom said that at fourteen he was testing the borders between boy and man.

"His J. M. Barrie stage," she said.

"What's that?" I asked.

"J. M. Barrie—the man who wrote *Peter Pan*, who never grew up."

"Peter Pan never grew up, or J. M. Barrie?"

"Both."

Dillon chattered in the wittiest ways, making up words or phrases that deserve dictionary status. Like *mobscenities*—mob plus obscenities, which means a bunch of cussing coming from a crowd—or *godzillion*—Godzilla plus zillion, which means lots and lots, or bigger than big. He calls it Dillingo, which is Dillon plus lingo.

He'd dance across the kitchen with bundles of carrots, or make embarrassing noises at just the right moments, like the time the lady in the bank bent over. He was really funny, but since I knew what lay behind it all, while my face was laughing, I cried inside. He would not discuss Mom's condition. If the subject was raised, he would shut right down.

I started journaling.

In the first few weeks of writing, I discovered something. I discovered that pain is like a pencil tip: The more you write, the blunter it becomes. The pain is still there, but you can divert it onto a page, break it into little stabs and penpricks that help carry the pain for you, like lines of ants sharing the load.

I'm on my third journal now. My second one's packed in the trailer. My first one's inside my pillowcase on the backseat of the car. I don't want anyone to see it.

On the first page, there is only one word.

Mom?

"YE," I SAID. "DEAR DRAGON—"

Ye could have dealt with his loss like a storybook beast. He could have rampaged, shooting flames of vengeance and wrath. Instead, he had burrowed down deep to sleep with his ancestors, the golden relics of his past. He had accepted his fate.

The last dragon on Earth. He would lie here, too, someday, as dragon gold.

Suddenly, I pitied him. I respected him, liked him, *adored* him.

But there was nothing I could do. I was sorry I'd disturbed his sad sleep.

"Ye," I said. "I need to go. I need to go now."

I think he was lost in a dream.

I had nothing more to say. I started to walk away. Out, back into the blackness. Where I'd end up, only heaven and Ye would know. Probably down some blind tunnel, nothing left of me but bones, like the skeleton in the trench. I was overcome by sorrow, guilt, compassion—an avalanche of feelings. I was an intruder, hardly a footnote in his long history. I wanted to leave him to his memories and his gold.

I still had his gold in my pocket.

His gold, not mine.

It could be his mother. It could be her heart.

I was too ashamed to return it. Too ashamed for him to know I'd picked it up. I knew what I would do. I would drop it as I went, somewhere in the shadows.

Stepping over the turquoise stream, I thought I heard him snuff. I turned, and he started to cough. A hard, harsh, hacking cough.

My mother had a practice of ending her talks—whether with a stranger or friend or foe, whether there'd been an argument or agreement—with a kind word. She would offer a smile and say something like, "Stay well," "Be blessed," "Peace." I wasn't going to smile—I was too sorry about the gold in my mouth, the gold I'd once been so proud of.

So I waved, but I don't think he saw me. So I called. "Take care of yourself, Ye! You've got a nasty cough." It wasn't the greatest farewell, but I hadn't practiced like Mom had.

He looked up. "I am a dragon," he said. "It is good to kindle the embers . . . *hrm-hrmm-hrmmm!*"

Then he had a convulsion of coughing, hacking, and choking that was far worse than before. It went on and on and on. I stood helpless, watching spasm after spasm jolt his rugged body.

"*Hrm-hrmm-hrmmmmm-hrmmmmmm!*"

If Ye was the last of the dragons—the *last* of the last of the dragons—I couldn't leave him like this.

Suddenly, his coughing stopped.

So did my heart.

He was still as stone, his head fallen, his eyes closed. The silence was deathly.

"Ye?" I squeaked.

No response.

"Ye?" I said louder.

Nothing.

Stumbling across the cave, I shouted, "Ye!"

He heaved a hollow sigh and opened an eye.

My heart beat again. All I could think to do was what my mother had done, whenever I had a bad cough.

"Let me listen," I said, and moved around to place my ear against his bulging, leathery, industrial-size furnace side. He did not protest. I listened, and heard a rumbling wheeze within—like a strong wind with debris in it, or a rockslide down a canyon.

"Is it serious?" he whispered.

"Shush," I said.

"What is it?"

"Shush!"

If I listened long enough, I hoped, I could pick up a pattern, see if his breathing was regular.

Right. About as regular as a cyclone. Not that I could do anything about it.

I pulled away with a roughened cheek and blistered ear. "I'm not a doctor," I said, "but it doesn't sound good." I came around to his head. His eye was at half-mast and had lost its fire. I laid my hand on his muzzle. I wiped some soot off his nose.

As I did, a change came over him. He lifted his head, his eye got big, and the light within it grew, like the light of the rising sun. His dragonlight became bright.

"Where did you get that?" he sang.

"Get what?"

"That pearl."

———⊰⊱———

THIS PART I CALL THE SHOWDOWN. HIGH noon on Main Street at the bottom of the Mollie Kathleen.

Ye was facing Me.

Neither of us was a gunslinger, but the lines were drawn.

Ye wanted the pearl. He didn't say so—but I could tell. Girl, was it obvious. He was transformed. It was as though centuries of his life had sloughed off like a snake shedding its skin. The light in his eye was now sweet as day.

So was his voice. "May I have it?" he asked.

"Have what?" I said dumbly.

"The ring. That pearl."

"Whatever for?" I had the feeling a weight was about to drape across my back.

"Is it yours to give?" he suggested.

"Why should I give it to you?"

"Do you like me?" He cast his words carelessly, as if this wasn't critical.

I narrowed one eye at him. All right—he may have a real bad cough, but he was using his aw-c'mon-insurance-salesman approach again. Was it another lariat? It was definitely unwinding, hovering above my head. I looked straight into his golden eyes to test his blinkmanship.

I said. "Why do you want it?"

He didn't flinch. "It is a wonderful pearl," he said. Deadpan, no emotion.

I stepped back, hand on my hip. That brought a wince to his face—the pearl leaving his sight. "Shame on you," I said. "I know why you want it."

"You do not."

"Do too."

"Why?"

"One word, Mister Ye. One short word."

"Kat," he scolded, "it is not greed. Greed has nothing to do with it." He coughed, and I questioned that it was real; perhaps it was forced to draw my sympathy.

"What is it then?"

Except for his wheeze, he was silent awhile, his eyes darting now around the cave, now to the hand on my hip.

It *had* to be greed. After all, everyone's greedy for *something*. Since it wasn't gold or vengeance or who knows what for this dragon, I figured his weakness was pretty pearls. Possessing mine would fill a yearning for conquest. Isn't that what dragons were known for?

While I was having these disenchanted thoughts, he broke his silence.

"The legend—" Ye began.

Ah-ha—the one question he hadn't answered. "The Serpent Mound?" I said.

"It represents the legend. Do you know what is in his mouth?"

"The serpent's mouth?"

"It is not a serpent," he reminded me.

"Sorry," I said. "In its mouth . . ." Not a gold tooth, surely. I couldn't recall it having *anything* in its mouth. I shook my head. "What?"

"A pearl. He is swallowing a pearl."

That set me back. Now I could picture the ancient earthwork, winding its way through the woods, its mouth open wide, a circular object inside it.

"A pearl?" I said, and slowly raised my hand, the one with my mother's pearl.

Together we gazed. And as we did, Ye told me of the legend, how its origin had grown out of great misfortune, far back in the dawn of time.

"When dragons first inhabited the earth, they were so numerous and strong, mortality was hardly a concern. They thought they would live forever. There were sea dragons and sky dragons, land dragons and subterranean. Each dragon shared the characteristics of each habitat— sea, sky, land, grotto—but each one had its own special strength. Then, quick as lightning, a cataclysmic event occurred. Something fell from heaven—Lucifer, for all I know, cast out. The impact shook the foundations of the earth, causing a flood and geological upheavals. In that single blow, nearly all the dragons were destroyed. Crushed, ground to bits, smothered, imbedded."

I pictured the poor dragons falling in crevices. "That explains gold veins!" I said.

"It does," Ye said sadly. "A few dragon eggs, called *hlams*, or silent dreams, survived. But ever after, dragons were weaker and far less potent. Whereas the first dragons lived indefinitely—though they eventually would die natural deaths—the remaining ones were shorter-lived. A few eons instead of millennia on millennia. Out of that extant brood, I came. Early on I was told of this legend, the way a human child is raised on nursery rhymes. Perhaps it was generated to give us hope, a recoil, you could say, against the unknown, the uncontrollable."

He took his eye off the pearl to look at me. "Do you understand all of this?"

"Most of it. Yes."

"I am using big words," Ye said. "Potent, extant, generated . . ."

"I'm getting it," I said, telling myself I'd look them up later. I was anxious to hear the tale, though anxious about where it might end.

"To make it short," he said, becoming somber, "the legend promises eternal life to any dragon who swallows a pearl."

I lowered my arm, and he followed it as if it were a falling star.

"I see," I said.

"Do you?" he asked.

"A long, long, *long, long* life."

"Forever."

"And ever."

His eye was back on mine. We were eye to eye.

"There is one condition," he said.

I wanted to blink, but couldn't. I was spellbound, waiting.

"The pearl must be given willingly, or it will not take effect."

⟶⟩⟨⟵

THE SHOWDOWN, SCENE TWO.

It was my turn to deliberate. (My turn for big words.) Deliberate: what the jury does when they're trying to make a decision. The opposite of being trigger-happy, which is what I was tempted to do, without further ado. Cut and run. Fire off an absolute "No!" and get outta there.

I deliberated.

If Ye hadn't been the last of all dragons . . .

If it hadn't been for his gold burning a hole in my conscience . . .

If it hadn't been for my need to get out . . .

The commonsense thing would be to exchange the ring for directions. I would help Ye in his hour—or whatever that would be in dragon time—of need, he would help me in mine.

If it hadn't been for my mother.

Promise.

But if I never got out alive, there'd be no way to keep the promise, or anything else for that matter.

It was what Dillon calls an oxydox: oxymoron and paradox combined. (More big words.) An oxymoron being two opposing things in one phrase, and paradox being something contradicting itself. Anyway, between a rock and a hard place.

There was no competition against my mother, even for a dragon. She would win every time, hands down. But I knew her well enough to know what she would do. I could hear her say, "It's simple, Kat. Which would you rather be—alive and free, minus the ring, or dead at the bottom of blackness, with the ring around your phalanx?" ("Phalanx" is the finger bone—Mom could be specific like that, and anyway, I learned it in science class.) Under the circumstances, she would release me from whatever promise I was sworn to keep.

There was something else, and I knew all along where my reasoning would take me. If I gave Ye the ring—

Wait. It had to be given willingly. A gift of the heart. How could I wrench it from my finger and give it to him willingly?

But if I gave Ye the ring—

All right, I'll admit it, because I've sworn to tell the truth—no gaps, no embellishments, no attempts at making myself look good.

If I gave Ye the ring, that would justify keeping his gold.

There you have it. I was a thief. Not a noble thing.

Ye was patient.

I was sure of this: He wasn't going to devour the ring then and there with me inserted in it, though he could have—in one gulp. No, that would not be willingly, that would be by force. And he wasn't that kind of beast. He was Ye the Dragon, with his own sense of honor. A noble thing.

He finally said, "Does it mean that much to you? Is it that valuable?"

I sighed. "You have no idea."

"I can judge that."

"It was my mother's."

"Ah," he said with an approving nod. "Given willingly."

"Passionately," I assured him.

"Hmm," he said. "How did *she* get the ring?"

"It was *her* mother's."

"Ancestral," Ye murmured.

"Yes." I turned her ring around. Around and around. Ye was silent.

I still had my dilemma: Die or give up the ring.

Finally, I said, "Ye?"

"Yes?"

"What chance do I have of finding my own way out?"

He glanced around the cavern. "One in a hundred or so, perhaps."

"Hmm," I said. "It'd take a long time."

"By your reckoning."

After circling back over my anguished, inner arguments and arriving at the same place, I said, "Ye, our wants are not that different—yours and mine. I'd like to live, so would you."

He studied me without a word.

"If you—" I hesitated under his gaze. "If you show me the way out—" I averted my eyes to the pearl, and imagined Mom smiling with relief. Yes, this would have been her solution. I took a deep breath and exhaled. "I'll let you have it."

He gave a smoky sigh. "That would not work."

I frowned. "Why not?"

"It would not be a gift."

"Well . . . it would be a barter, an exchange. An exchange is not exactly paying for your help."

"Neither is it a gift. A gift is given unconditionally, no strings attached."

Ye was making this hard—as if it wasn't already—but it hardly required thought: Of course, he was right.

I was back to square one. I'd have to find my way out. A near impossibility.

I hung my head and limped away. It was not an act—I was bone-weary spent, and my knee was starting to swell.

I was stepping over the turquoise stream for the third time when I heard him call. I stopped without turning and said, "What?"

He didn't answer, so I turned to look back.

He stirred himself, slowly swung his bulk, and lumbered into the dark. Then I heard his echo.

"Follow me . . . me . . . me . . ."

I tottered after him.

—❯❘❮—

CROSSING THE FAR REACHES OF THE CAVERN, Ye strode over stalagmites I had to clamber around. If not for my need to keep up, and my increasing numbness, I would have lingered over the splashes of beauty that appeared in the dancing dragonlight: translucent mineral curtains, thin hollow reeds of pale rock, gnarled formations creeping gnomelike along the walls, rhinestone rubble spilling across the floor, a fluorescent lime-green pool.

I halted at the pool, stunned by its vapory silence. What mysteries lay here? Did Ye navigate its depths, dive from cave dweller to sea swimmer and back again? Were there fish in it that he ate?

His muffled cough roused me. I turned in time to see him circle a huge stalagmite that towered like a Grecian column and enter a black mouth in the wall.

I hobbled as fast as I could, my thoughts bumping around in my head. We might have gone half an hour, but it seemed like half a year. How was he to know that an injured girl of twelve could hardly keep pace with a dragon of, what—three thousand?

Egypt . . . Babylon . . . Halley's Comet . . . What had he done all those centuries?

Where were we going?

Where would this stop?

. . .

We gradually ascended. I followed his tail, which wavered like foam on a moonlit shore and shone violet and green. With nothing else to see but his massive shape beyond, I kept my eyes on that slithery, shimmering wake into the dark unknown.

As we went, I realized the dragonlight Ye cast was for my sake: to prevent me from stumbling. But stumble I did, several times, and lost sight of him. I had to hurry to catch up, listening for his rambling rumble and occasional coughs, watching for his celestial scales, smelling his scent—for he had a scent. When I smelled it, I thought of fortune and ashes and spices and earth. It hurt me to smell him and soothed me, too.

At times, I wanted to crawl up his back to be carried and rocked.

When my feet had exhausted every excuse to plod on, I felt a whirl of air that was not dragon scent, and finally we stopped.

We had come to the end.

Ye listed to one side, backed into a nook that looked like another passage, curled his tail up around his chest, and declared, "Haven't done that in a dragon's age! A fanciful stroll!"

I nodded and gasped at him, unable to speak.

"Here we are," he said. "From here, you must crawl." He motioned to a hole in the wall behind me.

I stooped and peered in. A stone-gray spot of light beckoned to me from beyond.

This was it.

We would part.

I would go my way, back into the electric world of humanity.

Ye would languish in the dark until death.

I would see him no more.

I had a growing sensation this was all just a dream. But what a dream! Would I look back on it in disbelief? I glanced over my shoulder to be sure he was there. He was: gazing at me, expressionless, waiting.

"Proceed," he said.

I detected a wheeze. A golden string of smoke flitted from off his tongue. I looked closely at him, as if seeing him for the first time, believing it was the last. I tried looking into his soul, tried to take in his mystery, his reality.

I saw a scaly thing with four legs and a tail, wings folded, claws for digging and foraging.

I saw a fabulous mythical beast, who roamed the Wonder World, whose colors would sing in sunlight—whose wings would, too—whose blood beat with enchantment, whose powers could bind your heart.

Like a sleepwalker, I went to him.

I went pulling the ring from my hand.

"Here," I heard myself say. "I want you to have it. I want you to live forever."

He studied my face as if from far, far away, as if it was his first time to see me, too, and his last.

"Willingly?" he asked.

I could say no more. Gripped by a sadness I could not explain, I began to tremble.

I gave him the ring.

Then I got down on all fours and found the hole and crept in.

—⟫⟨—

AS I CRAWLED, I BEGAN TO CRY.

In this stuffy tunnel of time, I felt the weight of the world on my back. A messy, jabbering, greedy-fingered, snickering world that joggled your head and your heart and left you stranded.

Why should a world like that care for a daydreaming dragon, lying deep beneath human thought, out of sight and out of reach? Why should it care if the last dragon lived or died or blew pictures in the air and sang lines from "America the Beautiful"?

I had dragged that world through Ye's Dark Fantastic, leaving my own little snail trail.

Or did I have it backward? Was I crawling away from something so real, my own world was a myth? Was Ye the real, and the rest of us, clutching some handhold each in our own way, the unreal?

Were *we* the ones in the dream? And a bad dream at that.

Like my mother.

I saw her lying under a veil of gray, her face a blank.

Her hands empty.

I suddenly gasped. *Mom! Oh, I'm sorry! So sorry! I gave it away! Your pearl! Away! Gone! Gone . . .*

It had slid off too easily, had slipped away too fast. What was it I gave it to? A golden flight of fancy?

My finger felt so bare.

My soul so much more.

As I crawled molelike through the dirt, I sobbed, "Back! I want it back! It was everything! All I had left! The only *real thing!*"

—⟩⟨—

BY THE TIME I REACHED THE END, MY SAD-ness had lifted.

I wanted to be free of my underground dream, shake it off like a shell. I yearned to be with my family again, feel the sunlight on my face, breathe fresh air.

The end was not spectacular: There was no flower-scented breeze, no glorious light, no wide opening with the blue sky and the Rockies beyond. There was scarcely any light at all. The air smelled moldy, with a tinge of stink.

My mole hole emptied into an earthen compartment with a mound of crusty waste on the floor. Propped against the wall was something like a hen roost, posing as a ladder. I peered up. About eight feet up was a wooden boxlike cover with two watermelon-shaped holes that emitted gray light.

That was it.

OK. I was supposed to climb the roost and squeeze through one of those holes.

Which is what I did.

Not until I was halfway out, trying to avoid adding splinters to my assorted injuries, did I realize where I was. Vertical planks, a tin roof, a lazy, hinged door with a crescent moon . . .

An old two-seater outhouse! And I was climbing out the—

Grossville! I was free of the hole before you could say Johnny-Boy.

Later, when I told Dillon about it, he said, "That was a speedy *evacuation*. But hey, you should've been *relieved* it wasn't in *regular* use." Punny, punny, punny.

By the looks of the planks in the walls, full of cracks and bullet holes through which daylight leaked, I wondered how it could still be standing. What confounded me most was the double seater. Why would two levelheaded persons want to sit side by side in a privy doing their dirty work?

Suddenly, I had the urge to go, and this was the place to do it.

I would have, if it hadn't been for Joe. Fixed to the back of the door, just below the crescent, was a poster, brown with age. It must have been meant as a joke.

And there was Joe in a mug shot, glaring at me with one dark eye and one white. Among his listed crimes—some of which were really horrendous—was one that hit me in the gut.

THEFT.

I sat down (right where you're supposed to) and stared at the word. Now I was on the other side of the feelings I'd left behind. Guilt rose in me again.

"Kat," I said grimly, "you're no better than an outlaw. You could be the poster girl for theft."

Yep—Cotton-Eyed Joe and Jesse James and Billy the Kid and Li'l Kat Graham. My face burned with shame at the thought.

I took the gold rock from my jacket.

It was not too late to cast it off. Like casting off baggage, it would lighten my load. I could drop it down the hole.

It wouldn't be in Ye's possession, but neither would it be in mine. Back to the earth it would go, where it belonged.

I gazed at it awhile, blazing its image into my brain. How luscious and warm it felt! Like holding a chunk of the sun.

Wait . . . yes . . .

Things aren't always wrong and right, black and white. They can be gray, confusing, unclear. It depends on your motive. It depends on a lot of things. There was my mom, and we needed money.

I'd be out of my mind not to keep it. Anyone would. Besides, Ye wouldn't miss it. It'd be like, say, having the complete skeleton of your great-great-grandmother with one of her fingertips gone. Right?

When I put it in those terms, it didn't seem so bad.

It didn't seem so good.

Deep down, I felt it. Guilty, guilty, guilty. I had given Ye the ring voluntarily. But he had not given me the gold.

I had stolen that.

I sighed a deep sigh. "Well, Kat," I said, "you may as well get used to the feeling, because you know you're determined to keep it."

I dropped the gold back into my jacket, shook my head in self-contempt, got up, and shoved Joe aside.

THEIR NAMES WERE MAX AND MARLENE Warren, and they were the kindest old couple I could have stumbled upon.

Max was sweeping the back porch when I came wading through the grass, and dropped his broom and his jaw when he saw me. I did not see him until that moment, or I would have been more stealthy.

"Oh dear!" he said. "Where'd you come from?"

As I tried to think of an answer, something like, "Do you mean, what city and state?" my weariness descended full force and I nearly collapsed.

"Marlene!" he shouted. *"Marlene!"*

Marlene poked her head out the door and exclaimed, "Oh my!"

"Get the first-aid kit!" said Max. "And draw a bath! She smells like the dickens!" Then he winked at me.

• • •

Their faces were the sweetest I had seen in a long, long time, their kitchen smelled delicious, their couch couldn't have been softer.

While we exchanged names, I looked at them closely. Max had a round face with an upturned nose that habitually wiggled like a rabbit's, and a wispy cloud of hair. The undershirt he wore was a faded tie-dyed pink. Marlene's hair was as pale as corn silk and snipped short along her hairline. Her glasses magnified her slate-blue eyes. When her hands weren't busy helping me, she would tug in various places at her green-and-white-striped cotton dress.

As I lay on the couch, to where they had led me, Max held my hand and Marlene dabbed my face with a moist washcloth.

"Gracious!" she said. "Look at that!"

"It's all right," Max said soothingly, as if to counteract her comments. "You'll be fine."

"She's probably dry as a bone," said Marlene. "Look at her lips." She peered at me from behind her glasses. "Would you like a drink, honey?"

"Please," I said, realizing how parched I was and hoarse I sounded. "Water."

Max got up to fetch it.

"I'll get the bath going," said Marlene. "You need a good soak." She lightly stroked my arm. "How do you feel?"

"Not . . . too . . . bad," I said. Now that my ordeal was over, I could barely move or think.

Max came in with a big glass of water, which Marlene helped me hold. I drank it down nonstop, water running around the rim. It was heavenly.

"More?" said Max.

I gasped and nodded.

Max went to get more, and Marlene said, "We'll clean you up and check your hurts, and you can tell us what happened."

I was too exhausted to think of what I would say.

After I drained the second glass, Marlene said, "Now—can you stand? I'll help you to the tub."

"Wait." The water had revived me enough for me to think more clearly. "I need to make a call. Can I use your phone?"

"Of course," said Max, and got me a cordless.

I dialed Dad's cell—which was really Mom's cell—expecting Dillon to answer, since he's the one who carries it. No one answered. I got a recording saying something about being unable to process the entry. "Goodbye," the automated female voice said.

I stared at the phone. "I need to talk to them," I said. "They'll be so worried."

"Calm down, hon," said Max. "No need to panic."

Marlene asked, "Who?"

"My family. My dad and my brother." I sat blinking at her while she blinked back.

She patted my knee, then pulled her hand away. Her fingers were bloody. "We'd better take a look," she said.

I had to think, and thinking was hard. "All right," I said. "I'll try again later. I really need to—"

Marlene had gingerly lifted the torn denim around my knee and was shaking her head. "We should close up this cut."

"All right."

I thought I could stand on my own, but found it easier to give in to her help. As we made our way to the bathroom, Max spoke up. "You were in the mine, weren't you?"

I stopped. "Did you hear that on the news?"

"News? What news?"

"How'd you know I was in the mine?"

"Your jacket, sugar," he said. "It's the kind they use on the tours."

My jacket! Where was it? Marlene had helped me take it off as I lay on the couch. It wasn't there. I made some sort of sniffly snort, and Marlene smoothed back a strand of my hair.

"It's all right, sweetheart," she said. "It's in the wash."

—⊶)⊱—

THAT'S ME? I THOUGHT, WIPING AWAY THE mist and squinting into the bathroom mirror. Without my glasses, I was spared the sharp details, but still I was startled.

Except for the spots on my forehead and cheeks where Marlene had dabbed with a washcloth, my face was grimier than Ye's sooty snout. Dirt had collected around my eyes; dirt was even in my nose. My lower lip was cracked. And my hair—now I knew what the proverbial rat's nest looked like. I inspected the bumps on my head and found another at the back of my skull, squishy and sore.

As I glared at this shabby version of myself, I hardly cared what Max and Marlene thought. All I could think of was Ye, as if I was caught in his spell. Under the grime I blushed: I had appeared to him like this, representing the human race!

• • •

Marlene had added therapeutic salts to the bathwater that foamed up around me. I kept my injured knee, now covered in butterfly bandages, above the water. My cuts and scrapes stung at first, but the pains grew less the more I soaked. The suds felt so good I wanted to stay there forever, but worries and questions were bursting like the bubbles around my head.

Did Marlene find the gold in my pocket? Wouldn't she have heard a clunk when she dropped the jacket in the wash?

Where were Dillon and Dad? Back at the hotel, or still at the mine?

How could I get in touch with them?

What time was it? How long had I been gone?

Would it be on the news?

What should I do next?

The longer I stayed in the tub, the more anxious I became, until, with the grime barely gone and some cuts still oozing, I got out. Marlene had taken the rest of my clothes, too, so I put on the terry robe she'd provided. It was thick like a winter robe, smelled slightly of mothballs, and had a red heart stitched on the front. The fit surprised me: It could not have been Marlene's and it certainly wasn't Max's. Maybe they kept it on hand for guests. Or maybe it was Marlene's when she was a girl.

Standing, dripping in the hallway, I called to her.

No answer.

"Max?"

I could hear the washer going from somewhere in the house. I could also hear the TV in the living room, giving the weather for the Teller County region.

Should I try to retrieve the jacket—and the gold—or use the phone again? It was probably too late for my jacket. I would use the phone first.

As I came into the living room, Max came in from the kitchen.

"That was quick," he said.

"I need to call them again." I said.

"Help yourself."

I picked up the phone, dialed, and got the same message.

"This is what I've been waiting for," said Max, who came and sat on an arm of the couch, leaning toward the TV. "At first, I thought you'd been struck by a hit-and-run driver; then I thought . . . well, I won't say. Then with the jacket and all . . ."

It was the "all" I didn't like the sound of. But I didn't ask. The local news was on. A reporter was talking. The jacket would have to wait. I stood fixed to the screen.

The reporter—a woman who looked as if she'd spent all week in Chic Hair 'n' Nails—stood near the mine's hoist house, where a crowd of onlookers had gathered behind yellow police tape. I was suddenly short of breath and scanned the blur of faces. Were Dillon and Dad among them?

I almost missed what the reporter was saying.

". . . today in the Mollie Kathleen Mine. They're still looking and believe they're getting close. They've found evidence of a fall she might have taken, and rescuers are now descending an unused shaft. We'll keep you updated on further developments. Back to you, Chet."

In the newsroom, Chet continued with the state's economy.

"Well, Katlin Graham," said Max, turning to me with a look of awe and sympathy. "It's no wonder you're so banged up."

—◆)(◆—

WHAT HAPPENED FROM THERE RUSHED IN like a train.

Max asked whether I cared if he called the police, and I asked how far the mine entrance was from here. He said up several streets. I asked if he could take me to it. Marlene came in with an expression that I could only describe as astonishment, and she asked why I wanted to go there.

"To try to find my family," I said, giving her a worried look. It was genuine, but I worried more about the gold.

"Your clothes are in the dryer," she said quickly. Then she apologized for not mending the holes, and said if she'd had more time . . . "But give me a minute and I'll find some others for you." She gave Max a serious stare.

"I can wait," I said, just as the TV reporter came on again, chic hair and cheeky smiles.

"They've found evidence that the girl was in the shaft. We've heard mention of a hard hat. Whether that is . . ."

Hard hat! At the bottom, in the tunnel! I had probably left footprints, leading right to Ye! He would be discovered! They'd capture him—or worse!

Turning to Max, I begged, "*Please* call the police! Tell them I'm safe!"

With Marlene standing behind him, tugging at her dress, Max gave me a long, patient look, wiggled his nose, and reached for the phone.

• • •

Before the cops came blaring up to the house, we saw it unfold.

After a few commercials about cars, shopping sprees, and the state lottery, there was the mine again, with more people, more police, more excitement in the air. We saw emergency lights swirling in the background, heard sirens, saw cops conferring. In vain I looked for Dillon and Dad. The reporter, obviously loving her job, introduced an important-looking man as the chief of police. She held the microphone to his face.

Despite the man's steely voice, he seemed camera shy. I heard the words, *calling search off*, and *juvenile's been found*.

"How is she?" asked the reporter, chasing the chief's cautious mouth with the mic. "Did she survive?"

". . . think she's all right . . . not saying . . . until her father . . ."

The reporter looked incredulous. "He hasn't been notified?"

"As we speak."

Without another word, the police chief pivoted and left the scene, while the woman and two other reporters hounded at his heels.

• • •

A few minutes later, the neighborhood erupted with lights, cameras, action.

Max and Marlene and I stood in the doorway. I fretted more about getting the gold back than getting my clothes, and while scheming to figure out how, Max said, "Looks like the Fourth of July."

The cops were arriving—two cars, blue lights flashing. Behind them, taking most of the street, roared a fire truck, red lights flashing. Behind them, an ambulance—more red lights. Behind that, a red luxury car with the reporter I'd seen on TV, in living color, taking the neighbor's driveway. And behind her, in a mud-spattered Jeep, came more reporters; they took the neighbor's yard. Last came the old workhorse, trailer in tow, tattered American flag on the antenna, Dad at the wheel and Dillon half out the window. They almost took the neighbor's mailbox.

And the neighbors, coming from all points of the compass, with yapping dogs and screaming kids, filled in the gaps.

Everyone got out at once—four cops, three firefighters, two emergency technicians, three reporters, my brother, and Dad—scrambling up to the house as if they ran a free-style competition. The youngest-looking cop made it first, blocking Dillon and Dad from advancing, and me from going to them. His face was flushed and blotchy, which I judged as overenthusiasm. He whipped out his notebook and addressed Max.

"You're Maxwell Warren?" he said, louder than necessary.

"That's right," murmured Max, in easy contrast. "I'm the one that called."

Then, adding triumph to his tone, he looked at me and said, "You must be Katrina Graham."

"Katlin," I said, and took this as my cue. I stepped forward, brushed past him and whoever else got in the way, enveloping them in gusts of aromatherapy and bubble bath, and went to Dillon and Dad. Bathrobe and all—or I should say, bathrobe and nothing. But thick as it was, I looked more Egyptian mummy than water sprite.

With the whole world gawking, we locked in a three-some embrace.

"Kat! Kat!" Dad kept saying, and Dillon searched my eyes, trying to learn what he could in one steady look. I wanted to tell him everything.

Everything, that is, except Ye. He would be my secret for a while. Our secret—Ye's and mine.

Everyone was looking me up and down as if I belonged in a sideshow. They saw the scrapes and bruises, the lump on my cheekbone. But they could also see me standing on my own two feet, clean (for the most part), and whole. The medics were standing by, ready to check me over. The reporters were chomping at the bits to question me. They had their gadgets out, recording and shooting.

"Miss Graham! How-did-you-end-up-here-is-there-another-way-out-how'd-you-get-past-everyone?"

"Miss Graham! Were-these-the-folks-who-rescued-you-do-you-know-each-other-what's-the-connection?"

I ignored them.

Then the same metallic voice I'd heard on TV broke up our hug. It was the chief of police. What I had taken for nervousness on the TV, was a stutter.

"M-m"—he slapped his holster—"M-Miss Graham, we need to take you to the hospital."

I turned to him and stared, while Dad echoed, "Hospital?"

"To see that she's all right."

Nodding to him in assurance, I said quickly, "I'm all right. Nothing broken." I gave them all a smile, then clamped my mouth shut: I had new reservations about my gold tooth.

"We need to be sure, M-m"—holster *slap* again—"Miss Graham."

"No," I insisted. "I'm good. Really."

"Katlin Graham . . ." The chief was not budging.

I took Dad's arm and gripped it tight.

"M-m"—*slap*—"Mister Graham—"

Dad was beginning to stir.

"—we have no choice," said the chief.

The line between Dad's eyebrows darkened. "What do you mean, no choice? You can choose to go now. She said she's OK."

The chief held up his hand. "I understand that, M-m"—*slap*—"Mister Graham. But you need to understand—"

"Understand what?" demanded Dad, in his weary-dad voice. "That my daughter's been missing since ten o'clock this morning? That she managed to escape without *your* help? That we've all been to Hades and back?" (Dad had this thing about using bad words. But hell isn't a bad word: It's a bad place.)

The scene reminded me of the time he felt challenged by the insurance agents, who kept fending him off, hemming and hawing, giving him . . . well, Hades. "Who's side are you on?" Dad would ask them. "What kind of protection is this? What've I been paying for all of these years?" It takes a lot to stir him up, but like a hibernating bear, once rudely wakened—watch out.

He was glowering.

The other cops closed in as if to rally around their chief, as if we were criminals, ready to run.

The police chief stood his ground. "To be blunt, M-m—"

"Mister," I said helpfully.

"—Graham, it's not just about you and your daughter—" A quick glance at me, then the reporters, then back to Dad. "It's also about the M-m"—*slap*—"Mollie Kathleen M-m—"

"Mine," I said.

"This is serious. Your daughter needs to be examined by the m-m—"

"Medics."

"Then we can complete our report—"

"To avoid complications," inserted the younger cop (whose name tag actually said young) obviously eager to be involved. "To avoid litigation . . ."

Litigation was the wrong word. Dad flinched—along with the police chief. Definitely the wrong word. Dad had had his fill of litigation. Now he was growling.

"So *that's* what this is about! Money!"

The younger cop nodded. "We have to be sure—"

"Harold!" said the chief, sharpening the steel in his voice. "I'll handle this."

Harold the Younger retreated and began scratching in his notebook.

Dad was just warming up. "Money! Let me tell you about money! If they sue—"

"You have it wrong," said the chief. "The m-m—" He glanced at me and I suggested, "Money?"

"—m-mine is concerned that you'll sue *them*."

Dad halted, eyebrows up, pondering this new thought.

"Now," the chief said, turning to me. "Would you like to come along with us?"

"She would not!" said Dad.

"M-m—" He looked at me again, but I shook my head. How was I to know what word he wanted?

"Graham," the chief said, bypassing the *m* word. "Back off everyone. Back off! Now . . . *Graham*, don't make me call the child protection service."

"Child protection service!" fumed Dad. "*I* am the child protection service! I'm her *father*!"

It was Marlene who provided intermission. She had come through the crowd unnoticed.

"Katlin," she said in her gentle, domesticated voice, "Your clothes are ready." She held out a clean, neatly folded stack. The jacket was on the bottom. "You can change in the house."

I studied her rainy day eyes, trying to tell what she knew. They told me nothing. Nothing I hadn't already known, nothing but compassion. I took the clothes (did they feel heavy?), making sure they stayed in a stack, wishing I could check the jacket, pat it to feel for the gold. But I dared not—not in front of everyone, specially the cops.

"Thank you, Marlene," I said, and risked dropping the clothes by giving her a one-armed hug. To Max I said, "Thank you, Max. Thank you for all you've done."

Leaning toward me as if to kiss my cheek, he whispered, "We had a daughter once. She was worth more than all the gold in the world."

—⟩⟨—

THAT EXPLAINED IT. IT EXPLAINED THE bathrobe. It explained why they'd been so kind, why I had no need to fret. Unless I had straight out misread them, the Warrens were making sure I was taking everything I'd arrived with.

Even if it included a mysterious, unbelievably large chunk of gold.

Now my dilemma was how to keep it from being discovered.

If I changed into my clothes, there was still the jacket, which belonged to the mine. I could stuff the rock into my jeans, but it was pretty big, and if they rushed me off to the hospital for a medical exam . . .

I didn't blame Dad for not wanting me to go. He had passed an extreme stress test, had just recovered his missing daughter, and simply wanted to retire with his family and get back to being normal. Whatever that was.

And back on the road.

. . .

The verbal skirmish between Dad and the police chief was still in progress, stutter and holster slap on one side, arm flings on the other, and since I had triggered the whole thing by refusing the exam, I felt responsible. Something had to give, before we all ended up on the most wanted list.

Here's how it was going:

dad: Don't I have the right to resist?

chief: I'm not arresting you.

dad: Then I resist.

chief: Then I'll have to arrest you.

dad: Arrest me for a non-arrest resist?

For the sake of truce, I was ready to give myself up. Though compared to the condition I could have been in—like, broken in *umph*-teen places or silent as the skeleton stretched out in Ye's cave—I didn't think I *needed* a medical check.

The emergency techs had been murmuring between themselves, and one of them got the chief's attention. With an apologetic look, she said, "Chief Huffman, Mr. Graham? We can examine her here. It won't take long. If she checks out all right—"

"Here?" shrieked Dad. "In front of all these people?"

I looked around at their faces: cops, reporters, neighbors, dogs, even an old gray cat in a window next door. All anxiously waiting.

"No, sir. In our unit. We're equipped." Without waiting for anyone's approval, she motioned to me. "Katlin, can you hold off getting into your street clothes? It would be easier—"

"OK," I said, clutching the bundle as if my life depended on it. I stepped between the chief and my dad and as calmly and cheerfully as I could, said, "Dad, it's all right. They can check me over." To reassure him—and myself—I added, "They won't find much."

Why would I be so lucky?

—⟩⟨—

A DESPERADO. THAT'S WHAT DILLON SAID he felt like, that he couldn't improve on the word.

"Desperate in Colorado," he said. "It's perfect."

It was stampede and gold rush rolled into one split second.

It was Calamity with a capital *C*.

As I stepped into the unit, everything white and antiseptic, one of the attendants reached for my bundle. I gripped it so tight—I don't know, I must have squeezed the gold out of it, or maybe it was jostled. However it happened, the scene was shown godzillion times on TV and the Internet for months afterward. Hundreds of millions of viewers and still counting.

Here it is:

A glorious gold nugget, lying on the blacktop, circled

by groping, human hands, hands of all ages and sizes and shapes and colors, all of them contorted, like the tentacles of an octopus ready to catch its prey. I think a dog's nose was in there, too, sniffing to beat the band.

One of those hands was Dillon's, shooting out from of the rest. He grabbed the gold, grappled with a few fellow fortune hunters, and took off running. He held his fist high the whole way, yelling, "Pretty paperweight! Pretty paperweight!"

How he came up with that is beyond me. Later, he explained, "At first, I thought souvenir, then fool's gold, but 'pretty paperweight' landed in my head and stuck."

Now I know a recipe for instant mob rule:

• Take lots of people.

• Throw in a gold rock.

. . .

Dillon made it to the car, scrambled in, slammed the door and hit the power lock. One man had his finger in the door when it slammed, and performed a waltz before yanking it out. Blood spurted onto the window, which Dillon sat beaming behind.

It was a good thing the cops were there, or I think we would have declared the car totaled without being in a collision. Explain *that* to the insurance company. The medics took a moment to bind the man's finger inside the ambulance, while he stood scowling at me.

After they checked all my vital statistics and treated my cuts and scrapes, they had Dad sign a release and said I was free to go. By then, the crowd had increased. The reporters were grouped on the front porch, interviewing Max and Marlene.

As Chief Huffman accompanied Dad and me to our car, I heard Max say, "You can't squeeze blood from a turnip." And I thought, *Good for you, Max—tell them nothing, the snoops.*

No. 3

EMPIRE MIRE

Cripple Creek, Empire Hotel. Sun—day of ~~rest~~ unrest. A night long on fatigue & short on sleep.

I haven't climbed out of bed. Pulled open bedside drawer to get my journal, saw a Holy Bible, & picked it up instead. Stamp on the cover says, "Placed by the Gideons." I closed my eyes, stuck my thumb into the pages, flopped book open, ran my finger down a page, & stopped. Opened my eyes. My finger was on a quote in Ecclesiastes (written by Solomon, wisest & wealthiest of kings): "There is a sore evil which I have seen under the sun, namely, riches kept by the owners thereof to their hurt."

What! Just what I needed. A prophecy of doom.

Or, to look on the bright side, a word to the wise.

Namely, get rid of your riches. Or, more namely, your chunk of gold.

I'm anything but wise. I'll go down in local history as the Cripple Creek Clod or the Touched-in-the-Head Tourist. To be wise:

- You don't go falling down mine chutes.
- You don't go stealing gold from unsuspecting dragons, specially the last one on Earth, who's sweet enough to

show you the way out, if, during a momentary lapse of wisdom, you fall down a chute.

- You don't cause an uproar (including cops, EMTs, reporters, old couples, kids, dogs, & a guy who splits open his finger in your car door).
- You don't keep riches (says the Holy Bible).

I laid my journal aside and stared at the blank TV screen.

So what was I supposed to do? Give the gold to the poor? *We* were the poor. Though you wouldn't know it at first glance. I mean, our clothes were worse for wear and our car was a scratch 'n' dent, but we weren't in rags and begging rides.

Not yet anyway.

On second thought, maybe you *would* know it at first glance. As of yesterday, when I stepped out of the medical unit for all the world to see, the holes in the knees of my jeans mouthed words when I walked, I kept covering the bald spot on my seat with my shirt, I wore butterfly-bandaged glasses with sand-blasted lenses— which the rescue workers had found and exchanged for the jacket—and my shoes had been waxed with Mollie Kathleen Muck.

As to our car, it was the perfect metaphor. Due to

the abuse it had seen time and again, and neglect, it featured an outbreak of dings and scratches, a gold front fender that matched the gold of my tooth (thanks to a poor frenzied deer and the fact that the parts yard had no match for the gray), a pitted windshield, and rusted wheel rims. Sometimes it wouldn't go in reverse. The fan belt whined.

Yep, just like me.

But thanks to Dad's new employer, at least we had enough for the trip. I lay in a comfortable bed in a historic hotel. We'd had a decent dinner in the lounge last night.

I burped in bed just thinking about it.

With a little imagination (the burp helped, too), I could still taste the tender rib eye and all those fries. I must have drunk a gallon of sarsaparilla, which is kind of like root beer. Dillon said the reason I thought it tasted so good was I had gone so long without food. He had barbecued shrimp, and said the reason *that* tasted so good was because it *was*. Dad did not indulge but had a glass of milk. He might have been suffering indigestion, or felt he deserved nothing more, blaming himself for what had happened.

To escape the mom-'n'-pop-arazzi—which was Dillon's term for those homegrown, camera-toting stragglers who wanted another glimpse of the gold or of me and my shadow—the cops had escorted us back to the hotel. Dad suspected it wasn't really for our safety, but to keep an eye on us. Dillon said it was definitely the gold. The chief had grilled him on it while I was in the ambulance. With the car window open just low enough for talk—Dillon explaining to the chief the window would stick in a stubborn down position if it went any lower—he showed him the paltry "gold sample" he had got on the tour. Which, by the way, had as much gold in it as a cloud has cotton candy. Since the chief hadn't seen my nugget to begin with—he was talking with Max at the time—he had no way to disprove it. But judging from all the excitement, he argued, it couldn't have been that rock. Why would a rock like that cause such commotion?

When Dillon related all this on our drive to the hotel, Dad asked him where the gold was, if it truly *was* gold, and where he had got it.

Before I could speak, Dillon said, "Sorry, Dad. I'm not telling."

That jerked a stare out of me.

Dad said, "What? I'm your father—remember?"

"I thought you were the child protection service," Dillon said smartly, then hung his head.

Dad fell into a meditative slump. That's when I

realized he was blaming himself. He had not protected
his child: He had let me wander off. There was much I
wanted to say, to tell him it was my fault, not his, that
he hadn't failed me, that what had happened was for our
good, that we could pay off our debts . . .

That, in particular, I wanted to say.

I looked questioningly at Dillon. Why had he hidden
the gold? What business was it of his?

It was *my* gold, for golly sake.

I glared at him. If I glared hard enough, maybe he'd
feel a hot spot on his head, like aiming the sun through a
magnifying glass.

It worked. He turned in the front seat to address Dad
and me. "In case they interrogate either of you, or both of
you, I won't say where I put the . . . rock. That way, you
won't have to lie."

Dad pouted and hit the horn—which, like the seat
adjustments and dome light and AC, doesn't work.
"Lie? Why would I lie about something I'm in the dark
on? Why would we be interrogated? Gold? Rock? What's
this all about?"

Dillon was eyeing me, while I looked from him to Dad
and back again, my tongue caressing my tooth. I guessed
it was my turn.

"Uh . . ." I mumbled, and gazed out the window as the town bumped by. "When we're back in our rooms, I'll tell you everything."

Well, not *everything*. Not about Ye. He was too incredible. Too unbelievable. They'd think I'd been knocked in the head one time too many. I liked the thought of keeping him secret. It made me feel part of something. Something vast and ancient, like dipping my toe into the cosmos. Telling about Ye would be betrayal.

"But, Dad," I said, to make up for what I *wasn't* saying, "money won't be a problem for a while."

His eye shone at me in the rearview mirror with what looked like a spark of hope.

. . .

As soon as we had entered the lobby, reporters sprang from every direction. Three, four, five in all, notepads in hand, firing questions, shooting pictures. Why they thought I was so newsworthy I couldn't guess. It only showed how pinched for a story they were.

Chief Huffman was still with us, striding along as though he was home on the range and we were his herd. "Later!" he boomed at the reporters, but it had no effect. As we hustled our way through, their questions hit us like hailstones. All about gold.

*Where'd you find the— Is it real— Whose is the—
Where is the— Can we see the— Gold, gold, gold, gold,
gold . . .*

It probably *was* a good idea that Dillon had hid the
gold.

While the chief strode to the front desk—I think he
was after our room numbers—Dillon dug into his pocket,
raised his arm high, and flipped a shiny penny behind
him. This caught the reporters off guard. And while they
stopped, mesmerized by its flashing, head over tails arc,
we darted up the staircase, down the hall, into Dillon and
Dad's room, and slammed the door.

———∙)(∙———

Whew, what a night. I just came in after telling D &
D my tale without giving Ye away. NOT easy.

Felt good leaving Ye out—but it was hard connecting
the dots & making it sound believable.

Here's how it went:

Somehow I groped my way in absolute darkness to
a hidden passage that led to a weedy field behind the
Warrens. In the cave, I'd picked up a rock that happened
to be solid gold & kept it. You couldn't see it, Dad said,
so how'd you know it was gold? That was tricky, until I

thought of saying, It was heavier. Heavier than what? Than the other rocks, I said. You picked up other rocks? To stack up as markers. Hmm, said Dad. D was quiet. It was smoother too, I said, & warmer. Did you feel any others that were heavier & smoother & warmer? Not really. But there may have been others? Maybe. You just happened to pick this one up. Yep. Maybe there are <u>many</u> more that you missed, & it wasn't a matter of finding this one rock, but picking up one out of many? You have a point there, I said. When I said that, the Q & A session was over. Dad gazed at the wallpaper, as if each flower would turn to gold. Dillon said nothing, just got up & put his ear to the door, listening to the hubbub downstairs.

I lay my journal on the Gideon Bible and closed the nightstand drawer.

How I ached, inside and out! Every muscle and bone in my body must have met rock. When the medic said I'd feel it in the morning, I had no idea. I reached for the ibuprofen samples they had given me and swallowed one dry. The thought of getting up, let alone packing my bag, was too much.

I stared at a stain on the window shade. There was

no flowered wallpaper in my room, no wallpaper at all. Dillon and Dad got that and twin beds; I got the double bed and the high slim window that faced the street. Last night—this morning actually, around one a.m., after journaling about Ye—I had pulled the shade down, not wanting to be wakened by the sun as early as I had been yesterday.

Yesterday. Had it been only twenty-four hours? It seemed like a year, a dragon's dream.

I looked at my travel clock: 8:32. The shade hardly kept the morning out; it now shone primrose gold. I stared at the stain, letting my thoughts drift, wishing for more sleep.

I always see faces or animals in random shapes like clouds or spills or clumps of leaves. Specially when I'm not wearing my glasses. As I stared, the stain became a face, and I knew the face. Mom's—her hair spread out as on a pillow. Like the last time I saw her. When I had bent to kiss her cheek and say goodbye.

The ache that I'd felt on that day filled my head again. *Oh, Mom! Do you know that I am gone? Do you miss my face, my voice, my hand? Can you still see the times we shared long ago, the ones I hold on to with all my heart? Like our tickle tests, when you were always the first to* laugh? Or the meteor shower, when we lay on the roof and counted ninety-four? Or our beach vacation, when I hid you with sand and Dad searched and searched . . .

What will become of you?

Will you be there when we come back?

Or will you slip away and turn to dust?

I kept staring at the stain.

It was no longer my mom.

It was a winged dragon. Ye had eclipsed her, like a bird across the sun.

Ye, I thought, *what will become of you? Will you live forever? Will the pearl, my pearl, Mom's pearl, Grandma Chance's pearl, give you never-ending life?*

Or will you slip away and turn to gold?

Then, like the optical illusion that appears as either a hag or a young woman depending on your outlook, the stain became Mom's face again. Then it was Ye—and back and forth it went.

Ye . . . Mom . . . Ye . . . Mom . . . Ye . . .

• • •

A rustle outside the door.

That got me out of bed. Stifling another moan, I went to the door and peered through the keyhole.

There stood a man, a few steps away, bent as if listening

or looking for something. He thrust his nose forward, like a rat. He was small and bowlegged and very tan—I could hardly read his features for his tan. His high-crowned hat, which was black with black feathers stuck in a snaky black band, and his snaky black boots, made up for his short stature.

Though my room radiator sizzled with heat, I shivered.

He turned as if he had felt my shiver and looked straight into my eye.

I almost fell back into bed—but I knew if I moved he'd see a change of light in the keyhole. And he'd be able to see me—all of me—but I couldn't see him. So I stayed, still as stone, my senses on high alert with the creepies crawling over my skin.

Our eyes locked.

His eyes were black and beady, two dark dots in his sun-darkened face. He got closer and closer. It was like one of those scary stories, where you wait for the end with your heart in your throat. My door was locked and chained, but it felt as though there was nothing between us.

He came even closer. I was peering through a microscope with the controls set on zoom.

The window shade flew up with a bang behind me and I whipped around, my shoulder whacking the door.

Blinking with fright and the harsh morning light, I stood there, hand on my heaving chest. Surely, there was no connection between the stranger and the shade. A change in temperature no doubt, probably from the rising sun, had caused it.

I waited a moment more, held my breath, then peeked through the keyhole again.

He was gone.

I plopped onto the bed and wrapped the blanket around me. Then, thinking better of it, I put on my glasses, limped to the window, and peered into the street.

There he was, his black hat bobbing behind a small black car. He glanced up at me, climbed into the car, and drove away. I noticed his license plate: I2I.

—❯❮—

A TAP ON THE DOOR.

"Kat!" Dillon's voice.

Just to be sure, I peered through the hole and saw his faded red shirt. I unlocked the door and opened it with the chain still in place. He was wearing his morning hair and an anxious look.

"Kat, you dressed?"

"Wait a minute."

I hurriedly dressed and let him in. He set a tall Styrofoam cup full of coffee on the nightstand.

"Since when do you drink coffee?" I asked.

"Since now." He took a sip. "Anyway, it's a latte—mostly milk. Want some?"

"No thanks."

"How'd you sleep?"

"OK. What there was of it."

He went to the window. "Nice view."

"I've hardly had a chance to enjoy it."

"Why's that?"

I told him about the black-hatted man, though it freaked me out describing the last part.

"I passed him in the lobby!" said Dillon.

"He was parked across the street," I said. "In a black sports car. I got the license plate, in case—"

"What was it?"

"Nothing, really. One-two-one."

"One-two-one," Dillon said musingly. "One to one . . . One hundred twenty-one . . ."

I stared at him. "Dillon, I just realized. Those weren't numbers, they were letters."

He went blank for a second, then said, "You mean, the letters *I*?"

I nodded slowly, trying to ignore a wave of nausea.

"Eye-to-eye," he murmured. "That's eek-o."

"Yeah."

"Grags."

"Grags?"

"Gross and gag."

We sat still for a moment, trying to make sense of it.

"Wait," I said. "He might have been after the gold."

"Might have."

"Dillon, where is it?"

He came over, took another sip from his cup, and sat by me on the bed. Coffee breath was definitely better than morning mouth. "Safe," he said simply. "Now you tell me something."

I blinked at him. There was something in his tone I didn't like.

"Kat, what really happened?"

"Huh? You mean that guy?"

"Not the guy. Your story."

"Story?"

"I think you know what I mean."

I put on my innocent girl face, which I had used so often last night I could have auditioned for Joan of Arc. "I don't think I know what *you* mean."

"Something's missing from it."

I studied his face, noticing the bit of crusted sleep in his eye, the whiskers starting to introduce themselves. He looked old. "What would be missing, brother?" I said. The brother thing usually works.

"That's what I'm asking you."

Suddenly feeling the pain pill kick in, I got up and tossed my pajamas into my bag.

"Kat, if you were certain, really certain, that it was gold you'd found—after all, you pocketed it—why didn't you feel around for more?"

"Well . . ." I stammered. I shrugged a shoulder. "I didn't want to be greedy . . ."

He stared at me.

"And . . . I wanted to keep going . . ."

He kept staring.

"That nugget was heavy enough . . ."

Kept staring.

"I was in a lot of pain."

He acknowledged this with a nod.

Why was I so unwilling to let him in on my secret? What difference would it make whether he knew about Ye or not? On the other hand, if he didn't believe my edited story, why would he believe the unabridged version?

I tried a different tack. "Dillon, you want more gold, don't you? Just like Dad. You think there's more."

"I think there's more, and I think there's more to your story."

"What I'd like to know," I said, turning my volume up a notch, "is why you're keeping it hidden. You snatched it up and think it's yours now, don't you?"

He flinched, as if he'd had a sudden pain.

I stuck out my palm. "Just hand it over."

He stared at my scratches and bandaged thumb. He frowned over something and looked up at me. Except for a drop of bright blue, his eyes are just like Mom's, a blend of sadness and secrecy.

"You *don't* have to keep it hidden," I said, attempting a hardness I didn't feel. "The cops aren't after us."

As soon as I said that, there were voices in the hall. A knock on the door. I thought of the man in the black hat, and shuddered. I shook my head warningly at Dillon.

Another knock. It wasn't my door after all, but Dad's.

Dillon peeked through the keyhole.

"What is it?" I whispered.

He motioned me to be still.

One voice was Dad's. The other—I had heard it before: Chief Huffman's. Plus another I didn't recognize, higher pitched. Was it the mystery man's? I glanced out the window: no black car.

"Let me see!" I whispered, and nudged him aside.

He put his ear to the door while I looked. I saw a beefy hand—Chief Huffman's—handing Dad's hand a sheet of paper. Dad's hand was shaking, from either fear or rage. Dad wasn't one to show fear. The only time I'd seen him show fear was when Mom lay in the hospital, her head wrapped up, her face dead, her body hooked to tubes, a monitor beeping.

Rage, then.

"Search warrant!" Dad was saying. "Not on your life!"

"I'm sorry, Mr. Graham." The chief's stutter was gone. "We have reason to believe you're concealing stolen property."

"Stolen property! Whose?"

"The Mollie Kathleen's."

"I'm calling my attorney!"

Dillon and I looked at each other: Dad didn't have an attorney—he couldn't afford one.

"You have that right, Mr. Graham. We still need to search your room."

Dillon nudged me aside and took my place.

I tried to be patient, but my worries were mounting.

Where had Dillon put the gold? Would they find it? He was just a kid, and these men were experts. They knew where people hid things. Loot, drugs, weapons—they couldn't be fooled.

Yet, whatever the outcome, I appreciated Dillon's intent. I looked with admiration at the back of his head, his rumpled hair—dear brother. If Dad had known where the gold was, he'd have given it away, right off. All they'd have to do was watch his eyes. It would be like saying "Warmer, warmer—hot!" in the game of hide the thimble.

Maybe there was a chance. Maybe the gold wasn't here at all, but in the car, or the men's room off the lobby, or . . .

On Dillon himself.

Good thing they hadn't come here.

Dillon leaped up as a knuckle rapped the door.

—⟶⟩⟨⟵—

DILLON LEANED AGAINST THE WALL, ANKLES crossed, sipping his coffee. He said to me, "Aren't you going to open it?"

I stared at him. "Should I?"

"Of course. They're the law."

I unlocked the door and loosened the chain. Chief

Huffman towered in the doorway, and a woman in uniform stood with him.

Dad, craning his neck from behind them both, said, "I'm sorry, honey, but—"

"Miss Graham," said the chief. "How are you today?"

I was speechless.

He paused when he saw Dillon, then continued. "We're here on official business. This is Officer Hance." The woman nodded to me, poker-faced.

"We're here to search your room," said the chief, and he held up the paper I'd seen through the keyhole.

Despite my daze, I caught some of the words. *U.S. District Court . . . Teller County . . .* Affidavit and Application for a Search Warrant . . . *U.S. Magistrate.* At the bottom was an ominous signature as tangled as the gold-tarnished mess I had got us into.

They entered the room and began their search. I went to the window and gripped the sill to keep from trembling; Dillon slouched against the wall; Dad stood in the doorway, taking it in with a pale, grim face. They lifted the pillows, blankets, mattresses; looked under the bed, felt around the bed frame. They turned the stand upside down and right side up, and emptied the drawer of the bible, my journal, the pain pills, and the tobacco tin.

The chief got serious about the tobacco tin. He tried prying it open without success. He shook it, asking, "What's in it?"

"Dirt, probably," I said.

"Where'd you get it?"

"In a field where my horse used to run." I'm sure he would have kept it if I'd told him the truth.

He passed the tin on to the woman, who got it open with her fingernail file and handed it back. He eyed the black bits inside and sniffed. Dirt, probably.

When he flipped through my journal, I gasped. One look at the last entry and he'd know. "That's my novel!" I said.

He squinted at a page on which I'd copied a poem by William Butler Yeats—"The Folly of Being Comforted"— after Mom's accident. "'Your well beloved's hair has threads of grey'?" he read loudly, and handed me the journal.

I clutched it to my chest and exchanged glances with Dad, who had a momentary slip of grief in his eyes. Dillon was staring at the floor.

They went on searching: the upholstered chair, unzipping its cushion, prodding every inch of padding; the TV, which was mounted on brackets high in a corner; the space behind the radiator; peering into the tiny closet, which was bare; the tieback curtains on either side of me standing at the window. They went through my travel case, examining each pouch and pocket, and did the same with my clothes. Officer Hance raked her fingers through my underwear, which should have embarrassed me.

I was feeling anything but. I was beginning to share Dad's rage, and feel pride, too. Pride for Ye. For it was his gold, not the Mollie Kathleen's. The fact I had taken it from him was irrelevant.

They had no right to claim it.

I was proud of Dillon. He leaned against the wall as though this happened every day. I couldn't help thinking how I'd be reacting if I knew where the gold was, and again admired his foresight.

They searched the bathroom: I heard the shower curtain rustle, the toilet tank lid rattle, the cabinet door creak. I think they even removed the plastic light cover.

The toilet flushed, and Chief Huffman, his face as steely as his voice, came out of the bathroom and said to Dillon, "Now you."

Dillon took a casual drink, set the cup on the stand, and raised his arms for a pat down. As though *that* happened every day, too. I had no idea they'd be so thorough. The chief's thick hands worked up and down

Dillon's thin body, including places I hadn't seen Dillon himself touch.

Before I could think, Officer Hance was doing the same to me. I automatically raised my arms as Dillon had done, my journal in one hand. I was tempted to bop her stubby head with it when she got personal with me.

"Ha," she said when she felt the dice in my pocket. "What's this?"

"Not gold," I said.

"Remove it."

I did, explaining I carried the dice for luck, and her face slid into a smirk. When Dad said "I'll take those," she examined them, shrugged, and gave him the dice.

At last, the humiliation was over.

The officers stood silent in the middle of the room, the chief frowning at Officer Hance, her poker face gazing at him.

I was bursting with delight.

The chief then set his eyes on me and cracked a long-time-no-see kind of smile. I realized this was where he belonged, out of the range of microphones and cameras and crowds: He had no stutter and holster slap.

"Miss Graham—" he began.

I blurted, "I have the right to remain silent, don't I?"

His smile vanished. He jerked his head at Officer Hance, made one last scan of the room, and they left.

—⇥⇤—

DAD CLOSED THE DOOR BEHIND THEM. "Well," he said, sighing. "Maybe that's the last of it."

Uh-uh.

There was a rap on the door and Chief Huffman poked his head inside. "For your information, we're checking your car."

"Our car!" said Dad, looking at Dillon in panic.

"It's unlocked," said Dillon. "Nobody'd steal that junker."

"Locked or not," said the chief. "We're checking it." He shut the door.

"It's cool, Dad," said Dillon, and shook his head as if to say, *It's not in the car.*

Dad nodded slowly. "All right. Let's pack." He went back to his room.

I sagged to the floor, exhausted, but pleased.

Dillon came over and offered me his coffee again. "You might want this."

"Dillon, I do not like coffee."

"Neither do I."

"What?"

"I hate coffee."

"Then why—"

"Take it. But hold on."

Puzzled, I took it. "Hey," I said, nearly dropping it. "It's heavy. Really heavy."

"Yep," he said. "Heavier than the others. Smoother, too, and warmer."

"Dillon!"

He left me grinning like a Cheshire cat.

——⟩⟨——

AS I REPACKED THE UNPACKING THE COPS had done, Dillon came back in. He traveled light, with his knapsack slung across his back.

"Still in there," he said, lifting the cup of coffee, which I had set on the stand.

I nodded, smiling. "It's an awesome hiding place. Right smack in the open." I tucked my journal into a side pocket and zipped it up.

"Dad's on the phone with the Home," Dillon said. (The Home was what we called the place where Mom stayed.)

Anxious to hear some news about her, I said, "Any-thing . . . different?"

"I don't think so. The usual catching up. How about a bite to eat?"

"When's checkout?"

"Noon."

I picked up the travel clock—10:07—and snapped the lid shut. "You know, Dillon," I said, eager to forget the stranger, the cops, the drama. Everything, that is, but Ye. "We can still make it. Last night, I figured the miles and the time—three days—to get to San Francisco."

"Yeah, we can make it, Kat." He paused for emphasis. "If we don't have any more detours."

. . .

Bypassing the hotel restaurant, we went into the street. Casinos, antique and gift shops, jewelry stores, a small museum, trinkets in storefront displays—everything was geared toward tourism. We found a local-yokel café, ordered pastries and juice at the counter, and cozied up to a table at the front window, where a cat was dozing on a sunny ledge and a newspaper lay scattered.

Dillon devoured half his apple pie before he started up again. "Kat, why are you holding out on me? Did you or did you not steal the—" He glanced at the patrons nearby and left it unfinished.

I took a long drink of my cranberry juice, set it down, and said, "Yes . . . and no."

He blew out his breath in exasperation. "Yes and no. That's like saying you're lying and telling the truth."

"Isn't that what we usually do?"

"That would be a half-truth. Which would also be a half-lie."

"I mean, without realizing it. We don't one hundred percent of the time tell one hundred percent of the truth, do we? We're not one hundred percent knowledgeable about everything in order to always, one hundred percent of the time, tell it exactly—"

"One hundred percent," he said smartly, raising his index finger.

"—one hundred percent the way it is. Take that newspaper, for instance—"

He began gathering the pages.

"I don't mean literally, Dillon."

"I do." He started putting the pages in order.

"Do you think everything written in there is one hundred percent true? No way. Reporters are notorious for getting things wrong."

"That's the truth," he said with an extreme head nod.

I knew he was mocking me, but I wanted to make a point that was becoming clearer in my mind as I spoke. "They usually get quite a bit wrong. Remember when—"

"Kat—" he said. His eyes had got big, but I thought he was still jeering me.

"Remember when that—"

"Kat—"

OK, maybe he'd found an example to prove my point, so I allowed him the interruption. He folded the paper with the front page up and slid it over.

Little Girl Lost Finds Gold

CRIPPLE CREEK — A twelve-year-old girl was lost for more than two hours yesterday after falling down an abandoned chute in the Mollie Kathleen Mine, causing the mine to be shut down indefinitely. The girl suffered only minor injuries and miraculously found her way out. It is not clear how the incident happened, but a spokesperson for the mine said they believe she strayed from her tour group, which included her family, and entered a sealed area some distance from the trail. "We have reason to think this may not have been accidental," the spokesperson said, but did not expound.

After the girl was located in a neighboring home, several witnesses claim to have seen her pass a large gold nugget to her brother, who then sped away. The father of the girl, Howard Graham of Richmond, Virginia, was heard to have said he was in financial difficulty. He argued with the police over liability issues. "These people are gold-crazed," one witness said. "The girl even has a gold front tooth."

The current price of gold is at $835 an ounce.

The Mollie Kathleen was once one of the world's greatest-producing gold mines. Production stopped in 1961, and in the last several decades the mine has been one of Cripple Creek's unique tourist attractions, taking as many as 400 visitors a day a thousand feet down to explore its depths.

"Kat," said Dillon. "Your mouth's wide open."

I promptly shut it.

I was the girl with the gold tooth. I was the girl with the gold nugget. I was the *little* girl.

"Front page news," said Dillon. "Sunday edition. Congratulations."

I really should not have been stunned. After all, this was obviously big news for a small town. Still, I never dreamed I'd be in the papers.

"You've had your fifteen minutes of fame."

"More," I said meekly.

"Much more. And I bet—this is a betting town, isn't it? I bet you'll have more than you can stand before it's over."

"What do you mean?"

"Look at the story. They're questioning motives: People are putting one and one and one together." He picked up a sizable crumb from his plate and placed it on the table. "One. You just happen to fall down a chute and emerge, on your own, with a huge hunk of gold." He put another crumb alongside the first. "One. Your dad is overheard saying how cashed out we are." Another crumb. "One. We're 'gold-crazy.'" He gazed outside for a minute. "It's serious."

"Dillon," I said, rising from my chair, trying to make it *unserious*. "The time. We'd better go. Dad—"

He reached over and took the paper from me, folded it carefully, and set it between us. "Kat, not yet. Sit down. It's ten to eleven. Dad can wait."

"But we need to get on the road. Checkout time doesn't mean we should—"

"The dark cowboy," he said quietly, as though he was reading a sign outside the window. "Eye-to-Eye."

I turned my head to look.

"Look at me, Kat," he said.

I looked at Dillon.

"Did you see him?"

I nodded.

"OK. Like I said, Dad can wait."

——❯❘❮——

HE MADE HIMSELF COMFORTABLE BY stretching his scarecrow legs and propping his feet on the ledge, which gave him the advantage of facing the window naturally. The cat slept on, though her tail twitched. I took another look as I adjusted my chair, and wondered how our spy—or whoever he was and whatever he was up to—could keep his hat from smothering his face in that low little car.

"The rock," said Dillon, in his getting-down-to-business voice. "Tell me."

"I picked it up. As I said."

"Stole it."

I shrugged.

"And didn't steal it."

I shrugged.

He said nothing, just tried stacking the crumbs on top of one another. I knew he was waiting for an explanation. Maybe if I said just enough, just a little more, he'd stop bugging me.

So, in a monotone, not wishing to call attention to any potential eavesdroppers, I said, "When I picked up the . . . *hmm*, you know, I wasn't thinking in terms of *stealing*. I mean, I was how far under the earth? And here was this *hmm*." True, so far.

I stopped, trying to replace the real picture in my mind with a pretend one.

"Here was this *hmm*," Dillon echoed. "As though you knew ex-act-ly what it was—"

All I could do was shrug.

"—*in* the dark." He grabbed the newspaper and snapped the table with it. "I'm beginning to think this article is true after all. You knew *just* what you were doing. Robbed the Mollie Kathleen reserve for all I know."

"Dillon! It was an accident! I fell! See?" A bit of saliva came out on "*see*," and I shoved my hurt hands in front of his face. Then I glanced around.

People were staring at us, amused, curious, puzzled.

But Dillon was staring at my hands. His face went pale. He said hoarsely, "I knew I had missed something."

I took one look at my hands, gasped, and plunged them into my lap. "I . . . I . . ."

The sadness in his eyes darkened.

"I . . . lost Mom's ring."

He whispered, "How could you?"

"Dillon, I feel bad enough already. You don't have to—"

He was shaking his head in disbelief.

"Dillon, stop it."

He kept shaking his head.

People were still staring.

I calmed myself and tried to smile at him, but he'd gone rigid, staring at me, just staring, along with everyone else in the room and in the whole world.

"Well," I said lightly, scooting back my chair. My feet felt like lead. "See you later."

His stare was infuriating.

"I don't have to tell you everything," I said, keeping my voice low and maintaining an awkward smile. "You're not my conscience. You're my poor, skinny brother."

I stood up—not hastily, though I kicked his shin in

the process—and acted as if I were making a friendly departure.

He stood up, too, taller than I, gripping the newspaper as if to beat me with it. "OK." He was trying to keep from breathing hard. "You can pay your own way from now on, with the stolen *hmm* I hid, that would no longer be yours if I hadn't. They'll probably take you in for questioning anyway. Kicking and spitting." He leered at me. "And be a nice rich sister and buy more food to put on your poor, skinny brother's bones."

He walked out before I could move.

—⊰⊱—

GOLD HAS DEATH IN IT. IT'S IN ALL THE stories. The death of saints, sinners, pirates, Pony Express riders.

It's also the death of dragons.

What would people think if they knew that? Would they build special cemeteries? Shrines? Mausoleums? Would they construct gold dragons? Worship them with sacrifices, burn incense, chant prayers?

Holy, holy, holy! Lord Gold Almighty!

Would all the stories be retold? Midas and Scrooge and Long John Silver?

Or would it make any difference at all?

I had these thoughts as I walked back alone.

What I was really doing was trying to ignore Mom's pearl. But there it was, floating before my face. *You shouldn't have, shouldn't have, shouldn't have. You care more for a dragon than you do your own mother. She means that little to you.*

I don't know what had come over me, there in the tunnel. I had been in a trance. I don't even remember Ye taking the pearl. I think I shut my eyes. When I looked, it wasn't there. He must have swallowed it that quick.

How could I explain that to Dillon? Mom meant everything to him. He couldn't even say the word *Mom*, he hurt so much.

Mom meant everything to me.

So, how does that work? How could I care that much for her and that much for a dragon at the same time? Did I give half my heart to each? Or did my heart swell bigger to make room for both? I also thought the world of Dillon and Dad. Does your heart keep swelling to make room for all the loves you have through life, until it swells so big it bursts, and you die?

When I passed Eye-to-Eye's car, he was gone—he

may have followed Dillon for all I knew. Dangling from his mirror was a chain with a gold cross.

Because of Ye, wherever I go, wherever I look, I notice gold. Gold catches my eye like flames. Flames flashing from a woman's ears. Flashing from a man's neck. Flashing from the lettering on a loan office window.

All these little fires. It's like living with a horrible secret you can't put out.

Whether or not people change their view of gold, I am sure of one thing: Greed will never change.

I picture greed as a devouring beast, like the one I conjured up in the mine, the one that scared the scream out of me. Greed is the opposite of Ye. It has so many arms, groping about like tentacles, you can't count them; its bulk is covered in a hairy black gloom; it stinks to high heaven and creeps across the land like a shadow or a disease.

It *is* a disease: It burrows into your blood and creeps down your fingers and dilates your pupils.

Greed or need, I made up my mind: I would take the gold back to Ye. Whether he lived a day or an eternity, the gold was his. The cops wouldn't get it. The mine wouldn't get it.

No one would get it.

As I neared the hotel, I plotted my plan. I would persuade Dad to take me to the Warrens before leaving Cripple Creek. We'd stand in the yard and I'd say my goodbyes, then I'd excuse myself and run to the outhouse before anyone could stop me. I'd crawl through the hole and through the tunnel and toss the gold in. I'd call Ye's name. He may hear me, he may not—but he'd eventually find it.

I felt better already. I'd thrown worry to the wind.

——◦}◦{◦——

WORRY BLEW RIGHT BACK.

My door was open at the end of the hall. Open just enough for a snake to slip through.

Dillon and Dad's was shut.

Fingering the key in my pocket, I distinctly remembered locking my door on the way out.

Could it be the dark stranger?

Chief Huffman?

The gold! I had left it submerged in the coffee. Dillon and I had gone out together, and since it didn't seem to worry him, I hadn't given it a thought.

Approaching the door cautiously, I heard movements inside, humming like a hornet's nest. As I was about to peer in, a man came flying out, knocked me against the wall, and another man followed. The dark stranger! He tackled the first man, who went down on the chair cushion he clutched, and together they rolled down the hall.

A feather floated in front of my face, black with orange flecks, along with rustic-smelling cologne and something at least 80 proof.

Eye-to-Eye's hat was off and he was straddling the back of the other intruder, a long-haired man in ice-blue jeans and a white T-shirt, who snorted and squirmed. From out of nowhere, Eye-to-Eye yanked a rope and, quicker than a finger snap, tied the man's wrists to his ankles. Then he leaped up, saying, "Ye-haw!"

As he turned to retrieve his hat, which lay just beyond my feet, Dillon and Dad came up the stairs, astonishment and fear on their faces.

Dad yelled, "Hey!" and bounded forward.

I don't know what he would have done, but here was his daughter, and here were two thugs, and he wasn't going to have me mauled.

Swiftly grabbing his hat, Eye-to-Eye pulled a card from the inside band and offered it to Dad, saying, "Ain't you never seen nobody hog-tied?"

Dad looked at the card, looked at him, looked at the captive on the carpet, and looked at me. "Are you all right?" he asked.

I nodded firmly. "I'm all right."

Dad said to Eye-to-Eye, "What is this? What's going on?"

Eye-to-Eye grabbed the man's hair and thrust his face toward us. His face was nothing out of the ordinary— just plain-Jane, Joe-homeowner vanilla. Maybe *this* was the face of greed. Not a monster, just a guy off the street. Well, almost. As I looked into his eyes, I saw how hollow they were, like staring into drinking straws.

"Business first," said Eye-to-Eye. "Dude's breachy."

"Excuse me?" said Dad.

"Breachy. He's known for breakin' out." He tipped his hat, gripped the man's hair tighter, and dragged him down the hall.

Never have I heard such a colorful string of cussing— before that time or since—particularly when they hit the stairs. You could tell how many steps there were—I winced at every count: sixteen total.

We examined the man's card.

REX HAVICK
Private vigilante

civil & criminal cases / personal protection
surveillance / strictest confidentiality
licensed, bonded, & insured

=≈}{≈=

"THIS IS JUST THE BEGINNIN'," SAID REX. HIS
raised eyebrows put hound dog furrows in his forehead.
He had removed his hat respectfully, and his close-
cropped hair matched the tan of his skin. With his black
hat off, his eyes were the color of molasses.

He had returned in no time, and now sat on the
radiator under my window, which gave him not only a
view of the street but the highest position. Dad sat in the
stuffed chair, after having put it and its cushion back in
place, and Dillon and I sat on the box springs of the bed.
I clutched my bag on my lap, hastily packed for the third
time.

My room looked like a hurricane had swept through.
The bathroom door had a hole punched in it the size

of a fist, the mattress slumped against a wall, and the nightstand lay on its side.

Rex had apologized, saying, "Comes with the turf. You mess with someone, things get messy." Then he'd added reluctantly, as though he would have rather taken full claim for the damage, "But it wasn't all me."

As soon as we had entered the room, I noticed the coffee cup was missing, and yelped. Not looking my way, Dillon put his finger to his lips. I immediately went through my heap of belongings to see that my journal was safe, and it was.

"Yup," said Rex, surveying the room. "Keepin' the law . . . minus the order." He explained that he had been on the man's tail since the rumor of gold hit town. "That joker and me goes back a ways. He's the type that thinks crime pays so you gotta show 'em what the pay is."

He cracked his knuckles and I thought, *Broken ribs.*

"Crazies," he said. "You get a little fame, a little fortune maybe"—a sidelong glance at me—"you get crazies of all kinds scratchin' at your door." He leaned forward. "This is just the start."

Dad shifted uncomfortably, which meant he was about to speak. He looked at his watch. "Well," he said, "the crazies will have to keep scratching. They won't get anything from us." (Dillon and I exchanged looks.) "We'll be leaving shortly."

Rex held up a hand. "The cops'll have a few questions."

I rolled my eyes. Not again! I'd had it up to here with the cops. I said, "We've already—"

Dillon cut me off. "Mr. Havick—"

"Rex, please."

"Mr. Rex. How do we know you're not one of the crazies?" He let that sink in for a second. "How do we know this isn't your way of getting into the room without getting caught? How do we know you and that other guy aren't a team and just put on a command performance? How do we know you don't have the gold?"

Rex was grinning. Except for a tiny chip in the shape of a horseshoe on a front tooth, his teeth were perfect and white. "If I needed a partner, it wouldn't be that cow pie! Pardon the French Canadian. It'd be somebody coyote smart, like yourself."

"Flattery," Dillon said in his driest voice.

"What may be flattery is the fat honest truth." Rex darted his eyes to the street. "Huffman'll vouch for me."

"We've met Huffman," said Dillon. "He's not so clever that you couldn't fool him, either." He spoke with the confidence he had gained from his disappearing gold trick. But had it disappeared for good?

Dillon said, "Mr. Tex—"

"Rex."

"Tell me some more truth—skinny or fat, whatever. Was there a cup of coffee in this room when you stepped in on the French Canadian cow pie?"

Rex was still grinning. "I like that," he said. He dropped his grin. "Coffee cup . . . No, don't think so. There's trash in the bathroom. You could check that."

I beat Dillon to the bathroom and fell to my knees. The trash was mine, of course, and there was the cup.

Empty.

IT SEEMED NO MATTER HOW I TRIED, MY plans always fell like a house of cards.

The gold was gone.

Just like Mom's pearl.

I thought I was stuck with Chief Huffman for life. He walked in looking like he was trying not to look bored. Huffman and Harold and the uniformed lady: It was like the king, queen, and jack repeatedly popping up in your opponent's hand.

When the cards were down, it looked like this:

Rex, ever the vigilante with an eye out for trouble, had been trailing this man, alias the Ghost, nicknamed Earp (not Wyatt, but *earp* as in, Pazz me the—*earp!*—bottle), who'd been trailing us from the evening before. While Dillon and I were in the café and Dad was loading the car, Rex had followed the man to the hotel and to my room. The Ghost had convinced the housekeeping woman it was *his* room she had cleaned, and she had moved down the hall. Rex burst in as the man was rifling the room. They tussled, Rex put the hole in the bathroom door where the man's face had been a split-whisker before, the man dove for the chair cushion, and that's when I showed up. Meanwhile, Dillon had joined Dad at the car, and together they had returned to look for me.

Dad asked Rex the question I was trying to avoid. "Did he get what he was after?"

Chief Huffman was quick. "What was he after?"

"You tell me," said Dad, equally quick. He and the chief had a staredown, in which Dad was working hard at the fine art of firmness.

The chief broke the stare by saying, "I think that's for Katlin here, or Dillon, to tell." He was playing his cards carefully. "What was he after?"

We played dumb.

The chief turned to Rex. "Havick? Any ideas?"

Rex removed his hat and rubbed his stubble. "Usually, it's somethin' valuable," he said, playing innocent. "Jewelry or cash." He cut his dog eyes at me. "You didn't have none, did you, darlin'?"

I stuck my hands in my pockets and shook my head.

Chief Huffman cleared his throat. "Let's put it this way, then. Is anything missing?"

Before I could think up an answer, Rex asked, "What'd your search of the Ghost turn up?"

Harold the Younger spoke out of turn, saying, "Nothing at all," earning another notch on Chief Huffman's nightstick, I was sure.

"Harold!" the chief growled, then asked Rex, "Did you pat him down?"

"I did, and just like Harold here, found nothin'."

So. The man hadn't taken the gold. Or if he had, he'd hidden it fast. I looked at Rex, who was fidgeting with his hat. He had a spark in his eye. Was he telling all he knew? Could it be that he had taken it himself? I mulled this one over, knowing that corruption wears badges sometimes.

Dillon was thinking hard—I can always tell by the half smile on the left side of his face. Did he know where the gold was? Had he somehow hidden it again without my knowledge?

Did anyone know? Could anyone be trusted?

As Chief Huffman and his posse filed out the door, the chief beckoned Rex with a jerk of his head.

Rex took a look out the window and donned his hat. "So long, folks. Like I said, this is just the beginnin'."

"WHAT'S HE MEAN BY THAT?" I ASKED DAD when Rex was gone.

The answer came as a made-for-TV voice crooned outside the room, "A-a-and here she is! The gold-toothed girl!"

A TV camera peeked around the doorway, a young man came with it, and a small crowd collected behind him, cramming the hall.

"It's confirmed then?" asked the voice, a voice I'd heard somewhere before. "Mr. Graham? It was gold the thief was after?"

A face that matched the voice, lipsticked and rouged and gold-crested, sprouted from behind the man behind the camera. It was the reporter I'd seen on TV and at the Warrens, who drove the red luxury car.

She must have taken Dad off guard with her warbling, for he took a step back, fumbling his words.

"I . . . there was a . . . you see . . ."

"May I come in, Mr. Graham? You've been through so much, I know. I think you deserve to tell your side of it." She wasn't waiting for an invitation, but advanced while she spoke and began closing the door behind her. This raised a protest from the onlookers.

"If you all keep quiet while I conduct this interview . . ." she said to them.

They murmured agreeably, and she left the door open. Clearly, she was set on commanding the situation, sink or swim.

She swam, smilingly. "Mr. Graham, Kathleen—"

"Katlin," I said with my mouth nearly shut. Why she irked me I wasn't sure, but I was sure she was up to no good. If this was journalism—

"Of course. I'm Rose Robbins, KOLT-TV." She gave me a firm but feminine handshake, and I predicted her fingernails were thorns in disguise.

Dad offered her the chair.

"I'll stand, thank you. I won't take much of your time, which, I understand, is short."

How she knew that, I could only guess. Perhaps she

had seen our packed bags in the car. So far, all of her shots had hit something. One had hit Dad's voice box: He was as mute as mud.

"Kathleen, may I start with you?" Again, she didn't wait for an answer but dove right in. "Tell me: How did it feel to fall down a shaft in the darkness? You didn't have any light, did you?"

I looked to Dad for a last call for help. Too late: He had taken the chair himself, in silent submission. I think he was on the point of collapse. I looked to Dillon, hoping he'd come to my rescue, but he had blended into the background, perhaps brooding over this whole mess, specially me losing Mom's ring. I wasn't in any mood to spill my story, but the camera was aimed at me, and an audience was waiting. I had to do something.

I said, "It wasn't exactly a walk in the park, I can tell you."

"Yes," Rose responded. "Tell us, please. It was a walk in the *dark*, wasn't it?"

Yep—thorns all right, underneath her pink petals. Well, I could scratch, too. "A stumble in the dark." I said. "A rumble, tumble, jumble."

With a sly smile in her eye and her voice, she said, "Now, that's an apt description. As you stumbled, rumbled, tumbled, and . . . what was that other word?"

I was beginning to hate her. "Fumbled," I said forcefully.

"*Jumbled* in the dark, that far underground, what kind of thoughts did you have? How did you feel?"

"I had deep thoughts and I felt with my hands."

A few snickers from the hallway, and the camera panned the crowd. Dad squinted at me as if his daughter had become a complete idiot. Dillon didn't look at me at all.

"Is that how you found the gold? By feeling with your hands?"

Blam! Double-barreled, first shot. But a miss. I'd expected something like that, and figured she had another cartridge waiting. What she didn't know was that I'd been through this already with Dillon and Dad. I wasn't falling into that trap.

"Did I say anything about gold?" I asked.

"You don't have to, Kathleen. We've all seen it."

I raised my head. "Then why do you ask?"

"How you *knew* it was gold," she said. "And *where* you found it."

The camera was back on me, zooming.

I raised my head higher. "The how and the where is not *your* business."

"So it *was* gold you found," she said triumphantly. "Not a *pretty paperweight*."

Blam! Right in the face. And I'd tossed her the target myself. The silence that followed was the post-gunshot kind, which leaves your ears ringing, your eyes batting smoke, and your heart one beat short. I blinked through the smoke into Dillon's territory, but he was playing dead.

The camera was now on Rose, who beamed through the lens and right into the homes and faces of a wide-screen TV-land throng.

"Real gold, folks," she chirped. "One of the biggest gold nuggets on record."

I stopped blinking and collected myself. I pointed my chin at her. "How do you know that?"

She ignored the remark. "The Mollie Kathleen will be proud."

"Where is it?" I persisted.

The camera swiveled to me and I swiveled to meet it. All right, then. I would conduct this interview. I would work the camera and wrap up the show. I sharpened my pitch and pressed the issue. "Is it sitting on some bigwig's desk? Are they divvying up the spoils? Wouldn't you love to have some, Rose?"

Wide-eyed, she declared, "Oh, who wouldn't?"

Narrowed-eyed, I stood up, gripping my bag. "That's what's wrong with your world."

"What is, Katlin?"

Picturing Ye's scorn, I said with gritted teeth, "Greed."

I headed for the doorway. I'd had enough. It was time to usher this Rose Parade back out to whatever feeding trough it had strayed from. The herd in the hall parted willingly for me, and I hoped they would close the gap, corralling Rose and her cinematographer. Dillon and Dad would have to squeeze through somehow.

From behind me wafted her voice, melodic and clear. "Well, folks. You got it from the horse's mouth. Or I should say, the cat's. That's what's wrong with our world. Greed . . ."

I plodded on—past faces mirthful, mocking, confused, dumbfounded.

". . . something our little gold-toothed lamb knows nothing about. Not in *her* world. Funny how she and her family held on to their lie as long as they could."

I descended the stairs, one hot jolt at a time.

"It's not *their* gold," she taunted, following me. "*They* didn't take it."

I reached the lobby.

"You can't help but wonder," she crowed above the

crowd. "Mom's probably pacing at home, eager to open a new bank account—"

That did it. I dropped my bag and spun on my heels. "What do you know?" I cried. "With your TV talk, scratching like a chicken for some speck to stick in your craw and spit out for"—I swept the crowd with my hand—"for viewers like you!" I felt a surge of tears, but the heat of anger dried it up.

Rose planted herself on the bottom step, too lofty for lowly me to make any impression. I backed into a chair off the lounge. That would do—I needed some height. I hoisted myself up. Better, here was a table. Ignoring a few scoffs from the gathering crowd, I scrambled up. I knocked over the chair. I knocked over a saltshaker, too, and, reaching down to right it, grabbed a spoon instead.

I stood as tall as I could. The ceiling felt close and warm, and a brass light fixture crowned my head.

Now I had their attention.

"Take care, Kat," said Rose, in a I-wouldn't-do-that-if-I-were-you tone. "This could go national."

"All the better," I said, delighted with the prospect and the acoustics. If she could chirp, I could purr.

Leaving her stairway perch, she moved in with her cameraman. "There's something you'd like to say?"

Sometimes the best way to disarm your opponent is to tell a little truth. I wouldn't say much. Just enough to show her up. I straightened my back.

"Yes," I announced. "There is."

"You're on."

"The gold," I said.

"The gold?"

"You're right. It isn't mine."

A stage gasp from her. "Well, I'm glad you finally admit—"

"It isn't the Mollie Kathleen's."

Her face sank for a second. "How ludicrous—"

"They don't own it. They couldn't."

Silence, as they all chewed on that one. I smiled. Oops Number One.

I stopped smiling.

"She *does* have a gold tooth!" someone said.

"The gold! Show us the gold!"

Ignoring the calls, Rose coaxed me. "So who owns it, Katlin?"

"Well." I swallowed. "As I was going to say, since it's a natural—"

Oops Number Two.

I was going to say, Since it was a *natural cavern*, not

a hole some miners dug, it wasn't a part of the mine. But that would blow my "in the dark" fib. Because, how would I know it was natural or not, if I couldn't see?

But worse, it could jeopardize Ye. They'd want to go check it out.

Now what? I should have got down off my high horse and walked right out the door. But all I could do was stammer on.

"It's a natural . . ."

The crowd had increased—people jammed the lobby, the hotel staff was spotlighted along the desk, servants and diners were silhouetted in the lounge. The double doors swung open and a cluster of senior citizens stepped in and stopped, heels and bangles clacking.

The camera ran on, its red light glaring. Somewhere in the haze of faces must have been Dillon's and Dad's, but I didn't dare pick them out.

Think, Kat!

"It's a natural thing . . . to question whose gold it is."

"Of course," Rose said smoothly. "That's precisely why I'm asking."

"When . . ." I fumbled. "When you consider . . ."

Faces curious, expectant.

That's when it struck me. Eureka. The ah-ha moment.

Something amazingly smart, if not ingenious. Something that would get me off the "stole the gold" hook, now and forever. Why hadn't I thought of it before?

Why hadn't *anyone* thought of it before?

I looked down at Rose, then at all the people.

"Hup," I said, emitting a hiccup intended to be a short laugh. "When you consider it's too far down. My goodness, it's out of their reach! The Mollie Kathleen *couldn't* own it!" I shook my head in disgust, and the brass fixture backed me up. I knew I hadn't said it quite right, to get the full impact of this newfound truth, but my revelation was a work in progress.

Rose nodded thoughtfully. "I see. It's too far down for the mine to claim. How astute. So, would you say it was really closer to . . . hell?"

"Don't clown with me."

"And the devil himself owns it? But, *naturally*, since he wasn't looking . . ."

The crowd began to twitter.

Mockery skittered behind Rose's Mary Kay face. "Was it warm so far down?"

"Go there yourself and find out!" I snapped, and from somewhere near the stairs somebody screeched my name.

It sounded Dadlike enough that I sweated a little, but the audience was laughing.

Others threw me remarks.

"Did you walk on coals?"

"Did you dance with the devil?"

"Did you sell him your soul?"

I was in this thing deep. Way past my head. My heart was flopping around somewhere in the depths, and I couldn't bring it up to hold it still. I had to do something else, say something else.

I brandished my spoon and shouted, "What do you know? What do any of you know?"

A young man at my knees said slyly, "The Old Tempter knows."

I glared down at him. He couldn't have been older than Dillon. His eyes were mean, his cheeks pimply, his mouth was smug. He had no idea what this was about, what I had been through. We glared at each other, each from our own crazy quilt patch of perception.

I took a deep breath and yelled at the audience, *"You don't get it!"*

That quieted them down.

"The mine," I said, steadying my voice, "can own *only*

so much land." I waited until you could hear a penny drop, or dice, then continued. "Where does it say that people own the land *below* them? Like, over a *thousand feet* below them? You have to draw a line somewhere. How far down can you own? All the way to the core of the earth? All the way to Shanghai?"

More dice dropping.

Finally, Rose said, "Nice try, Kat."

I made a noise like a flabby balloon. I had her this time. "It's more than a try, Rosie. It's a legitimate, debatable question. A question that should be asked. *And* answered."

Rose nodded. "A question for scholars, Plato, Socrates, Al Gore, oil barons. But since you have no way of knowing how far down you were—"

"But she's right!" A woman spoke up. "The girl's right!"

A guy threw me a catcall. Hey, I had never been whistled at before. I was tempted to smile again.

"That means we can *all* search for gold!" someone said.

My inner smile died. My face went all tingly.

The room exploded in cheers. You couldn't have heard a torrent of dice.

Now what had I done? What would this mean for Ye?

"The gold! The gold! The gold!"

I looked out across the crowd. These people were more gold-crazed than I had ever been. But it was more than gold for gold's sake. It was the prospect of Get, the power of Win.

Gold flashed throughout the room. A woman toying with her splashy necklace. A man checking his swanky watch. The boy below me with a showy stud under his lip. Myriad flames whispering to me from ages past, *Dragon gold . . . dragon gold . . .*

My frustration suddenly turned to pity. If they only knew. If they only understood.

My pity turned to my second revelation, which canceled out the first. I had found my calling. I would tell the world the truth. The whole truth.

The truth about gold.

Rose had said it could go national. Well, it was bigger than that. Universal. The wide world over, people would see gold in a different light.

And dragons, too.

I could set the record straight. After all this time, I could clear the dragon name. Fate had led me here and given me a mission: I would be Ye's errant knight. I would be his mouthpiece.

And *not* give him away. Yes—I could do it without betraying him.

The crowd was going wild, the word *gold* circulating like funny money.

I could also put a hurt on greed. If people knew the truth, maybe they'd place their bets on something else.

I pulled the tobacco tin from my pocket, and, with tin in one hand and teaspoon in the other, I began tapping the ruckus down.

Tap, tap, tap. Tap, tap, tap.

Rose pumped the air with her hands to assist me, thorns hidden for now. The hotel staff joined the cause.

When at last the uproar died, I put away my drum set, made sure of my footing, and placed my hands behind my back. I wanted no distractions. Rather than search hopelessly for one compassionate eye in the lot of them, I looked beyond their faces and into a teeming mass of humanity. I spoke low and distinct. The room leaned forward. The camera honed in.

"I don't care where you come from," I began. "Or how good you are, or how bad, or how greedy. I don't care how much money you have, how many riches, how much gold. There's something you all should know. There's something the *world* should know. I don't expect it will change anything—" I said that to challenge them. Reverse psychology.

Then I halted. I had found a face like Mom's—her age and coloring, her eyes on soft-focus. My heart began pushing against my chest. It moved to my throat, my eyes.

I looked away from the woman and into a blur. I said, "But miracles happen sometimes . . . and some people have honest hearts."

I exhaled my next words, rather than spoke them. "All the gold in the world . . ."

Eyebrows lifted, lips parted.

"All the gold in the world . . ."

Bodies tensed, ears tingled.

". . . belongs to . . ."

Yes? Yes?

". . . dragons."

⟞⟝

I WISH I COULD TELL YOU I FELL, HIT MY head on the chair, and blacked out—the way you're supposed to after a scene like that. It would be so easy and anticlimactic. I'd wake up in a quiet place and peer into kind faces with caring voices saying, "It's all right,

Katlin. Here, drink this." They would calmly relate what had happened, and I'd be spared the agony of it all.

Nothing doing.

I was wide-awake conscious, sky-high alert, when the whole house erupted. Laughs, jeers, whistles, snorts, howls, boos, even belches. The rafters rang, the table shook, a biscuit whizzed by my head.

A young man appeared at the table—not the one with the golden lip-stud, but one with a soulful face.

Dillon!

He reached up his arms as I went limp, ready to be swept off my soapbox. We swirled past wagging tongues and pointing fingers, past the party of jeweled and perfumed senior citizens, which shuffled out of the way, and through the hotel doors.

The workhorse brayed at the curb. Dad was at the wheel.

"Go!" yelled Dillon, as he yanked me inside.

We went.

No. **4**

IN MEDIAS REX

I HUDDLED IN SILENCE AS WE RODE OUT OF town—storefronts, signs, pedestrians, dogs, history, promises, drifting away.

Goodbye Cripple Creek, Colorado, elevation 9,494, population 1,012.

And one lone dragon.

My heart split in two at last, like an eroding cliff that cracks until it falls. The first half I had left with Mom. The remainder was now with Ye. I ached for him as much as I'd ever ached for my mom.

What was left was a vacancy.

I couldn't even cry. I've never been much of a crier, but this was one time I wanted the tears to flow. Instead, I was dragging this sack around, stuffing it with all my thoughts and questions and feelings and fears, and they were slipping out a hole in the bottom.

No wonder I couldn't keep hold of anything.

I began counting my losses, and finally gave up, overwhelmed.

Dillon and Dad were silent, simmering over the calamity I had caused. We each had things to tell, to explain to one another—I in particular—and the time would come soon enough. But I dreaded it.

It wasn't the telling I dreaded, but the disbelief.

Funny how you can unlock a precious truth, a sacred secret, hold it up high and say, Look, look! And though people look, they don't see. It's brushed away like a gnat.

I could share my thoughts with no one—no one that would believe or understand.

. . .

The highway had opened and there was Pikes Peak, basking bare and unconcerned above the tree line. We were back on the course of reality, and Cripple Creek was a small eddy into which I had spiraled for a moment. I and a few others, colors spinning in a whirlpool.

I looked over my shoulder. The town lay like scattered dice on green felt. In one die were the Warrens, living their day-to-day lives, mourning the loss of their daughter. In another was Rex, peeking through a keyhole or stalking a thief or . . . or perhaps he was the thief and zoomed around in his slick black beetle with a bigger grin than before. In another were Chief Huffman and company, working their cases, including the Case of the Mollie Kathleen. Rose Robbins and her cameraman—who were they shooting now?

Underneath it all was Ye, counting the years the way we count days, musing in the mist.

I had much to write about. Write about . . . write . . .

I lunged for Dad. "My bag! I left it in the lobby!"

Dad threw back his head and glared at the sagging headliner, while Dillon slithered low with a hiss.

"My journal! It tells everything! It tells about—" I slapped my hand across my mouth.

Dillon finished it for me in a raw, ragged voice. "Dragons?"

—◆◆—

AS WE HEADED BACK INTO CRIPPLE CREEK, a shiny black hum pulled up alongside—Rex's hardshell beetle! Rex looked our way, raised something off the seat, and held it to the window.

My bag!

Then the critter took flight, and Dad flew after him. Dad didn't just follow him, he rode him. You'd have thought we were roped nose to tail. Every turn Rex took, every tap of brakes, every acceleration, Dad was right there. On entering the town, we slowed, passed the Empire Hotel, took a few turns, and ended up somewhere near the Mollie Kathleen. I could see the top of the hoist house, poking above a roofline. We were doing fine until our car sneezed, sputtered, and gave up the ghost. The gas gauge needle, which was reading half full, fell.

"Vapor lock," said Dillon.

Dad, white-knuckled and gripping the wheel, looked grim. His foot was pumping the pedal. We were coasting.

"Or it's taking well-earned retirement," Dillon added, in his usual attempt at humor at times of distress.

"Quiet!" yelled Dad. He turned the key, the car sneezed again, neighed, and began to hum, back from its near-death experience.

A block ahead of us, Rex was darting into a driveway between two buildings.

We did likewise, as Rex swung into a private space in a dusty courtyard.

We did likewise.

Rex was out of his car and up some wooden steps, toting my bag, and we all got out and followed, right on his black boot heels.

His motive for this had better be good, I thought. We still had two and a half days to get to San Francisco, but Dad's patience for shindigs, scalawags, and other detours was growing skin thin.

The steps led to a wooden deck, and the three of us

caught up with him just as he entered a door. He left it wide open, and that's where we halted.

Was it a trap?

Was Chief Huffman inside, ready to clamp on the handcuffs? Or was Rose Robbins, equipped with lights and camera, waiting for action? Was there some varmint we hadn't had the pleasure to meet? Dad, breathing hard but first in line, stuck his head inside, not knowing if he'd be lassoed, splashed with whiskey, or yanked by the hair.

"Well, you gonna come in?" Rex piped from the shadows. "Got somethin' to show you."

In we went.

———)(———

REX, BACKLIT BY WINDOWS THAT LOOKED out on the street, was sprawled on a shaggy brown sofa as if it were a favorite dead horse he hadn't been able to part with. His hat was off and he held a glass of something dark. On one wall, long steer horns stabbed the air above a cluttered rolltop desk, and skewered on their tips were papers large and small, hand-scribbled, typed, or computer-printed. On a coffee table made from an old lacquered door, complete with iron hinges and a mouse hole chewed at one end, was a laptop with a tiny bat fluttering on a midnight blue screen.

"There's hardly no room," said Rex, shaking off his boots. "But you're welcome."

We remained standing.

In a voice he would use in a harsh wind, Dad said, "What is it, Havick? Why'd you do this?"

"Have a sit," Rex said calmly. "Have a drink." He sipped the dark stuff.

"Just hand over the bag!" Dad was now leaning into the wind.

"OK, OK." Rex jerked his thumb to a stool behind the door. "There it is."

I snatched up my bag and checked the side pocket. My journal was safe. I said, "Thank you, Mr.—"

"Rex," he said. "Now before you go . . ." He threw a look at Dad that said, *Don't interrupt.* "I got an offer you can't refute. But first, Girly May, take a look-see inside."

"Me?"

"You."

"My bag?"

"Look inside!" said Dad, his patience now in shreds. He was close to conducting a lynching—I could tell by the way he eyed the ceiling fan, which had only one blade. He was probably wondering if it would hold Rex's weight. Or mine.

I unzipped my bag and looked.

There, on top of my clothes, the gold nugget gleamed.

. . .

Rex had persuaded us to sit, and we felt we owed him that much. Dad had never seen the gold, which remained in my open bag on the floor, and could not take his eyes off it. He had settled down considerably and had called off the lynching. From a big leather beanbag chair, I watched the little bat on the screen that was happily chasing stars. Dillon gave his full attention to this man called Rex Havick, who seemed part lunatic, part fox, part buckaroo. We all had glasses of the same dark stuff he drank, which turned out to be cold sweet tea, though oversteeped.

Rex began by saying, "Little darlin'"—I don't remember him ever using my name—"you've started a stampede, single-handedly. I've been speculatin' on what they'll call it, and here's what I think: the new millennium gold rush. How's that sound? All shiny cap letters. The crime rate'll jump, of course. Won't hurt me none." He chuckled to himself. "So will the stock market. We'll have a heyday." As he drained his glass,

I wondered who the "we'll" was. Then, as though he'd heard my thought, he said, "More on that in a minute."

He got up, went to the fridge in the corner kitchenette, retrieved a second pitcher full of syrupy tea, and topped off our glasses.

"The gold—" he said, taking his place back on the couch.

"Yes," said Dad. "Who—?"

"The maid."

"The maid?" Dad and I sang in unison, disturbingly off-key.

"At the Empire Hotel. Cleanin' woman. Found her at home, packin' her bags and her baby. Just wanted a knock-'n'-talk, I told her. Before I could start, she broke down, shakin' with guilt. So much gold! she says, So much gold! Told me when she dumped the coffee down the sink in your room, there it was, with the words *take me* sketched on it."

"Really?" I said, and joined Dad in studying the gold.

"That's what I thought," said Rex. "Really? You saw them actual words? 'Yes,' she said. I think she meant she saw 'em in the little crevices. 'You takin' anything?' I asked. 'I took the gold! I took the gold!' she said. 'Never mind,' I said."

Dad was getting fidgety. "Yes—well then. So, why

give the gold back to us? And why the trouble to bring us here? Why not the hotel, or the side of the road?"

"Good questions all. For one thing, the hotel, right now, is the wrong place you wanna be."

"Why's that?" asked Dillon. Those were the first words he said since this powwow had begun.

Rex looked like a bee had stung him. "Didn't you notice? Place is bustin' with gold seekers. The rooms is maxed out. No vacancy for the next ten months, I figure. Anyways, you'd be mobbed." He said this to me, but I was busy digging a crater, postrear, in the beanbag chair.

I stopped digging for a moment. "Me? Mobbed?"

"'Xactly you, darlin'."

"That's impossible."

"You, Missy Sue," said Rex, with a tipsy shake of his head, "got the Midas touch."

"I beg your pardon," I said, digging again. "People are crazy."

"That's right." He reached down and tapped the nugget. "Gold crazy. See"—his manner changed to schoolboy, and he leaned back on the couch—"history never dies, it pops up now and then for us to take another shot at it. Don't tell me I don't know. I was raised on knowin'. My daddy'd tell me what his daddy done—"

"And what was that, Mr. Havick?" Dillon's second speech.

Rex squinted thoughtfully into his tea before he spoke. "Every anniversary of my granddaddy's death, he'd tell me. Granddaddy was mindin' his own business, playin' down at the pool hall one Friday night, hopin' to add a little profit to his little bag of gold so's he could buy a house for him and his bride and their new baby boy—my own daddy—when here comes Sharp-Eyed Joe and shoots the legs out from under him, sayin', 'Gimme what gold you got.' Granddaddy says, 'You're goin' to hell.' Sharp-Eyed says, 'Not yet, I ain't,' and shoots him in the intestinals. Granddaddy hunches over, but he's got enough blood left in him to scrabble up and jab his pool stick hard into Sharp-Eyed Joe's eye. Near took it out; broke the socket bone. Joe shoots wild and stumbles back, squealin' like a stuck pig."

Rex took a long gurgling drink and wiped his mouth.

"Well, to make a slow story quick, Granddaddy died, Joe took the gold, and changed his name to—"

"Cotton-Eyed Joe!" I exploded.

Rex blinked at me for a while, and Dillon and Dad were doing double and triple takes. I grinned at them with my best Girl Wonder grin.

Finally, Rex said, "If you grind them beans any harder, sister, the leather's gonna bust and we'll be swimmin' in bean soup. I'll be pickin' beans outta my socks from here to eternally."

"Sorry," I said, letting go of my grin and my wigglies.

"'S OK, darlin'."

His face a blank memo pad, Dad said, "Kat—" but apparently couldn't remember whatever it was he'd forgot.

Looking me over as if I'd just introduced myself, Rex said, "That's right. Cotton-Eyed Joe, it was. His eye went white—the blind one my granddaddy gave him. That was the last crime Joe ever done. While he was servin' sentence, somehow he broke out. Never was seen from again. Some folks say they heard his voice yellin' deep down in the Mollie Kathleen."

It was my turn to take a long drink, for his last words made my head tingle. The skeleton in Ye's chamber. Was it—?

Dad had quit his quadruple take on me and began talking quietly with Rex.

But I could not contain myself. I asked, "Is there any way to identify Cotton-Eyed Joe? I mean, after all these years?"

"Now, you're a strange one," murmured Rex.

—⟩|⟨—

"C'M'ERE." REX WAS AT THE WINDOWS, parting the sheer curtains. "Crank your head that way," he told us. "See them folks?"

Through a space between buildings, we saw several people who appeared to be protesters, carrying signs. I tried to read the signs, but my glasses were fuzzy.

"What do the signs say?" I asked.

Rex handed me some small field binoculars that were lying on the sill. "Have a look-see yourself."

After focusing the lenses, I read, "'That's . . . far . . . enough. How . . . low . . . can . . . they . . . go?'" I turned to Rex. "What's it all about?"

"See where they are?"

I looked again; they were near the hoist house. "The Mollie Kathleen!"

"That's right, sister. And what's the Mollie Kathleen got that they ain't got?"

The answer was obvious.

"How low can they go?" said Rex, raising an eyebrow. "Seems *somebody*"—the word came out singsong— "started this fancy talk about the mine not ownin' the gold 'cause it's outta their reach—legality-wise, that is, and geographically-wise, too. Bein' people's always tryin' to find a way around things to get what they want, the idea caught like wild fire, and they run with it. *How low can they go* and *That's far enough*, meanin' if there's gold way down deep, it's first come, first served."

I was stunned. As wide open as my mouth fell, I'm sure my gold tooth was showing up loud and clear. I was that somebody. I had come up with the idea. Just a short while ago.

"Look at it this way: If a juvenile can find a chunk of gold, anybody can. *Everybody* can."

"But . . . but . . ." I shook my head in a daze.

"Ain't you heard the news?" Rex asked us.

Our faces told him otherwise.

"I'll be a paisley-patterned horned toad." He dropped the curtains, picked up the TV remote, and hit power. A cartoon came up; he scanned the channels, got the weather, a black-and-white western, a few soaps, a hallelujah gold-and-glory sermon, a crime solver, a jewelry commercial, a football game, and three talk shows. Leaving the TV on one of the talk shows, he hit mute and said, "That there's a local channel. Just missed the top-of-the-clock news. It'll come back around."

He straddled an arm on the couch. "Yup. Thanks to that gimme-the-gold flix, the one with all them itchy fingers reachin' for their golden opportunity. And thanks to Rose Thorn-in-the-Bud Robbins."

"Her!" I exclaimed. "What'd she do?"

"Not much—yet. She's been after the big story for years, the one that'll send her to the broadcasting big top. She'd do anything to get there." He paused, looked at the time on the microwave, and said, "Y'know, folks, the questions are stackin' up. What're you doin' for dinner?"

Dad said, "You still haven't explained why you brought us here. It's getting late—"

"You'll be needin' dinner sometime or another, right?"

Dad frowned. "We haven't even had lunch yet. Really, Rex—"

"It's on me, then. I'll call in the order. Take just a minute. You can eat whilst I explain."

• • •

The Digs, Grub 'n' Grog, was right next door, due east, as Rex put it. To the west, on the other side of his apartment, was Mile High Ice Cream, where he said we could go for our "just desserts." And directly below was an antique shop—he pronounced it "antikky"—called the Owl's Nest. Dillon asked if he owned the shop, and I wondered the same, considering all the old stuff in his apartment and the fact he lived above it.

"Hail Mary, no! That's Ken Carpenter's. But I barter there on the whimsy."

The grease-stained bag that a ponytailed guy delivered to the door had the digs printed on it in sand-colored ink and a symbol of a miner's pick.

Rex plunged in his hand and pulled out four big burgers, one by one, and passed them around. Then, gripping his own, he said, "Bless this humble abode and this awesome, mouthwaterin' chow," and chomped down.

The three of us ate in silence. I was back in my crater, worrying about Ye.

With chock-full cheeks, Rex asked, "Whad-da-ya think?"

Dad nodded, while Dillon said, "Kind of chewy . . . long-horned steer?"

Rex shook his head. "This," he said, swallowing his last bite with a satisfied rotation of his head, "is the Bill Cody Camptown Ladies Sing This Song Doo-Dah Doo-Dah Buffalo Burger."

We stared at him.

"Big furry backs, beady black eyes, itty-bitty horns." He stuck two fingers behind his head.

Dillon said, "They still kill buffalo?"

"Hey, bigger beasts have died."

Bigger beasts. That slowed my appetite way down. Brought it to a halt. I couldn't swallow. I couldn't finish the poor buffalo. Ye was bigger than a buffalo. More threatening by size alone. Not to mention his smoke and wings and claws and tail. The look in his eyes goes straight to your soul.

Would they kill a dragon? Like all the other dragons?

You bet they would.

—⇥ ⇤—

"BACK TO RAMBLIN' ROSE," REX WAS SAYING, while I was trying hard to untie the knot in my stomach. He tucked his chin and looked at me from under his burnt brown eyebrows. "Promise me you won't beat her with your spoon?"

"I . . . How'd you know about that?"

"Saw it stickin' out your back pocket like a jackrabbit's tail."

I'd totally forgot it. That made me a thief all over again, though taking a spoon from a hotel was nothing compared to taking gold from a dragon.

Or putting his life in danger.

"I'll start with your satchel," said Rex. "Which you left it behind."

That didn't help me any, either.

"I'd heard about the hoedown at the Empire, " he said, "and by the time I walked in, which was through the delivery doors off the back of the restaurant—"

"That's how we got out," said Dillon. "After taking the elevator. The stairs were impossible."

Rex nodded to him, then continued. "Here's Rose, sittin' in a low-light corner of the bar, kinda' slinky, readin' this"—he threw a glance at me—"book."

"No!" I could have blasted out of my crater.

"Page after page—I was watchin'. So, I sorta' sidles up and says, 'Howdy, Rose,' and she drops the book outta sight and gets up. She says, 'Rex, do you have the gold?' And I say, 'I was thinkin' maybe you did.' 'That's a joke,' she says. 'Well,' I says, lookin' down in the dark underneath where she'd dropped the book, 'considerin' you seem to be up on the latest . . .' 'What do you mean?' she says. 'You been mindin' your own business,' I say, 'or somebody else's?' 'My business *is* mindin' somebody else's,' she says, and storms out, leavin' the book and your satchel behind." He stroked his chin casually. "I guess she got what she wanted."

"Got what she wanted?" I asked.

"It's on the news."

"Exactly *what* is on the news?" said Dad, who was eyeing the fan blade again.

Before Rex responded, we heard voices outside. It sounded like a chant. Rex went over and raised one of the windows an inch. The chant became clear.

How low can they go! How low can they go!

"It ain't over," Rex said somberly, looking at each of us in turn. "It's just startin'."

That silly phrase of his, repeating itself like one of Mom's old broken records, wasn't sounding so silly anymore.

—⟩⟨—

"THE PLOT DEEPENS . . ."

Rose Robbins of KOLT-TV, in garish, high-definition color, red lips shining, hair sprayed gold, was looking straight into the eyes of viewers like me. Rex turned up the volume.

". . . unfolding like a fractured fairy tale. Poor deluded girl! Dragons, of all things!"

There, posed on a table like a happy nitwit, was the poor deluded girl, waving her spoon and flashing her gold tooth whenever she opened her mouth, with the light fixture skipping around her head. Fortunately, there was no sound to the video clip, though Rose had gladly filled in the blanks.

"But one thing is undeniable," she said. "There's gold in them there depths!"

The horrifying table scene changed to the hand-groping one at the Warrens, with arms like spokes in a wheel and the gold at the hub. That scene would circle the globe before it was all over, to become the icon of the twenty-first-century gold rush.

"Everyone wants a piece of this pie," said Rose.

Now we saw the protesters at the Mollie Kathleen, wandering back and forth with their signs. One detail I had missed from Rex's window was the signposts: They were inverted picks and shovels. You could hear the chant on TV, which syncopated with the real-time one coming from outside.

How-how low-low can-they-can-they go-go!

"They're lining up," said Rose, "ready to claim what they can. Many witnesses, including yours truly, have seen the gold nugget. It's the size of the American dream." (Back to the hand-groping scene.) "Little Girl Lost admitted to finding it, more than one have tried to steal it, but one of several questions remains: Where is it now?"

Her words made me so nervous, I scrambled from my crater and zipped the clothes bag shut. The nugget had teased our senses plenty, and I feared Rose would spot it through the TV screen if she looked hard enough. Pivoting in her seat, she grinned at us from a dramatic angle.

"After the break, we'll let you in on some astounding interviews, and let you be the judge."

Dad leaped up. "I've seen enough! It's time to go! Kat, get your bag." He extended his hand to Rex. "Appreciate the—"

Rex had leaped up, too. "Hold on there, partner! We ain't talked business yet!"

"I'm well aware of that," said Dad. "But I can't imagine it's something I'd agree to. If it's a finder's fee you want—"

"Whoa!" Rex pulled on invisible reins. "Whoever said somethin' about finder's fees? Keep your hunk of gold. More power to you. I just happened to be at the right locale at the right o'clock."

"Well, thank you—"

Rex held up his hand. "Don't mention it." Then he cleared his throat purposely. "But there *is one* thing you *can* mention." He went over and lowered the window, hit the mute button on a tooth-whitener ad that featured scores of smiling people, and came back. "Here's the deal."

—⟩|⟨—

THE DEAL WAS NO DEAL. NONE THAT DAD or I would agree to.

After some fast talk with Dad and some slow winks at me, Rex brought it down to this: Where there was one gold nugget, there were sure to be more. Whether or not I had actually *seen* more didn't matter. Just head him in the right direction, and what gold he'd find he'd split with us, fifty-fifty. Others were bound to find it sooner or later, he said, but since I knew the hidden back door, so to speak, we had the upper-vantage. We even had the upper-vantage over the mine's owners. I think he meant *upper hand* or *advantage*. It was almost a Dillingo.

But I was dismayed—I expected better things of Rex. I expected him to be different than all the other gold-hungry beggars.

"Just a few more of them rocks like what your daughter found would do you for life," Rex rhapsodized. "You can kiss your old job goodbye."

Dad, allowing Rex to gallop up to that point, finally spoke. "I don't have an old job. I'm headed for a new one, if I can ever get out of this place. As to telling you what you want to know—" He turned to me. "Kat, what do you say? Want to reveal the whereabouts of the—"

"No," I said. "Never." I picked up my bag and went to the door.

Rex looked hurt and started playing with his hat. "Well, now, sister. Ain't you shootin' yourself in the foot here? Ain't you doin' your family a mis-service? Think of your hardworkin' daddy . . ."

My hardworking daddy was right by my side, looking quite satisfied.

"I'm sorry, Rex," Dad said, offering his hand again. "I appreciate all you've done. But Katlin answered just the way I thought she would. She has her reasons. I have mine. I don't believe in get-rich-quick schemes. Hard work is what more people in this country need to be doing. Earning their keep."

Rex had lost his shine, like a dried hot pepper. I felt a little sorry for him, but I was feeling a whole lot sorrier for Ye.

I said, "Thanks again, Mr. Havick," and opened the door.

I stopped.

A sleek silver car had just pulled up behind ours,

blocking us in. We all watched as a man in a pin-striped suit got out. His silver hair was combed straight back and cascaded over his collar.

"Quick!" said Rex. "Back in the room."

"Now what!" said Dad. "Who is that?"

"The wrong man you wanna meet." There was an oxydox mix of respect and disdain in his voice. "Slickest lawyer in all Teller County. Rich man, baby. Sterling Blair." He turned to me. "If my nose is sniffin' right, it's all about you, Goldilocks. You and your little wheel o' fortunate."

———⸼⸼———

"LEAVE THE DOOR OPEN A CRACK," SAID Dillon, but Dad had already done so.

We were in Rex's bedroom, off his main living area. He had ushered us in using more fast talk, saying it would be tragic if we met Sterling Blair, a man capable of milking us for all we were worth, which, in my view, not counting the gold, was nothing. Later, I realized he meant information. Dad debated whether to go along with yet another of Rex's harebrained escapades, but by the time we were through the bedroom door, he seemed to be willing to do so one last time. If what Rex said was true, the man with the silver hair could be a subtle enemy, and Dad avoided lawyers like lice.

Rex had latched the deck door behind us, and took his time answering Blair's knocks. He sang, "Dinah, won't ya blow! Dinah, won't ya blow! Dinah, won't ya blow your hor-or-orn—"

I looked around the bedroom, which captivated me more than his other room had. His bed was made from a buckboard wagon, complete with wood-and-iron wheels standing shoulder-high and bolted to the floor. A bearskin blanket and two quilts lay on the mattress. On a nightstand armored with hammered-in bottle caps was a yellow lava lamp, where contorting shapes glowed eerily inside. Standing in one corner of the room was some kind of cactus, which had been lacquered and converted into a floor lamp, and light sprouted from holes up and down its height. In another corner stood a hat rack made of all types of horns—cattle, deer, antelope, even one that looked like a unicorn's, which Dillon said was a narwhal's—and on them hung Rex's many hats, all of them black. A goldfish bowl sat on a piano stool by the door, filled, not with water and fish, but with hundreds of fortunes he'd apparently saved from fortune cookies. Hanging on the door where the three of us were gathered were rattlesnake skins, which rustled and hissed whenever we moved.

We heard Blair's voice, commanding and confident. "Caught you at last. In medias res—"

"In *what* kind of *what*?" I whispered.

"It's Latin," said Dad, "for 'in the middle of things.'"

"—where are they, Havick?"

Rex's voice was confident, too, though a little quick-on-the-draw. "Now, wouldn't you like to know."

"Their car's here. Virginia plates. Are you hiding them?"

"They could be out havin' dinner."

"Could be?"

"Could be."

Some papers shuffling.

"My client is insistent, Havick. They won't press charges, provided one thing . . ."

A pause. Blair was waiting for Rex to ask what the one thing was. He didn't.

". . . provided they hand over the gold and say where the exit is."

No comment from Rex.

"Well?"

"Well's deep."

"You know where these people are, Havick. You know where the gold is—"

"Hold on, there, Solicitor!" I could picture Rex pulling on reins. "Your client'll let the Grahams off, you say. Won't press charges. How about if you turn that gun around?"

"Gun!" I whispered, alarmed.

"He means metaphorically," Dillon whispered back. "Figure of speech."

"The *Grahams* won't press charges," Rex was saying, "provided one thing."

Silence. He was playing the lawyer's game—provided what one thing?

"Provided," said Rex, when Blair didn't respond, "they keep the gold and get on with their lives."

"They wouldn't stand a chance in court."

"Oh yes they would, and well you know it."

More shuffling of papers.

"We have a reliable witness who claims *you* have the gold, Havick."

"As reliable as a lame horse."

"She's been with the Empire Hotel ten years. She's an upright citizen of Cripple Creek."

"As upright as a wet spaghetti noodle. Sees messages on rocks."

"Oh? What kind of messages?"

Dillon shook his head at that, and Dad's mouth went tight. I wasn't sure what the problem was, but there was something in Rex's statement they didn't like.

Rex didn't answer the question. "Faces in clouds . . ." he rambled. "You know the type: Saint Anthony and UFOs and Strawberry Fields . . ."

"What kind of rocks, then?"

Now I understood. When Rex had said "messages on rocks," it was too close to admitting that the cleaning woman—the witness—had seen the gold nugget. If she had seen the gold nugget, Rex had, too.

"Rocks in the head," said Rex.

• • •

They went at it a while, Rex dodging the lawyer's questions, Blair jabbing away. When Blair suggested he might wait around for the Grahams to return from dinner or from gold digging, Rex said, "Not on my turf, you won't."

We heard the door close and their muffled voices continuing outside. Dad eased open the bedroom door and stood there, looking this way and that, and staring up at the ceiling fan. He looked at his watch, blew out his breath, and said, "We're stuck here until that sneaking attorney goes. He's stalling to see if we'll show up."

≈⊰ ⊱≈

WHEN, AT LAST, THE SILVER SHARK SLID OUT
of the driveway, we were breathing a little easier.

Rex poured himself another dose of syrupy black tea.

"He's ready to serve," he told Dad. "He had papers."

"On what grounds?"

"Conspiracy. Theft. It's the usual preemptive strike.
Sterling ain't satisfied with silver, if you get my drift."

I asked Dillon quietly, "Serve? Grounds? Pre-
whative?"

"Serve means take us to court," he explained. "Grounds
is what they'd blame us with. Preemptive means ahead of
us, before *we* sue *them*."

I remembered now—I'd heard those terms being
tossed around after Mom's accident. I shook my head.
"But we wouldn't sue them. Hey—who's *them* anyway?"

Rex had overheard me. "The Mollie—" he began,
then gave me a startled look. "Where'd you get your
brain waves, child?"

"You mean I'm stupid?"

"Just the opposition of that, smarty gal!" He was
beaming at me. "Sterling didn't name his client. Didn't
show me the papers, neither. He may be makin' the
whole thing up. For his own self inner rest." He looked

at me a while longer, but his eyes started to deepen. Then he turned to Dad, he lowered his voice, and switched his tune—something about another offer, a *better* offer, an offer we couldn't "refute."

Dad, surprisingly, disappointingly, was listening.

Dillon was wearing his sideways smile, which meant he was conjugating the verb *to think*. He whapped my shoulder, motioned me to follow him, and went out onto the deck.

I hesitated.

This could be it. My time of reckoning. But I'd been considering for some time that I should tell someone the truth. Dillon was first choice. He may call me insane, but he'd already heard the "D" word—I'd said it in a room full of spectators, right into a TV camera, and he knew it was written in my journal.

To tell of Ye, or not: That was the question.

I stepped outside.

• • •

He had plopped down into Rex's sagging cowhide chair and propped his feet on a small, stone mushroom-shaped table.

I went to the railing. The sun was lowering its face below the mountains, the hours were dropping with it.

Two full days remained, and the last of today. Twelve hundred miles. Still possible, but not favorable.

Not favorable for Dad. Therefore, not favorable for us.

Favorable for Ye.

Provided . . .

Provided I could persuade Dad to stop at the Warrens. For I had expanded my plan. I wouldn't just return the gold; I would crawl back to his cavern. I would warn him of the danger. It wouldn't be long before hordes would be swarming his tunnels, destroying his chamber, stealing his gold. Perhaps even—

Slaying the dragon.

Yes, I needed help.

I turned to Dillon and said, "About the dragon—"

"I was waiting for that."

—◦)(◦—

"YOU NEED A BACKUP PLAN," HE WAS SAYING.

"I'm not good at backing up," I said. "No better than our car."

"A backup, you know, as in, If at first you don't succeed . . . try this."

"Try what?"

"The backup plan."

Dillon had accepted my story and hadn't called me crazy. As I related it all, he listened respectfully, attentively, if not a little intrigued.

But better than that—

When I got to the part about Mom's ring, he hung his head and closed his eyes. It was hard for me to watch, just as it was hard for him to hear anything about Mom, so I watched the sun set as I talked. When I had told him everything—my burden gone at last—his head was still down, his eyes were still closed. I was sure he was shutting in more than he was shutting out.

"Dillon?" I asked.

A pause, then, "Yeah?"

"Do you believe me?"

A longer pause, then he raised his head. "Kat, if I'm going to believe that somehow, by some slurpy kiss of fate, we'll be spared the poverty we're in, I may as well believe in dragons—this dragon, anyway—and I may as well believe he can live forever."

I sighed, then slowly said, "Dillon?"

"What, Kat?"

"Do you believe Mom could wake up?"

An even longer pause. So long I watched a cloud turn from gray to golden by degrees, absorbing the light of the sun, now out of view. I turned back to him, blinking away the brightness, wishing he would remove the boulders and beams he had heaped up inside himself.

Then he spoke. "If I'm going to believe in dragons," he murmured, his eyes reflecting the gold of that cloud, "I'll believe anything for Mom. I'll believe she rides the stars at night, the winds at day. I'll believe she's never been happier in all her life. I'll believe the angels sing all her favorite songs. I'll believe she's carried in arms of love."

The sadness and joy I took from his words filled my head and spilled out my eyes. The word *Mom* had not passed his lips since that dreadful day.

He had said it. He had said it just once, but he had said it.

Then he ducked his head again, his shoulders began to shake, and a tear darkened his sleeve. I reached out to him, but he waved me away. I went inside and watched from the kitchen window. His body shook for a long, long time. He fell to his knees and rocked back and forth, moaning and clutching his head.

At last, after an agonizing, soul-thirsty dry spell, my brother wept.

—)(—

Still in Cripple Creek. Worried big-time, as Rex would say. Worried for Dad, for us.

Workhorse won't start. Nothing. Not even a whinny. They tried everything—sarsaparilla on the battery, shock treatments, kicks & shoves. She's probably dead, just hasn't rolled over yet.

Rex put his hat over his heart & said we should give the old gray mare a "decent & honorable burial." A glint's in his eye, that tells me he thinks he may get his way after all.

Dad won't talk, won't eat, sits & stares. His eyes are bloodshot & flat, as if he's dragged himself across Death Valley. I laid my hand on his, then took it away, afraid he'd see the ring was gone. I told him, Dad, we'll make it somehow. Not a blink.

I have two plans:

- Plan Forward: See Ye. Tonight.
- Plan Backup: See Ye later tonight.

I crossed out both plans, buried my journal in the bearskin blanket, and sat up in bed. Buckboard wagon, I should say.

Yep—we had spent the night with Rex.

"Hand me the fortune fishbowl, will you?" I asked Dillon.

It hadn't been a bad night, considering. Considering the yellow lava lamp made me think of dragons writhing, turning to gold. (I switched the lamp off.) Considering the rays of light coming from the holey cactus cast a creepiness over the room. One misty ray struck the snakeskins, which shivered like skinny ghosts. Another hit a blood-red jewel on one of Rex's hats. Another highlighted a black knothole in the paneling.

When I studied that knothole, I could swear an eye studied me back. I got up to examine it—nothing. I stuck my finger all the way in—nothing. Then I felt a slight breeze. I thought of Rex and our first encounter in the Empire Hotel. Eye-to-eye. I decided I'd ask him in the morning, "Rex, did you see me looking at you through that hotel keyhole?" and I'd watch for a flinch.

But morning had come and Rex had gone. He'd left us a note:

help yourselves.
raid the fridge.
remember the Alamo.

He hadn't talked Dad into staying—with the work-horse not running and all the lodgings filled, we'd hardly had a choice.

Rex said if I reconsidered his offer, he'd fly us to San Francisco. Fly! Hours instead of days. That was the offer he'd been working on. An offer you couldn't refute.

I looked up the word in the dictionary on the shelf near his desk. *Refute—to prove to be wrong*. I couldn't argue with that. His offer sounded right to me. I'd reconsider it, say no, and *still* he'd have to fly us to San Francisco.

My two plans hadn't worked.

With Dad tinkering on the car far into the night, and Rex bagging down on the deck—to keep an eye on things, he said—we couldn't sneak out.

When Dad finally gave up, he got the dead-horse couch, Dillon the beanbag chair, and I the buckboard bed. In my condition, they said, I needed a bed, and I admitted every inch of me still felt the hard-edged law of gravity.

. . .

So, there we were, mid-morning. Dillon was alive and talking, sitting sidesaddle on one of the wagon wheels with his feet locked in the spokes. I sat with the fishbowl in my lap, pulling up fortunes and reading them out loud.

"'You are beautiful and—'"

"Kat," said Dillon. "I've been thinking. Because you're *not*."

"—bright.'"

"You say you're afraid—"

"'You jump at every opportunity.'"

"—you're afraid this dragon—"

"It's *Ye*!" I fussed. "Not *this dragon*!" I pulled another fortune. "'You are calm and serene.'"

"Ye, then. You're afraid he'll be shot or trampled or hung—"

"Hanged," I corrected. "'Life—'"

"Killed, anyway."

"—is what you make it.'"

"—but can Ye be killed? If he's going to live forever?"

I dropped my fortunes.

"Think about it, Kat. Will the pearl spare him from dying only a natural death, or *any* kind of death?"

I dropped my jaw. "Dillon . . . I . . ." Why hadn't I thought of that myself? Why did he always see things I overlooked?

"'There may be no cause for worry," he said. "If this dragon *cannot* die."

I was too bewildered to correct "this dragon." I was

too bewildered to think. I ran my hands through the slips of fortunes, looking for an answer.

—⇥ ⇤—

THE *DENVER POST* WOKE DAD UP. LITERALLY.

He had fallen asleep in the cowhide chair, deck side—at peace with the galaxy for one brief moment. Dillon, working on what he called Plan Sideways, was looking through Rex's cubbyholes for a flashlight. I was standing at the kitchen window, munching some trail mix I'd found, when a beat-up little car sputtered down the drive. From the car's window, an arm flung out a newspaper, which smacked Dad in the head.

He jerked upright, shouting, "It's over!"

We were out the door in a snap.

Dillon retrieved the paper while I consoled Dad, saying, "It's just the paper."

Just.

Dillon glared at the headline, slapped the paper and said, "This is the *Denver Post*. The *Denver Post!*"

I peered past his shoulder and read:

Who Owns Gold: Mollie Kathleen, Everyman, or . . . Dragons?

I didn't read any further. I didn't want to. *Little Girl Lost* and *gold-toothed girl* and *poor deluded girl*—I'd had enough of that. Rose's thorns cut deep, and Reporters Roundup was well into the game.

How far would it go?

"It's just startin'," Rex had said.

Well, I thought, *how 'bout if it just started endin'?* I wanted to go home, have my own bed, my own pillow—

It hit me like a dump cart in the Mollie Kathleen.

There was no home to go home to. Not even a stable.

We were homeless.

—❧ ❧—

"IT'S GETTIN' BIGGER."

Rex was back.

Just as Dillon and I were about to enact Plan Sideways, which involved slipping out the door for a "stroll," Rex strode in. He wore a new hat, which he patted, saying, "Like my somber-O?", went straight to the TV, and hit power.

". . . and in regional news," a newsman was saying, "today at the Mollie Kathleen Mine, more gold seekers gathered for another day of protesting. A spokesperson for the group asserts that the mine does not own gold outside their designated property." The spokesperson's head came up, spotlights gleaming on his face. "It's our belief that the hidden exit is on public land," he said, "and is therefore open to any who wishes to search for gold. By law, there are limits to vertical property, to a mining claim. Check it out. How low can they go?"

There were supporting cheers in the background.

"Meanwhile," continued the newsman, "the owners of the Mollie Kathleen have released a statement claiming the mine is family-friendly and safe, and are currently making plans to expand it for a deeper, grander tourist experience . . ."

A clip of Sterling Blair moving his silver-mustached mouth came on.

Rex kicked off a boot that landed squarely on Blair's face. "That's a cover-up if I ever heard one! *Expand*, my achin' foot! They'll scour them tunnels till every last stone is left unturned!"

". . . not altered their decision to keep the mine closed, however," the newsman said, "pending a complete investigation of Saturday's incident, in which a girl strayed from the tour . . ."

Rex hit mute.

"That ain't all," he said, turning to us. "There's

KYDS—Keepin' Youths Defended and Safe. They heard about your fall, Missy Sue, and wanna hold the mine responsible. There's the Green Group jumpin' into the feud, sayin' no more diggin', no more minin', leave the land be."

He worked the other boot off and pitched it near the first one, underneath the TV.

"There's the Romancin' Arts Mytho-illogical Society—that's a mouthful to get out. RAMS, they call it. Sayin' if there's a dragon down there, we wanna see it. They've joined the picketers." (He rhymed it with racketeers.) "Dressed to kill, in sparkly green shirts and long tails—"

I said without thinking, "But the dragon's not gr—" and stopped myself. I went to the windows to look at the gathering crowds.

"Then the *Denver Post*—"

"We saw that," said Dillon.

". . . the *Business Journal*—"

"*Business Journal*? What'd *they* say?"

"Predictin' a new gold rush, like what I predicted myself. Whispers on Wall Street already. Price of gold goin' up. Say you heard it from me first, partner."

The sun was filtering through the curtains, shimmery

like fish scales. The crowds were growing. I heard shouts, a siren, people singing, a car horn, a laugh.

It was unreal. As unreal as Ye himself.

———>)(<———

"DAD'S CAVING IN," SAID DILLON.

Plan Sideways was well in motion.

We were strolling along, each wearing a hat from Rex. He'd said if we went around town, we should be "in-clothes-neato," which, he explained, meant "dressed as who you ain't." (He meant *incognito*.) After the scenes at the mine and the Warrens and the hotel, he explained, not to mention the TV and newspapers, we should avoid being recognized. The hats were not bad fits. Mine was a black flat straw with an orange bandanna, Dillon's a black felt cavalry with the brim flipped up on one side. We got a few odd looks, but no one troubled us. I kept my mouth shut—which is not easy when you need to talk.

"Now that Rex has Dad, together they'll work on you," said Dillon.

"No way," I mumbled.

"Didn't you see the looks on their faces? As if their pockets were already gold-lined."

"He wouldn't do that. Not Dad. It's against his religion." I stopped at a corner as the light turned green. "Anyway, he's got to be in San Francisco."

"He probably thinks he can do both, at this point. Get some gold *and* fly to San Francisco, all in one play."

He steered me across the street. "You'd think Rex would have a map," he said. "I still need a map."

"I bet he's got the whole place memorized. He lives here." If we had been at the Empire Hotel, I could have backtracked our way to the Warrens. But from this part of town, I couldn't get my bearings.

"And string," he added.

"String?"

"You know, like Theseus and the Minotaur. To find our way back out."

He stopped abruptly, adjusted his hat, and pulled me into the recess of a place called Sad Willie's Curios and Collectibles. "There was a woman staring at us, Kat. Don't look."

I didn't. I looked at a sign on the door that read, be back at—with a cardboard clock someone had drawn a sad face on, set at six. Who'd open a shop at six?

Just as Dillon was saying, "OK, she's gone," Sad Willie showed up. It was obvious. He couldn't have been anyone else, with skin like dough and watery eyes and a flannel shirt with a pocket handkerchief that was way past reviving. In other words, the kind of person that finds even laughter a pain.

"Wait one minute," he said, unlocking the door.

Dillon said, "Oh, we weren't going to—"

He looked at us with such mournfulness, we went in anyway.

· · ·

It had to have been serendipity.

There was a free tourist map, which showed the town and the mine and part of the outlying area, and there was string, lots of it, rolled into a haphazard ball. But there was one hitch: The string came with a kite, a long, serrated, serpentine orange-and-pink kite. A dragon kite. Willie wouldn't give us the string without it. Said he was trying to downsize, get rid of everything in the shop that had been there forever.

"You'll be the envy of Cripple Creek," he wheezed. "Dragons are the next big thing."

—⟫ƕ⟨—

THE STREETS WERE LOOKING FAMILIAR; the faces, fortunately, were not.

"We'd better hurry," I told Dillon in my closed-mouth way. "We don't want another search-and-rescue melodrama."

He nodded. "Even if Dad gets Nellie running again, the old gray mare ain't what she used to be. We have, like, fortysome hours left. Into twelve hundred miles that's—"

"Still possible."

"Depending on how long-winded your dragon is."

"Dillon, it's not—"

"Pardon me," he said with a tip of his head, which was too Rex-like for my comfort. *"Ye."*

We weaseled through traffic.

Then he said, "You know—"

Funny how two harmless words can sound suspicious. I gave him a warning look.

"—Dad doesn't believe in dragons," he said. "Rex doesn't, either. They've both heard the wacky word circulating and haven't asked you a thing about it. It's total nonsense to them."

Tightening my mouth, I waited for his conclusion.

"It's the gold that's real."

I stopped. "Are you implying that Ye is not?"

"Gold is golden," he said with a sudden ugly delight.

"Admit it, Kat. It would solve it for us. Rex is right: We'd be set for life."

"Dillon! I can't believe you're saying this! The gold is Ye's!"

Glancing at the pedestrians he reached out and pulled down my brim. "Your tooth is showing."

"Your *greed* is showing. Who's side are you on?"

"Kat. Don't get shook. I'm just being sensible."

"*I'm* being compassionate. And moral. The gold is *Ye's*. Gold that once was a dragon! Don't you *get* it?"

He shrugged, and if there's anything I hate, it's a shrug of indifference. I was furious. I felt like getting physical, so I pulled out my spoon.

Then he said something that came out much too easily. "What good does the gold do him? According to you, he just sits there day after day after day."

"What is wrong with you!" I yelled.

"I'm beginning to wonder the same of you. Because, really, what good does it do him?"

Ignoring the fact we were now in the center of the street—there were no cars . . . not yet—I fumed, "All right, mister sensible *idiot* brother!" I stressed "idiot" to make sure he knew it was italicized, underlined, and in capital, bold red letters, with arrows all around it.

I pointed the spoon at him, my voice rising like a bird. "What good does it do? *What good does it do?*"

He tried to be playful, lifting his arms in surrender. "Is that spoon loaded?"

"Tell me—what good does it do you to sit day after day after day with Mom?"

Playtime was over. Dillon's arms fell. His face went bone-white under his black cavalry hat.

"That gold could be Ye's mom!" I said. "Or his granddad! Or—"

"OK, Kat," he said quietly. "I get it."

We moved off the street and onto the sidewalk.

But it was too late.

⬳ ⬳

HAROLD THE YOUNGER WAS PLEASED WITH himself. That's pleez-duh, as in, pretty, with sugar on it, and, duh cop finally done sumthin' right.

We, of course, couldn't have been more *dis*pleased, and that included the dragon kite perched on the seat between us, who was all bent out of shape. A ride in a patrol car would have been exciting under other circumstances, but as it was, I was feeling anger, humiliation, and anxiety for Ye. I was also wondering, *Would we go directly to jail?*

Harold assured us that any suspicious-looking characters—and that included paper dragon contraptions and people in black hats—who jaywalked or violated a city ordinance, or were engaged in any other dubious activity, were to be taken in for questioning. The dragon kite would be used as evidence.

Using Dad's reappearing attorney trick, I said our attorney would be the one to define *who* exactly was engaged in dubious activity. But when Harold asked if we paid our attorney with gold, the attorney disappeared.

Harold was returning by way of the mine district, slowly cruising along as if he had nothing to do till kingdom come.

"I think he wants to show us off," Dillon whispered. "Catch of the day."

"No talking back there," said Harold.

The scene outside was as thick as thieves, and Harold's pleasure faded. The crowds had become so dense that his cruising came to a halt. I jumped when someone slapped the trunk of the car, and Harold said, "Hey!"

Another slap. Some laughter.

Turning to us, Harold said, "Keep your seat belts fastened," and got out. He went around the back to confront the hecklers. I thought it was nothing serious until he shouted an order, whipped out his book, and stormed into the crowd.

Dillon was unbuckling his seat belt, saying, "Get out, Kat!"

I needed no prodding. I unbuckled, got out, and ran.

—⟩✦⟨—

THE MOLLIE KATHLEEN GOLD MINE HAD gone from missing-person crisis to county fair. The yellow police tape I'd seen on TV had been replaced with heavy white rope, and a gold banner waved from the top of the hoist house.

I pushed back my hat to read it.

OLD WEST GOLD MINING ADVENTURE!!! ABOUT TO GET RICHER!!!!

I guess the more exclamation points you put after something, the more exciting it's supposed to be.

We felt reasonably safe in the mix, and decided we'd head back to Rex's for refuge. Harold, as far as we knew, wouldn't know where to look. His car was down the road and one block over, and we would ditch our hats and the kite—which Dillon had become fond of—if Harold came into view. I was glad to be out of the cop car but sad to be above ground, as far from Ye as ever. I was blaming Dillon for the failure of Plan Sideways. If he hadn't challenged me in the middle of the street . . .

Most in the crowd were would-be gold diggers—men, women, and even children—carrying the how low can they go? and that's far enough! signs tacked to shovels and picks. There were the ever-present mom-'n'-pop-arazzi and a pesty TV crew. Vendors sold wares from vans, trailers, pickup trucks, and scooters. Besides shovels and picks, they sold bandannas, flashlights, water bottles, candy bars, bags of nuts, copies of a *Field Guide to Rocks and Minerals*, coils of rope, topographical maps, and a photo-op with a burro. The burro wasn't smiling— that was just his way of trying to remove the gold foil someone had wrapped around his tooth.

There were environmentalists, identified by their lime-colored caps with the name *Green Group* on them.

There was the Romantic Arts Mythological Society, whose members wore unbuttoned shirts covered in green glitter with the tails cut to a tapered point. Under their open shirts, black T-shirts showed a medieval-looking beast with a spiraling horn coming out of its head and the acronym RAMS, printed in white.

Sitting at a card table on the sidewalk were a man and woman, representatives of KYDS, Keepers of Youth Defenses and Safety, offering pamphlets that addressed child-safety issues.

"Here you go, miss," the man said to me, holding out a pamphlet. "This explains our organization."

The woman said, "What would you do if you fell down a mine?"

"Hurt myself," I said.

She looked at me tenderly. "Yes, dear. I know exactly what you mean. We live in a dangerous world."

Dillon took the pamphlet, saying, "Thank you," and nudged me on, trying really hard to be *incognito*.

"Nowww . . ." said a gangly, gawking man who had stepped alongside us, ". . . you look like the type who believes in dragons!" His glittery green shirt fluttered in the breeze he created, and he strode as if to avoid scampering rodents. "Quite the kite you have there!"

Dillon tried scrunching "quite the kite" into "not quite the kite."

"Ever read *The Hobbit*?" the man asked cheerfully.

"Saw the cartoon," I said.

"Saw smog in Kansas City," said Dillon.

"You saw . . . ha! That's funny—Smaug, smog!" He slapped his thigh, which seemed to wobble. "Good enough!"

"Good enough for what?" I asked.

"To qualify for membership in RAMS! I can tell that you're fantasy people!"

"I'm sorry," I said. "You're mistaken. Dragons are real."

"Kat!" Dillon rasped between his teeth while trying to steer my elbow away.

"Dragons are . . . ha! That's the spirit! We need people like you!" With two thin fingers he pulled a purple card from his green shirt pocket and gave it to me, bowing. It was a form to fill out for membership in the Romantic Arts Mythological Society. "Join the local chapter! You'd love it. We get together and dress up as fantasy characters— you know, orcs, ogres, and other phantasmagoria. We have RAMS festivals twice a year. We munch jelly beans!"

"I told you. I don't believe in fantasy, thank you." I handed the card back.

He looked confused. "But you said dragons—"

"Are real."

We had stopped. Dillon was now trying to steer my elbow into a U-turn.

"Dragons are real," the man echoed, his expression gone sour. "You really mean that."

"Come on, Kat." Dillon had found my crazy bone.

"Not till you release my arm," I told him. "That's my sore arm—one of two. Now it's my sorest arm. I'm not made of Silly Putty."

"Sorry," he said, and let go.

"Have fun playing fantasies," I said to the man.

"Right."

"I really mean that."

We left him muttering to himself. "Dragons are real . . . what a stupid girl . . . no imagination . . ."

"Kat," Dillon warned. "You're going to give us away."

"If you tell people the fantastic truth," I explained matter-of-factly, "they *won't* believe you."

The noise of the multitude increased. As we made our way through, someone from the Green Group shouted, "No more digging! No more mining! Let her rest! Let her rest!"

"Let who rest?" I shouted back, thinking—*Mollie Kathleen?*

"Mother Earth!"

Dillon began wrestling with the dragon and my arm again. The shouting stirred the gold-seeking crowd, who started up their chant, "How low can they go! How low can they go!"

Clashing with that came some singing from the RAMS group. The thin man had rallied his members after our little dispute and stood, head and shoulders above singers and kazoo players, his hand over his heart, bleating, "All you need is lore"—*brrra-ta, ta-ta-ta!*—"All you need is lore"—*brrra-ta, ta-ta-ta!*—"All you need is lore, lore! Lore is all you need!" Mom would have recognized the melody, which was an old Beatles' song on one of her records.

Dillon hurried us away.

• • •

If it hadn't been for the kite, parading its carefree self. No matter how Dillon carried the crinkled beast, it unfurled some fanciful part that would go fluttering past our heads or playing at our feet. Dillon threatened at one point to wad it into as small a ball as possible, which still would have been the size of a rain barrel. But there was a silent understanding between us that meant crushing it would somehow jinx Ye. So, avoiding the eyes of fellow pedestrians, we bore up under our paper pet's frolics.

If it hadn't been for us looking like loonies, despite Rex's hats. Or perhaps because of them.

If it hadn't been for my familiar, media-unfriendly face, the one with the famous gold tooth.

If it hadn't been for the kid.

We were one street short of Rex's when the dragon sneaked its tail across the sidewalk and into the plumed rump of a dainty dog that was prancing on a lead. At the front end of the lead was a woman who, in my view, could have used a caution: wide load sign.

The dog yipped and the woman whipped around, unleashing a bristling spray of words—quite purposely—along with her little furry terror—quite accidentally.

I knew the fiend's name.

Duchess.

The woman didn't recognize me, but from behind her popped—give me a dice roll and a pie in the face—the kid who did.

"That's her!" Lucas yelled, pointing his all-day sucker at me. "That's the girl that took my money!"

"What!" blurted his mom.

We halted—our in-clothes-neato, not-so-neato any-more.

"Hey!" said someone else. "That's the girl—"

"The gold-toothed girl!"

"Hey, everybody!"

"The girl that started it!"

"*Yip-yippity-yip! Yippity-yip-yip!*"

Dillon yanked the unruly dragon back into some degree of submission and stood up straight, expecting the worse: to be mobbed, tarred, feathered, drawn and quartered, drummed out of town, or otherwise persecuted.

I pulled out my spoon.

"We're just . . ." Dillon stammered. "She's my little . . ."

"I want my money!"

"Show us the gold!"

"Grab them!"

"Make 'em talk!"

We ran.

With the pink-and-orange dragon crackling and snapping above our heads, we ran. With Duchess yipping in and out of our legs, we ran. With a scramble of gold-crazed chasers who were followed, I was sure, from somewhere back there, bringing up the rear, by Lucas and Wide Load, huffing, we ran.

And a Snickers bar wrapper was stuck to my shoe.

—⊰|⊱—

FORTUNATELY, OWL'S NEST ANTIQUES, RIGHT below Rex's, was open.

Unfortunately, Dillon had let the kite go but not the string. Theseus wanted the string. The dragon, free at last, went zooming over our pursuers' heads, dazzling them momentarily.

The string led right into our hideout.

When we crossed the threshold, Dillon realized his mistake. Not wanting to lose the string, he tried biting it, breaking it, and burnishing it on the doorjamb. He ended up chucking it, ball and all, into the faces of our frenzied followers.

The dragon zipped and dipped, and I saw it no more.

We pulled the door shut and meandered, hearts pounding, among the antiques, looking, under the circumstances, as ho-hum as possible. Duchess had slipped in, sniffing mineral deposits and other delights from my shoes and throwing another yippy fit. We ducked behind a mirrored whatnot standing at the back of the shop, and as the first trick-or-treaters arrived, the shopkeeper met them at the door. We caught a glimpse of the man—a big glimpse, for he was a mountain. If there had been three of him, he would have been the Tetons.

"No dogs!" he bellowed. "No running!"

The doorway was filling up.

"He's . . . not my . . . dog!" someone panted.

"Then whose is it?"

"Don't know! We're looking for—"

"Who?" he asked, and got a volley of answers.

"Two kids!"

"Thieves!"

"Black hats!"

"Girl with a gold tooth!"

"Up front!"

"Bandages on her hands!"

"Broken glasses!"

"Armed with a spoon!"

"Say what?" said the big man. "A spoon?"

"Never mind that! They're wanted—"

"Stole a *spoon*?"

"No!"

"Yes!"

"She has my money!" said Lucas, who had just run in.

The big man turned. He wore suspenders, a walrus mustache, and looked legendary. "*What* was it they stole?" he asked, his black eyes narrowing.

"Gold!" said one.

"Shh!" said several.

"Two dollars!" said Lucas.

"Ah-ha," said the man. "Let me go check." He hove out of sight behind a Louis-the-some-teenth armoire.

Somebody blabbed, "I know I saw the—"

A figurine crashed to the floor.

"You break it, you pay!" boomed the man from somewhere in the southwest corner, and a few cowards left the shop whining.

Despite the owner's thunder and size, however, more folks filed in, suddenly in the mood to buy antiques. A woman tugged her partner's sleeve and pointed to a soup tureen. A man examined a fire poker.

We watched in the mirror's wavy reflection as we crouched low on the floor. They'd point to this item or fondly touch that, while darting their eyes around. We heard Lucas's mom call from up front, "Duch-"—*puff*— "ess!" and Duchess obediently trotted out from between a footstool and a chamber pot and down the main aisle, having performed below and beyond the call of duty, her feathered tail flagging in triumph. It had been a good chase.

"You Rex's guests?"

The mountain man was nearly straddling us, his boots like boats, his mustache clouding our vision.

We nodded eagerly.

His voice was a gentle roar. "Then quick! Get up! The stairway's behind that wall!"

We found the stairway behind that wall and climbed into the darkness.

—⟫⟪—

REX SAT AT ONE END OF THE COUCH AND Dad sat at the other, smiling from the heights of their secret agreement. An agreement that, if Dillon was right, churned in my suspicious stomach.

Dad patted the place between them. "Sit down, Kat."

It was the ol'-buddy, ol'-pal system, where the sucker sits in the middle. Nothing doing.

"Dad," I said. "I'm exhausted."

We had come up the stairs and entered Rex's apartment through a door off the bathroom.

"Then sit."

"I'm in pain."

"Sit."

"We won't bite," said Rex.

I glared at him.

"Well, maybe one lick," he said, trying to soften me up.

I glared at them both. Dad's eyes, normally hazel, were dollar-bill green.

"Katlin," he said. He hit the cushion hard, and a cloud of dust escaped.

Dillon said, "Dad—we've just been through an Ordeal, with a capital O." To me, he said, "Why don't you get a drink, take a breather. . ."

"Dillon." Dad was losing the sale along with his temper.

Dillon said, "Dad, can I talk to you?"

"I'm all ears." But not all smiles—those had vanished.

Dillon glanced at Rex. "In private, please."

Rex threw up his hands. "All right, all right! I know when I ain't wanted." He got up and went to the deck door. "Howard"—it was first name basis now—"call if you need me." He went out.

After disfiguring his typically John Doe face with sternness, impatience, and parental authority, Dad said, "OK. What?"

"Kat's not well."

"Fine."

"Fine?"

"What else?"

"I'll get right to the point."

"Please."

"It's a sharp one."

"Ha, ha."

Dillon sighed as if he was trying to clean a spot on a kettle, to see if was worth shining, and knowing it wasn't. "She wants to give the gold back."

You could have heard a grain of sand drop.

Dad sat stone-stiff. He would be needing a chisel. "Why?" It was the only word in his vocabulary, and he had pulled it out like an impacted molar.

I had not moved. "Dad," I said, "You don't believe in get-rich-quick schemes. Remember?"

—⟫⟪—

REX RUSHED IN, SLAMMED THE DOOR, AND shot the bolt. "The green coats are comin'!" he said. "The green caps, the picketeers, and who knows whose brother's uncle's niece!" He added a few dashes of French Canadian.

"Why?" said Dad, using his newly acquired one-track line.

A knock on the door.

Pounding on the door.

Yells.

Something peppered the front windows. Dillon went over and peered through the curtains. "They're throwing gravel," he said.

Something thudded on the glass.

"And a cucumber."

Something thumped.

"That looks like a buffalo wing."

Suddenly, he ducked, saying, "Watch it!" A hard crack on the glass. "That was a rock," he said in sad wonder. "Left a ding."

Meanwhile, back at the deck door, where Rex bobbed with agitation, a note came shooting through the mail slot. He snatched it up, took one look, wadded it, and tossed it behind him.

I retrieved the paper and smoothed out the wrinkles.

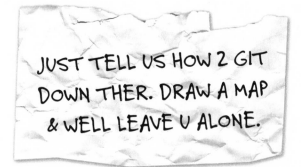

JUST TELL US HOW 2 GIT DOWN THER. DRAW A MAP & WELL LEAVE U ALONE.

Dad's face was back to its customary blankness.

Rex was back in the saddle, spurs a-jingle. "Pardon

my admiration," he said to Dillon and me, "but what'd you two do?"

Dillon looked around the room for a moment, searching for suggestions. "Nothing really. We ran."

I looked at Rex. "You said yourself it was getting bigger."

He nodded solemnly. "So I did, sister." Gravel hit the front windows again. "It's well into the third half."

Dad woke up from his other self. "I think we should call the police. Chief Huffman."

"No!" I said. "I mean—"

The shouting and pounding increased. There were sirens.

Rex said, "I got me a better think."

"What's that?" said Dad.

"She could use a breather." He turned a thumb at me. "Save us all some trouble." He knuckled the top of his head and said apologetically, "I can handle 'em if she ain't around."

Taking me politely by the shoulder, he led me to the bedroom and to the paneled wall. He hooked his finger into the same knothole I had explored in the night, and pulled. A door that was cut into the paneling swung open. I peered in and saw stairs going up.

"That way, darlin'."

——)(——

A DOOR AT THE TOP OPENED ONTO THE roof, where the scene took me totally by surprise. It was a garden. It had a potted tree and planters of flowers. A small fountain rose from a water-filled trough where goldfish flashed. A satellite dish stood next to a sundial.

Gazing at the scene, I realized how Rex's little kingdom had all these little secrets. How many rooms were in his place? How many doorways, stairways, hidden panels? A main room, a bedroom, a bath. A stairway to an antique shop, a stairway to the roof. Simple. Why did it unfold like a Chinese puzzle?

I sat down in a lawn chair and turned my gaze beyond the roof. A townscape of chimneys, antennae, wires, pipes, signs, air-conditioning units, pigeons. The topside, backside of things; the complex with the plain.

In the distance blazed a bright spot of color like a butterfly on the grill of a car. It was the paper dragon, caught and flapping forlornly in a network of power lines.

I wished better things for Ye.

Yet seeing this view of Cripple Creek removed me from the fears and frets I lived with at ground level. It was like looking in on a sleeping, naughty child. From this perspective, it was easy to be forgiving.

I forgave Harold the Younger, who was just trying to do his duty, overkill though it was. I forgave the mob below, even as they groped toward me with their gold-greedy hands. I had done no better, down in Ye's cavern. I forgave Rose Robbins for her rude, intruding way. If I pursued journalism, that could be me in twenty years. I forgave Rex for wanting his due at my expense. He had also been helpful and generous. I forgave Dillon for his momentary madness, wanting the gold like everyone else. I forgave Dad for his lapse of respect for what he knew was right. He was under a lot of pressure to provide for those he loved.

I looked up at the deep, deep sky.

In that moment, I saw my deepest mind. Like a shaft of light that burns a hole in the clouds before they close up again, I saw it.

There was one person I couldn't forgive for all the trouble she had caused.

Calamity Cat.

⟶⟩ ⟨⟵

I WAS DREAMING. IN MY DREAM, I WAS walking along a path and dropping little gold nuggets from a bag. Ye was following, gently murmuring as he went, but I couldn't hear his words. He seemed pleased with something, nodding his head as if he had come to a decision. I kept dropping the nuggets and looking back at him until, out of the gloom above me, blackbirds came. They began pecking up the gold as though it was crumbs or seeds. I ran after them, screaming, and they beat their wings against my face. I swung the bag at them, but it was empty. I let the bag go, and it blew away down the path. The birds were gone.

Ye was gone.

· · ·

I opened my eyes to a tangerine sky. Pikes Peak shone sunset-stained. And all that lay beneath it, below the reach of light, slumbered in blue. A haze blanketed the east.

My belly hurt with hunger. I got up and saw Dillon sitting in the stairwell, his head on his arms. He had brought me dinner. I lifted the napkin on the plate to find cheese and crackers, and under the plate was a big bowl of soup. I didn't see a spoon, but I had one already.

Dillon woke when I spoke his name.

"Hi, Kat," he said lazily. "You've been asleep."

"So have you." I started eating.

"How is it?" he asked.

"Did you make it?"

He nodded. "Sort of."

"It's good. Soup's a little cold, but I'm hungry." I wiped my mouth on the napkin. "Did you eat?"

"Yeah. We all did."

We talked. He told me that when more cops showed up the crowds thinned out. He never saw Harold or Huffman, and no cops had come to the door.

"It's on every news channel, Kat."

"The riot?"

"No, the gold. Your gold. Everybody's gold."

"It's not my gold. It's not everybody's gold."

"People are coming from all over," he said, ignoring my words. "As far away as Florida. One guy flew in from England, enamored with the American West, he said."

"What!"

"Denver airport is packed. Flights are overbooked. It's a mess. So are the roads."

The low drone I heard in the background—was that traffic, rolling in from all corners of the country, and beyond? For what?

The dream I'd had appeared behind my eyes. But I couldn't see the gold. All I could see were the birds. I watched the fountain for a moment, until my gaze shifted to the poor dragon kite. My hand trembled as I set down the dishes.

"Kat, are you OK?"

I sighed. "Dillon, I don't think I gave Ye the pearl willingly. I was under a trance. I wasn't thinking anything, or feeling anything. I just . . . gave it to him. The way you'd give a cashier your money."

"In other words," he said, "you don't think he'll live forever."

"I just don't know. I *want* him to live forever."

"Then if you want that for him, he probably will."

I turned to him, wanting him to prove my worries wrong. "I bet Ye *can* be killed. Like the elves in Tolkien. They'll live forever as long as they're not killed."

"Kat—"

"What if they cage him? What if they put him in a zoo? I can't bear the thought of some snotty-nosed kid smacking on a snow cone and gawking through the bars at him. Ye's too precious." I knew Dillon couldn't relieve my mind— that was asking too much. I headed toward the stairs.

"Kat, wait." He picked up the dishes and stood, gazing at the sunset. He breathed in the air. "Sure is beautiful." He turned to me. "Dad's not budging."

I was listening.

"He's given Rex his word. Kat *will* show Rex the way in, he said, and take him to the gold. Tonight."

I was stone silent.

"Rex is flying him to San Francisco. And he's flying *us* home, at Dad's request. Tomorrow."

"What?" I blurted. "That's . . . that's—"

"Crazy," agreed Dillon. "It is."

"Where will we stay?"

"The Home has a vacant room right now. Someone apparently—"

"Not Mom!"

"Not Mom."

"But why?"

"It's part of their deal. Dad thinks he'll lose his chance. We keep getting in his way."

"You mean me."

"He said . . ." Dillon paused, obviously hesitant to tell.

"What did he say, Dillon?"

"He said, he's beginning to think you're bad luck."

—⟩⟨—

DESPERADO WAS TOO GOOD A WORD. I searched my heavy head for something that described the way I felt, and came up empty.

Dad and Rex were on all fours behind the couch, calling out numbers and rolling dice. My dice, the pair Dad had taken from me.

The shades were drawn at each window. A small desk lamp and the TV, which was on with no sound, were the only sources of light.

As we entered the room, Rex was saying, "You owe me, brother. Big-time." When he saw me, he jumped up. "Here she is."

Dad got up slowly and guiltily—by the look on his face I knew he'd been losing. By the look on Rex's face, I knew he hadn't.

But the stakes were a lot higher than a petty game of dice.

Dad picked up the TV remote and turned the volume up. He must have been waiting for this.

"Thank you for joining us."

An interview was on. A woman was talking to a man in a cushy studio setting, where a glass wall displayed the same evening sky I had seen from the roof, with the Rockies in silhouette.

"We have Professor Chester Lowe, senior scientist at the Division of Mining and Geology in Boulder, Colorado," the woman was saying.

"My pleasure."

"Professor Lowe, you're a leading authority on mineralogy." A nod from Professor Lowe.

A nod from Dad.

"Tell us, is there just cause for all this excitement? Is there really more gold, lots of it, to be unearthed?"

Professor Lowe smiled as if he wasn't feeling well. "One gold nugget was found. Perhaps the largest ever seen in the Rocky Mountain region. It has not been classified or even identified, except by sight alone. Naturally, a nugget of that size—"

"Can we rely on that? Sight alone?"

"A nugget that size can be identified by sight alone, yes." His eyebrows went up.

Dad's eyebrows went up.

"Is it true that where one nugget is, there are more?"

"Any geologist would expect to find more."

"And that's what folks are counting on."

"Literally." Professor Lowe smiled broadly.

Dad smiled broadly.

"Tell us, if you will—is there enough to go around? Or will this be a repeat of the first gold rush in . . . when was it . . . nineteen—"

"Eighteen. Eighteen forty-nine." His smile faded.

Dad's smile remained.

"Thousands headed west at that time—"

"Hundreds of thousands."

"—enduring great hardships, only to return with nothing."

Dad's smile faded.

"Right. The early birds got the gold. I'm not an economic geologist, but it's my guess that more gold will be collected, whether by mining or—"

"Professor Lowe, our time is up, thank you for coming in." Turning to the TV audience, she said, "You heard it! All that glitters *is* gold!"

Dad's smile returned, and he looked boldly at me as if to say, *See? There's more gold, and you, my daughter, know where it is.*

I went to the kitchen for a drink. A bouquet of daisies stood on the counter, rising cheerily from a foil container— out of place in the gloom. The florist's card said, *To the gold-tooth girl, from an admirer. Don't ever change.*

Dillon came to my side. "We had a couple of visitors after the mob left," he explained, and he placed his hand over something that lay beside the flowers.

"What's that?" I asked.

"Nothing."

"It's a rock, isn't it?"

He removed his hand. "It flew in when Rex opened the door for the florist."

It was a smooth gray rock that had words written on it with a black marker.

**Leave before Sundown.
we Dont want you hear.**

———)|(———

"MIDNIGHT," I WHISPERED.

Dillon gave me one slight nod.

I was ready. The blood in my veins rushed with readiness. Godzillion wild horses wouldn't hold me back. And if that wasn't enough, all the forgiving I'd done on Rex's rooftop wouldn't. I wanted to be rid of this monstrous gold rock that clung to me magnetized, that circled the world for everyone to crave.

I was sick of the gold.

I was sick of greed more. I'd go barefoot in the snow, live in a wigwam, eat radishes. I'd be the poorest of the poor before I'd hold onto that gold. I'd have my tooth pulled first chance I got. Even if we couldn't afford enamel.

My disgust sweetened my love for Ye. I'd be seeing him soon. In just a few hours. At last.

Ahead of Dad and Rex.

Dad had given me my marching orders as I sat sullen on the buckboard bed. "We are going to the mine," he said with finality. "Before dawn. Rex is coming. You will show him the way. Ahead of the masses."

Staring at him was like staring at a beloved pet that got hit by a car: Suddenly, it's a useless lump of fur. The life is gone and the raw law of nature has replaced it. Dad wasn't breathing anymore. He wasn't my father.

Seeing something that must have looked like repulsion in my face, he said, "I'm your father."

Dillon, who had been listening, came in close. "I'll say it this time without an ounce of guilt, Dad: I thought you were the child protection service."

A wrinkle of regret scurried across Dad's face and dissolved just as quickly. His mind was set in cement, his eyes were the color of future wealth. "Three a.m., Miss Katlin Graham. I'll come wake you." He went to the door and added, "You *will* obey."

Nobody said good night.

No. 5

DAWN'S EARLY LIGHT

"KAT!" SOMEONE WAS SHAKING MY FOOT. "Kat!"

I rolled over and blinked through the spokes of a wheel. The cactus in the corner was leaking light.

"Kat!" Dillon stuck his head inside the wheel.

"Meow," I said, and threw off the bearskin blanket. I was fully dressed, ready to prowl. Ready to enact my new plan.

This time, it would have the right name. We had named the others all wrong: Forward, Backup, Sideways.

This was Plan Downward, because that's the direction we needed to go.

"The bathroom window," I said.

"Right."

Earlier in the night, I had crept around, checking on things. Rex was bagged down on the living room floor, not outside. Dad was dead on the dead horse couch. Originally, we were going to use the fire escape, which I had noticed on the rooftop, but this was better: The window was right off the deck.

I climbed out of bed. "You have everything?"

He patted his pockets. A small flashlight in one—he had found it in a kitchen drawer—and the street map in the other. "Everything but string."

"I don't think we'll need it," I said, pulling the pillowcase off my pillow.

"What's *that* for?" asked Dillon.

"You'll see." I stuffed it into my sweatshirt.

"It's not . . . you're not . . . that's not for . . ." He suddenly looked like a child, hugging himself with a chill. ". . . gold?"

"Dillon, you're still an idiot—but I forgive you."

Recovering his valiant self, he reached into the fishbowl and pulled out a fortune.

"What's it say?" I asked.

"Outhouse or bust."

· · ·

The night was silent for a town overrun with newcomers. We kept to the darkness when we could, against all street-wise codes; it was that or risk being seen. With every passing car, we hunkered down. A police patrol cruised by, raising a surge inside me. Was it Harold? What would he do *this* time? Would he clap handcuffs on and give us the third degree? Would he at last win his promotion, have Chief Huffman dub him "Sir Harold the Younger" with his nightstick?

Would we be sentenced to life? Or be blindfolded and hanged?

When we were free of downtown and heading through the residential area, the only other alerts we had were a barking dog and a man smoking on an unlit porch. Cutting my eyes his way, I saw a red tip flare and fade.

We neared the Warrens. I spotted their place, sleeping in the dark. We rushed down their drive and stepped through trampled weeds, where Dillon nearly tripped.

"Look at this, Kat!" he whispered, flashing the light across a broken shovel with the sign still attached. how low can they go?

That accounted for the trampled weeds.

"It makes sense," I said, "that people would search the area where I showed up after the accident."

We arrived at the outhouse. It looked untouched except by time, which had its handprints all over it.

"This wouldn't last another winter," said Dillon. "It's the leaning tower of poo-poo."

"Dillon—"

"You sure this is the place to go?"

"Dillon, stop! My sides ache bad enough."

The outhouse door creaked a warning as we clambered inside.

"Huh," said Dillon, aiming the light. "A double ringer."

Then the beam caught Cotton-Eyed Joe, who glared at us with murderous disapproval. I noted which eye had been damaged—his right.

After a quick read, Dillon said, "I see."

I took his flashlight hand and guided it down the toilet seat hole. "There," I said. "I'll go first."

"Now who's telling bad jokes?"

I descended without a hitch. But Dillon snapped the first rung and down he went, bypassing the rest of the roost and landing at my feet in dried muck.

"Sorry," I said. "I should have told you. The first rung's a doozy."

"Not anymore."

. . .

Crawling with the mini-light in my mouth, I led the way through the tunnel. When it emptied into the main passage, we were able to stand. Dillon reproached himself for having pitched the string away, but I explained to him my use of rocks as markers.

We had a choice of two directions: the branch to our left, or the one straight ahead. I was sure the left-hand one was the one Ye had backed into when we'd said good-bye, so I took the straight one.

Not questioning my navigational skills—which were as developed as my attempts at public relations—Dillon followed. I had no dragon to lead me, the spotty beam of the flashlight was small, and I hoped there were no confusing branches off the passageway. But it went easier than I expected, and I realized that being rested and well fed, rather than lame and stressed, made a difference. We descended the entire way, and my confidence increased. After a time, I smelled a draft that brought the green pool to mind, and I knew we were drawing close.

Smiling to myself, I quivered with anticipation. Ye would soon see I was better than a scruffy, dirty, hobbling human. I looked respectable and clean. I would make a good second impression. Plus, I would place the gold at his feet, with sincere apologies, and kiss his royal snout.

"Watch your step, now," I cautioned. "It gets a little rough."

Crossing the gnarled entrance, we entered the crystal cave. We came to the murky pool. Unlike the warmth of Ye's dragonlight, the flashlight cast a creepy effect on its surface, one of certain doom. We skirted the pool. We were past it. Formations bobbed in and out of the blackness like balding gnomes. Skeletal columns wandered by.

My expectations sank. The cavern was cold, the mist evaporated, the magic unmade.

I flashed the light randomly. The gleam of a bottle, the dust of the game board, the chalk of a stalactite, a few golden glints.

Dillon gasped at the gold, but I gasped in despair.

Ye was gone.

—⟫⟨—

"YE?" I CALLED. "YE?"

I'd been calling for some time, my voice hoarse and spattered with tears.

Dillon was quite the opposite: He was enthralled. He sauntered here and there, trying to mask his glee by remarking on ordinary things. "Who played, I wonder? Hmm, black resigned. The pawn would become queen. These explosives: How long are they active, I wonder? Pretty small boot for a man . . ."

Finally, he could not hold it in. "This gold! It's unreal! I cannot believe this gold! Godzillions!"

I had called myself sick. I slumped to the floor.

"Just think what you could *do* with all this gold! You could go private jet! Sail the world! Own an island! You could—"

"Dillon!" I cried. "Stop! It isn't yours! It's not what you think it is!"

"It's gold . . . looks like gold to me . . ."

His voice became fainter and fainter. As I moaned in my anguish, I sounded like someone else. Either the flashlight went out, or my vision did.

· · ·

I must have dozed or fainted, for I realized I'd been hearing my name. Echoes rose from my subconscious. Even then, I didn't answer. What was there to say?

"Kat."

Dillon was nearby.

"You OK?"

I shook my head.

"Kat." He came close and squatted down. He touched my shoulder. He touched my hair. "Have you ever—" He halted.

"What," I said absently. "Ever what."

"Don't get upset." Again he touched my shoulder. "Come on. Get up."

I could not move. Feeling the flashlight in my hand, I

shone it on the crevice I had wiggled through, so long ago now, though really only days, when I first saw the last of the dragons, the beautiful, ancient dragons.

Could Ye have squeezed through there?

"Kat, have you ever—"

"Ever what."

"Doubted."

"Doubted what."

"The reality of Ye."

—◦)(◦—

DILLON WAS BABBLING ON AND ON ABOUT whether dragons existed or not, and if they did, turned to gold or not, but that one thing was sure, that gold was rare, and rare things were precious and therefore valuable, and since society valued rare and precious things, whoever *owned* rare and precious things could live any way they wanted.

Babble, babble, babble.

I had given up on arguing that not all rare and precious things were something you could plop into your pocket or onto the betting table or into a bank account, blast it all, and that dragons were rare and precious things and *that* was why gold was rare and precious, bless it all, and since dragons turned to gold, and since Ye was a dragon, the gold was *his.*

Why bother?

I shone the flashlight on an impression in the dirt. "That's his footprint," I said. "You can believe me or not."

"It could be a fossilized leaf."

"A leaf. Down here. You idiot."

"Or a starfish."

"A starfish. Ha."

"They've found seashells in the desert."

"This is not the desert!" I shone the light rudely into his face, to see what he looked like to make such stupid remarks. His face looked just like Dad's. I shone it back on the four-point impression, which was shaped like a playing card club and spade combined. "That's his footprint. Ye was here. I can smell him."

The debate left me cold, the kind of cold you'd feel if you were stuck on the moon.

"I'm leaving," said Dillon abruptly. "Print or no print, smell or no smell, dragon or no dragon." He walked away, muttering, "There is no dragon, but there's *all this gold.*"

I let him go. Into the blackness. Without a light of his own.

I got up and went over to the ditch where the skeleton lay.

Let Dillon stumble. Let him whack his head on a rock.

I shone the light on the bones. The old rotten bones.

Let him know what it's like to stumble in the dark.

The old rotten bones that had died, when flesh hung on them, with blood on their hands.

Let him slip into the pool like a stone. He asked for it.

The old rotten bones of Cotton-Eyed Joe. Yep— there it was. His eye socket, his right, bashed in. I took out the pillowcase and shook it open. I took out my spoon and hooked it into the good socket and dangled the skull.

It comes down to this, I thought. *A grinning globe of calcium and dirt. The tongue no longer cursing, the eye empty of greed.*

I plopped it into the bag.

I pulled the gold from my pocket and gave it a sad kiss—the kiss I had saved for Ye.

I gave it a benediction. "May this gold, Ye's ancestry, lie here long after these blasphemous bones have turned to dust. Long after the town of Cripple Creek cracks, withers, and fades. Long after I'm grown and gone and my kids have kids and their kids have kids, and so on and so forth, time without end, amen." I dropped the gold into the ditch. It broke through Joe's ribs, rolled an inch or two, and lay still.

But it would be stolen before the night was out.

—⇥ ⇤—

DILLON WAS NOT THERE.

I stood at the pool, shining the light onto its ghastly surface.

"Dillon?" I said feebly.

Nothing.

"Dillon!" I said loudly.

Nothing.

"Dillon!" I screamed.

Echo . . . echo . . . echo . . .

How could I have been that cruel, that harsh, that . . . *murderous?* After preaching on things rare and precious, things you can't buy—for example, sisterly love—how could I have let him wander away?

It wasn't *his* fault Ye was gone. He had never seen Ye's magic, heard his voice, touched his shimmery scales. What else was Dillon to do?

What good was preaching if you didn't practice what you preached?

Well, Kat, what good was preaching when you have a brother to find?

I turned to run, skidded in cavern clay, pitched forward, splashed through split pea soup, righted myself, kept going. It was all uphill. I tried not to think. I only breathed—that was enough. I supposed I cried, because I tasted salt.

Then I smelled smoke. Smoke!

Ye!

I quickened my pace, hope skittering inside me. Ye would help me find Dillon. He would know what to do. Now I was crying from relief.

But the smell of the smoke was not as I remembered. It was not dragon smoke.

A spark flared up ahead.

An orange mask.

A face in the light of a match.

"I was worried," said Dillon, approaching. "I came to find you."

• • •

In case the flashlight should go dead, he explained, he

had brought a box of matches he'd picked up from the Empire Hotel.

My crying hiccupped into a laugh. I had my brother back.

"Look at you, Kat," he said. "You're a mess."

I straightened my glasses and turned the flashlight on myself. He was right. Several times, I had fallen and now had a generous coating of subterranean browns, on top of the soaking I had got from the green goo near the pool. Several times, I had shed tears and smeared my face—I felt the clay caking up on my cheeks. Also, I listed to the left: My knee injury had opened.

I looked no different than when I had met Ye. Probably worse.

But what did it matter?

I looked glumly into Dillon's face. "Plan Downward has failed, too," I said. "And it's no good trying to persuade you—"

He lit another match, illuminating his face. The illumination went beyond a mere kitchen flame: He shone like the gift of the magi. And I knew. I knew it was the glow of enchantment. I knew he was under the spell. It wasn't fantasy. It was reality, history, prehistory, stretching its strange beauty across the millennia and into our pitiful, scrambled-up world.

I knew he had seen a dragon face-to-face.

Dillon had met Ye.

———⟩(⟨———

WE WALKED HAND IN HAND. HE HAD PUT away the matches and carried the flashlight. I had my pillowcase.

As we walked, he told me. Burning match after match, he had made good progress and was rounding a bend when he heard me scream his name. It had to have been a scream, he thought, at that distance. She's in trouble, he concluded, and immediately turned. As he did, something shoved him from behind. The mass behind the force was so tremendous, he knew it could have ended his life if it had wished. But there was grace in the act. Dillon had rolled, heels over head, his match extinguished, and lain at the mercy of the presence looming above him in the dark. Then the eyes, golden and deep, surfaced in his blindness, burning from their own inner source, like light from a well of wisdom. "I smell girl," the dragon breathed. "Someone I know." "That would be my sister," Dillon gasped. "Ah," breathed the dragon. "I also smell gold, something I know intimately well." "That would be this," Dillon confessed, and emptied out his pockets. ("Dillon!" I interjected.) After that, Ye had let him up.

"Isn't he marvelous!" I said.

Dillon didn't answer. We had rounded the bend. And there he glowed, like a cumulus cloud after a storm.

"Hello, Kat," Ye said cordially.

"How," I said, and pushed back a strand of my hair.

—⟩ ⟨—

THE MOMENT IS PRESSED IN MY MIND LIKE the forget-me-nots in my first journal, that stain the page with blue and gold and bittersweetness. I peer from another time and place into that little scene lit by dragon glow and battery-operated beam, and see the three of us, contemplating fate and one another. It's Dillon and Ye poking along the edges of philosophies and dreams, while I probe translucent wings with a flashlight.

It's both of us telling Ye about the trouble that brews above.

• • •

We painted the bleakest picture for him, describing the magnitude of it—the involvement of media, the mine, the general public.

"It won't be long," I fretted, "before they come. They'll penetrate your world with picks and shovels—"

"With drilling machines," said Dillon.

"They're going to expand the mine, Ye. They'll find you. Maybe you'll live forever, or"—I looked away—"or maybe not."

He was studying me intently.

"And if they can't hurt you," said Dillon, "they might try to capture you."

Ye mulled over our words, puffing out a pillow of smoke now and then, wheezing a little. "I have heard scratchings," he said. "They are rats, human rats. I have heard them before, over the centuries."

"Things are more sophisticated now," said Dillon.

Ye gave him a look of disgust. "More sophisticated? How can that be? Man has not changed since he first set a rude blade into this soil. He is a common knave."

"I don't mean—"

"There are a few exceptions, as a matter of course," Ye added, and gave us a contented growl.

"I don't mean man himself," said Dillon, "but his inventions."

"These people are determined," I said. "Desperate.

Please, Ye, find yourself a new home. The Andes . . . or the Himalayas . . . or . . . the Blue Ridge Mountains in Virginia! They're nice." I smiled to confirm it.

"The Blue Ridge," Ye murmured. "Quaint and homely . . . a pleasant place . . ." He coughed somberly, shook off his reverie, and said, "No. I was younger then. Now I am old. This is my home. This is where I have settled. And—" He swung his head in the direction we had come. "I have made precautions. I was shoring up beams and boulders at the far end when I detected you."

"What about your cavern?" I interrupted. "The crevice. That's how I first got in."

He eyed me patiently. "That is my squint." When he saw this didn't register with either of us, he explained, "Castles have squints. You would call it a peephole."

"I call it a weakness," Dillon said bluntly. "If a girl could slip in—"

Something rumbled inside of Ye, like thunder preparing for a storm. Dillon took a step back, but Ye only coughed.

"I am a dragon," he proclaimed. "I was here when mammoths roamed free. I have witnessed great sweeps of nature, the polestar shifting from Thuban to Polaris, glaciers gulping mountainsides like snakes swallowing toads. I have seen civilizations rise and fall. Battles come and go—"

"And dragons," I had the boldness to remind him. "They've come and gone, too."

He stopped and stared at me thoughtfully, as if I'd made a strategic move in chess.

"Mammoths," said Dillon, "are no more."

Ye's eyes wavered. He sighed smokily and cleared his throat.

Then a change rippled through him, like a shift in the wind. His head lifted, his nostrils flared. "Rats," he said, and blew a stream of smoke that started to make a fist but curled instead like a fiddlehead fern.

I held still, testing the void with my senses, and only imagined what Ye must have heard or smelled or felt.

"These rats will stop at nothing," said Dillon.

"Oh?" said Ye. He prodded the air with his nose, as if rooting out the threat, and the rumble inside him rolled again. He blew more smoke and sidestepped like a swordsman, swiping the air with practice. Then he growled, expanded his chest, coughed and spat more smoke, and lumbered away in the dark.

We hurried after.

—➤⊱⊰◆—

DILLON SAYS IT WAS DESTINY. I SAY IT WAS the huge stalagmite, the Grecian column. Whatever it was that spared him, Ye survived the explosion.

And Ye saved us.

Once again we entered his chamber. I was trudging alongside his right flank, Dillon strode near his right foreleg, when Ye halted and studied the gloom of the hall.

Scrapings came from the crevice—his squint—across the way. A thin blue beam flashed into the cavern.

Someone was trying to squeeze through, just as I had.

We heard a man say, "Can't get it," and another man say, "Get back."

"Ye!" I whispered.

Ye was as still as stone, though his rumbling continued to roll. For a fractured moment, the blue beam spotlighted Ye's nose, showing two simmering coils of smoke.

More mutterings from the intruders.

"Ye!" I whispered. "Shoot some fire!"

He broke mid-rumble to swing his head down to me. "Shoot fire? I am not that kind of dragon."

"But you can't let them steal your gold!"

He gave me a look that puts an ache in my soul when

I recall it—a look of both pity and perplexity—but I had no reason then to understand why.

Nor any time to try, for an orange spark blossomed in the dark.

Ye heaved his bulk to shield us from the blast that roared across the hall. I was knocked flat. Dillon cried out like a bird lost in a blizzard, and the room billowed with a sour stench.

I lay shock-still, blinking the flash from my eyes.

Then Dillon had me by the arm, shouting, "You all right? You all right?"

I rose, and Ye began nudging us both, guiding us into the tunnel. We stumbled along, silent except for our panting.

When we reached the wide bend, Ye, steaming and huffing, reared like a rainbow and pivoted, his eyes glaring golden and dragon-keen into the ugly ruin behind us.

Dillon and I sank to the ground—two shaken humans, huddling, gritty, damp.

"It's too late!" I gasped. "Ye's cavern . . ."

Dillon nodded.

"The crack," I blubbered. "Explosives . . . to widen it."

Ye said, "Be still."

I tried to be still, but my insides were tumbling, my heart wouldn't slow, my senses stung.

Suppressing a rumble beneath his breath, Ye peered at us and asked, "You have not been hurt?"

"No," said Dillon.

"I don't think so," I said.

We watched him pace. It was not the kind of pace people make, wearing out a stretch of floor or rug until a judgment is made. It was winding and curling the way a dog does for the perfect position, unwilling and restless with every move. It was a sluggish tail-chase of indecision. He wove this way and that, slow and tormented, making groans now and then, while Dillon and I sat unmoving.

I realized Ye was at a crossroads.

His cavern was no more. It was no more his cavern. Its beauty had been erased, the delicate with the grand, destroyed. He could no longer barricade his bedroom; it was too late for that. Like a leak in a dam, the break had opened. He'd be overrun with rats. Whoever set the explosives could be gathering up gold this minute.

I closed my eyes. What was he to do?

Dragons are creatures of contradiction. They're either earthbound or airborne, slithering or soaring, swimming or spitting flames. After slumbering for centuries, cloaking himself in darkness, turning his eye, his memory, from the pain of all things lost, could Ye now sail the sky? Could he turn his face to the sun, tip his wings to the clouds, glide above the land instead of burrow beneath it?

Could he choose waking over dreaming?

I looked up.

He had stopped pacing. His eyes were lacquered rust. He reached back his head and licked at something. Frowning, I got up to examine him. But I had no light—I had lost it during the blast.

His dragonlight was dimming.

Something was stuck in his side, like a huge splinter.

"Oh, Ye!" I said tearfully, and put out my hand.

"Do not touch," he said grimly. "Let it be. I would rather it stop the hole it made than leak blood over the land for men to trail. For dragon's blood, too, turns to gold. Gold dust."

Resisting the urge to protest, I stepped back, horrified.

"It will be my thorn in the flesh," he said.

"What is it?" asked Dillon.

"The cursed pick, shrapnel from the blast."

"The miner's pick?"

"No!" I sobbed.

"A souvenir to my foolishness."

"What do you mean?" I cried, wiping away fresh tears. "It's not your foolishness! It's mine! I started this whole disaster! Instead of saving us, I've ruined us! Everything's ruined!"

He waved my words away. "No. I have been foolish to think I might dwell here forever."

What was he saying now? That he would not live in the cave anymore? Or not live forever?

What about the pearl?

—⟫⟪—

IN THE DUST-FILLED GLOOM OF THE DRAGON-light, Dillon and I watched as Ye removed the beams and boulders he had shored up earlier in the evening. We were at the far end of the branch opposite the hole that led to the outhouse.

The branch was the original tunnel. Ye had enlarged it long ago after discovering a natural entry. He had sealed it, he told us, before the Mollie Kathleen had been established.

"You mean," I said, "you haven't been out since then? You haven't breathed fresh air?"

Heaving the biggest timber from its place, he grunted, "Stay back!"

We stayed back.

"I have not"—he puffed—"seen the Milky Way for well over a hundred years. Perhaps two hundred." He started prying a slab of stone.

"Oh, Ye," I said, fanning clouds of dust, "it's fabulous—the Milky Way! You couldn't guess!"

Ye said nothing, just wheezed and kept working. After a while he said, "I remember. A dragon's memory is as good as gold." He worked the slab loose, stopped, sniffed, peered over at me, and said, *"Fresh air?"*

I had no answer—I thought the mountain air was divine.

"Stand back, now," he said. "Watch out." He broke an even larger stone from its roots, the earth shook, rocks and dirt fell, and a hole appeared. He stepped forward, nosing the night.

Dillon and I joined him in the doorway.

"Yes," he said, gently plucking something caught between his claws. It was a wildflower. But he was looking upward. "So there it is. Now I know my dreams are real. I have dreamed this, the dimming of the heavens." He set the wildflower aside. "Your ways have dimmed more things than just Earth. Like the man who goes a little more blind each day and does not know, until the day he wakens in the night and feels the sun on his face. Now I know."

I touched a tender place on his neck, under his jaw, where my mother would place her hand on me. I said, "You dreamed about this?"

"Sleeping and waking." He said it as if he were dreaming still.

"Did the stars go out completely?"

"Before I went below," he said, "I witnessed the northern and southern lights on a single night. The aurora. There, on Sun Mountain. That was the Ute people's name for it—a name that honors its glory—before Pike named it after himself—a name that reveals the pride of man." His voice went stale. "The dreams are black shadows in my eyes."

I knew then that he wept, for starlight glistened on his cheeks. We were quiet awhile, out of respect for his sadness.

Though the heavens looked brilliant to me, I said sympathetically, "I guess it has lost some of its spangle. Smog and stuff—"

"Industry," said Dillon, trying to be helpful. He wiped some grit from around his mouth. "Automobiles. Air pollution."

"Yes," replied Ye. "Fragments of it have trickled into my sanctuary."

Suddenly flinging off his grief, Ye turned to the northwest sky, and my hand slid away. With a kind of tipsy reverence he gazed, and in a voice only a dragon could make, which I would later try imitating on sleepless nights, he said, "I am but a spark in time to that."

He blew a beautiful smoke ring that glowed lavender in the dark and wandered up, up, beyond the tips of aspens, wavered a long moment, and spread like a halo around a shattered spear of stars.

Dillon and I watched in dizzy wonder.

"Draco," Ye said solemnly. "The Dragon. Thuban, once the polestar, shines in his tail. Five thousand years ago you could see it from Khufu's burial chamber in the Great Pyramid at Giza."

"The Great Pyramid?" I asked. "You were there?"

"I have been everywhere," he murmured. Then he added so quietly I thought I must have imagined it, "Except at death's door."

⟶⟩⟨⟵

THE WONDERMENT WAS OVER.

Ye was leaving.

Somewhere on the fringes of town, in dense dark foliage, we made our way. Dillon and I followed as best we could, barging through brambles and branches and stands of aspens, while Ye passed through as cool as moonlight. Only once was he hindered, when an old rusty rod driven into a tree snagged his wing. He had to back away from it to free himself.

We were headed down a gulch, where a stream sloshed and sighed.

"That rivulet flows into the creek that gave the town its name," Ye said. "Watch your step. Beasts have broken their legs on these slopes, coming to drink."

"Oh!" I exclaimed as I yanked my shoe from a tangled root. "Is that where they get the Cripple in Creek?"

"Smart girl."

We drank the cold water. Ye remarked how its sweetness was gone, and I rinsed my face.

Then he pulled the pick from his side and washed out his wound. Darkness ran from it. As we crossed to the other side, I looked over my shoulder.

Far downstream swirls glittered starlit and golden.

The opposite bank was not as steep, and eventually leveled out. Civilization crept forward through the patches of brush: a pile of trash, a stray croquet ball, a barking dog, the distant drone of a truck. It was long past night, but too early to be called morning.

The trees thinned and Ye stopped. Something flew past us, a black shadow on a silent wind, and I cried out.

"Only an owl," said Ye, laughing softly to himself.

Dillon, still walking ahead, was busy plucking twigs from his fleece jacket. Then he knelt to tie his shoe, lost in the shadows.

Like a butterfly emerging from its sleepy wraps, Ye opened his wings and closed them again.

I couldn't let him go without a proper farewell, though I knew I would crumble at a mere whisper. I went to him and gazed, trying to recall the smoldering, subterranean creature I had first met. His shimmering scales were like autumn locked in ice, his wings like parchment stained purple. His pupil was huge and his thin golden iris broke around it like a sun in eclipse. The patch along his throat, the colors of ivory and nutmeg, raced with his pulse. That's where I had laid my hand.

I wanted to cup this moment like water in my palms, already thirsting for it.

With no warning, Ye spread his wings and the wind blew me back.

I fell to my knees and dropped my pillowcase. I

covered my face and wailed. I had wanted to kiss him and bless him, the way my mother would have done. But I knew I did not matter. He lived and dreamed outside the window of my world, drifting on a wide universal tide.

I lowered my wail to a whimper and looked up—he was still there.

He yawned, released a spiral of smoke from off his tongue, and folded his wings. He coughed once, and said, "Rise, Kat."

Weakly and meekly, I rose.

He held out a hand—all satin and leather and claws— for me to grasp. "Forever is a long, long time," he said sadly.

I nodded, my eyelids beating like birds caught in a rain.

"Too long a time," he said, "to run from hole to hole in this hostile world—to run until all the holes are filled or cleared or taken. Do you understand?"

I nodded, thinking I understood, wanting to understand.

"Who knows what the world will become?" he said.

I nodded again; all I could do was nod—it was the least painful thing for me in that moment—nod and gaze. His pupil had got so big his eye was a mirror of the softening sky, a blend of mystery and recognition. I saw myself in it, miniature and wide-eyed.

"What is your mother's name?" he asked abruptly.

"My . . . my mother?" I whispered, startled by the question.

"The pearl was your mother's, you said."

"Oh. Yes. Yes, it was." My thoughts went topsy-turvy.

"Her name?" Ye repeated.

"Oh! Pearl. Her name is Pearl."

"Ahhh." He sighed a ripple of smoke that lapped along the leaves, and he studied me with an aching, satisfied gleam in his eye. "How beautiful, how tragic."

When he lifted the claw on the warm finger I was clutching, I frowned at it stupidly. This was not good-bye: On the point of his claw was the ring, with the pearl glowing moist as a November moon.

"Take it, Katlin."

"I . . . But I thought . . . Don't . . . don't you want to live forever?"

"There is more that shines in this pearl than a dragon's forever dream."

I hardly knew what to do. I started to tremble. "Ye?" I squeaked.

"Go on."

I touched the pearl, my fingers cold and quivering. The ring was wedged tight. I could do nothing but stare at it. I could not see my mother's face, or Grandma Chance's, or my own.

I could see only the death of Ye.

He would not live forever.

He would die.

I buried my face in my hand.

"Hush," he said, and nudged my ear with his snout, like a clumsy first kiss.

I turned my wet face to him.

"And, Kat," he said knowingly, "keep the gold nugget."

His eye swam in my vision, and I tried to blink it still. "The gold nugget?"

"Take care how you use it."

"You knew! You knew all along!"

"A dragon's senses are keen. His mind more so."

"Ye, I'm so ashamed! I stole it from you, yet you treated me so nice!" Then I gave a silly laugh. "I put it back!"

His dragonlight flickered. "You put it back? The gold?"

"Yes! When I returned to your cavern."

He blinked—a slow pink veil over an evening sun—

and he laughed, only it wasn't a silly laugh like mine, but serious and kind. "True to your name you are, *katharos*—pure."

I smiled dumbly at his words and touched my ear where it tingled from his nudge.

"That is all I could ever want from anyone," he murmured. "A pure, honest heart. Keep your gold tooth, too, with my regards. It makes you *xiao long*"—he gave a dramatic growl—"a little dragon."

Then his mirth melted away and he raised his head. Dillon, who was crouched near some high-standing brush, had called out a warning.

There were voices nearby, movements in the leaves.

I grabbed my pillowcase, but I could not move.

Snapping twigs, trampling boots.

Dillon said, "Hide, Kat!"

I didn't care about me, as long as Ye was safe. I looked around.

He had slipped away, silent as the fading stars.

—⟫ ⟪—

A GROUP OF MEN EMERGED.

One of them grabbed Dillon, another blinded me with a strong flashlight.

"Wal, looky what we caught," said a voice behind the light. "Greedy varmints."

A squat man with bulgy eyes came forward, inspecting me in the glare. He twisted his mouth into a liquor-laced whistle, and said, "What *doooo* you know." He grabbed my face and turned it. "Who do we got here?"

A tall, bearded man with a shotgun stepped forward. "Don't hurt them, Haddock," he said. "They're children."

"'Course they are, Crane," said Haddock, the man who gripped my jaw. "But more'n just children, they're the cream of the crop! See this here face? This is *thee* girl! Lemme see your tooth, honey."

I tightened my lips as Crane came close. "You sure?" he said. And with disgusting fingers, he pried open my lips. Then he stepped back and stared. "Well. Would you believe it."

Haddock was practically drooling. "We're out here lookin' for the hidden hole, and we find the key to it all. Killer luck!"

To distract myself from fear, I started a slow swing with the pillowcase, imagining what sort of collision a dead skull would make against a live one. Would the teeth still have bite? Would a brain make a difference?

"She *knows* what she's doin'," Haddock gurgled. "She got more gold."

"Right there in that bag!" called one.

Haddock's breath was definitely stronger than beer. "Don't you, sugar?"

"Open it up!" called another.

They hovered buzzard-busy around me now. The man who held Dillon marched him over. Dillon had made no attempt to escape or rescue me—he must have thought the same as I: What mattered most was Ye's safety.

Where was Ye? Had he flown away? I couldn't sneak a look for the pinching of my face, and decided that if Haddock let go, I would literally give him the sack.

Glory days, he did let go! And lucky strike, I smacked his ear, the red-hot fat one, before Crane could stop me. Yelping and slapping the side of his head, he played hopscotch on the grass. Someone pinned my arms from behind me as Crane grabbed the sack.

"Don't touch her!" yelled Dillon, his voice catching in the middle.

"Go fly a kite, Dragon Boy," said Crane.

They all laughed at Dillon and made a few remarks about paper dragons owning all the gold in the world. The man with the flashlight went up to him and said, "Ain't this sweet." He raised the middle finger of his left hand. It was mushroom white, wrapped in gauze and tape. I knew that finger, having seen it up close, treated in the ambulance. "Every girl oughta have a big bad brother," the man said.

The guy holding Dillon made a movement, and Dillon winced.

Crane silently gave his shotgun to another to hold. He held the pillowcase up in momentary suspense.

Everyone leaned forward.

He jerked the pillowcase open.

Everyone was trying to look, their heads in a jumbled circle, saying, "Gold! Gold! Gold!"

Crane said, "Get back!"

"Just empty it!"

"Pour it out! It's gold!"

He turned it upside down. Out wobbled the crackled remains of Cotton-Eyed Joe's quietly howling skull.

⸺⸙⸺

A WIND WAS UP. THE ASPENS WERE BLOWING, and Crane was raising his voice.

"You're in big trouble now!"

I was sure he'd haul us in for trespassing, humiliating

grown-ups, possession of a loaded pillowcase, assault and battery, and disturbing Chief Huffman's beauty rest.

He produced two pairs of handcuffs. After clapping one set on Dillon, he jerked my arms behind my back and clapped the other on me.

He shouted, "That'll do them!"

"Don't we have rights?" I shouted back, trying to ignore the pain.

"The right to shut up! Now what we're gonna—"

A sudden gust whipped Crane around, and we all saw that the wind was not caused by atmospheric pressure. It was not light to variable.

It was Ye.

He hovered above us, bronzed and glinting. His wings rose like thunderclouds, sweeping the sky. For a dragon who had languished for two hundred years, he was glorious and terrifying.

He smiled at the men, a volcanic fissure in the dark. He blew smoke that peeled like an orange.

He was not made of paper.

The men had turned to lead. One of the leaden figures gasped, "What in hell's kennel—" One broke rank and fell to his knees, babbling, "Our Father, which art in heaven . . ."

Something creaked in Crane's body. He grabbed his shotgun and aimed.

I stared in solid panic, unable to move, while Dillon whammed the back of his head into his captor's nose, broke loose, and lunged.

Too late. The gun went off.

I screamed.

Ye's smoky smile continued for a moment, then he rattled his head, swung it around, and frowned at his right wing. In its upper bend, a tattered hole shivered in a dying breeze. A star shone through it.

"Missed!" bawled Crane, and he began to reload.

Ye gave them all another molten grin.

"Fly, Ye!" I screamed. My captor covered my mouth with his sweaty hand, I chomped down, and my gold tooth hit pay dirt. He barked and let go. I screamed, "Fly! Fly!"

Ye's wings were up, gathering a flurry of new strength. But I heard a thin whistle, and his right wing went slack. He glared again at the hole.

I screamed some more, and no one stopped me.

Ye coughed. His nostrils flared. He glared at the men, his eyes hot ice.

Then a flame sprouted off his tongue. It was a little

flame, more of an arrow than a spear, a warm-up exercise, enough to roast a dozen marshmallows or crinkle Crane's beard. But it was fire—and I wanted to yell *Yay!* I was yelling something—I don't know what. It had Ye's name in it.

Crane was raising the gun.

Dillon was trying to stand; I was scrambling toward Crane's feet when the gun boomed again. The shot went wild, scattering the leaves above us.

Ye's molten grin turned perilous. He met the threat with a volley of flames that flew overhead like killer bees.

Some of them found targets. Crane pitched his gun into the air, grabbed Dillon by the arm, and stumbled backward. Flinging mobscenities right and left, the twig-breaking, boot-tromping band reversed itself.

I hugged the ground as Ye fired a third time. The blast spewed from his mouth, lighting up the landscape and sky in naked truth. One man's hair went up in smoke, and another man's hat. But more than hair and hat was singed: So was their pride and faith in reality.

That did it. All the king's horses and all the king's men fled.

I was laughing and sobbing and crying Ye's name. Through the falling cinders, he gave me a look of surprise, like a clumsy giant who has knocked over a castle by mistake.

He looked longingly then at the stars, and my heart stopped.

He unfurled his damaged wing, worked it gently, stretched it, withdrew it, stretched it again. As his confidence grew, so did the light in his eyes.

He fanned his wings and worked his tail and hurled himself skyward.

Branches shuddered. My mouth gaped in wonder and yearning. I was desperate to say something great, something good and important, when Ye tipped like a fledgling. He tread the wind his wings had stirred, his tail wagged for balance, his feet raked a branch. With a blow to his belly, he snapped a dead pine, gave a laughing cough, and recovered himself.

He rose once again, up through the aspens, which waved him on, bending and bowing. He rose free and sure, his head to the heavens, his tail making waves.

I leaped up, crying, "Bless you, Ye!" and my cry glanced off him like a little bird, for he swiveled an ear my direction.

He sped higher still, like a swift updraft, his wings singing hosanna in the highest.

Up the mountainside he flew, over Pikes Peak, into the spacious skies. He crossed a jet's vapor trail, soared higher, and touched a fainting star. Morning lay low and sea green in the east, and he soared so high he flashed golden in the unseen sun.

He banked to face it.

Draco had dissolved with the night.

Ye was gone.

⟶⟩⟨⟵

THEY SAY IT'S DARKEST BEFORE DAWN, AND they are right.

I don't mean the color of the sky.

Dillon was gone, and I hadn't even noticed. Crane had taken him. I guess I'd been too close to Ye to be taken, too.

I was sleepwalking, wandering in a mental night, aimless. A mosquito worried my head. I shuffled through a yard, brushed past a bush, stepped over a curb, down a sidewalk, around a light pole, crossed a street. But I walked in a dream. The dream was part memories, part my own making, part delirium.

I was flying with Ye. The wind whisked the tears off my cheeks. Ye pointed down and I looked. Beneath us were wide fruited plains and amber waves of grain and purple mountain majesties and a vast wandering wilderness. The wilderness flattened into a road-mapped carpet where red and blue lines crossed and crisscrossed and constellations were marked with gold stars for every hotel. Sometimes we flew, and sometimes we ran down an ever-winding hallway with the road map blurring below. The map dropped away, and a shining sea spread out before us. We were airborne. Ye pointed ahead and said something that the wind whipped away. The pearl ring gleamed on his pointing claw and shone a thin silver beam to the distant horizon, and to our journey's end, which was an alabaster city standing tall like stalagmites or angel's wings.

The mosquito I'd heard became the sound of sirens.

They were headed my way.

I trudged forward, my arms still handcuffed behind me. I had tried cracking them open against a fallen branch with no success. I'd managed to get the skull back into the pillowcase and dragged it along like a favorite teddy bear.

I began mumbling something about dropping the tobacco tin somewhere in the cavern, or in the outhouse, or while climbing down, or climbing up, or in the tunnel, or outside the tunnel, or in the green pool, or in the woods . . .

I was talking to myself, talking to the vacancy inside me.

"It's only an old tobacco tin," I said in a voice strangely sour, like sickness. I argued back, "It's the only thing I had of his. It was my kapeseek. It had Ye's claw mark."

I was slowing down.

"Keepsake," I corrected, murmuring. "He's gone. You have your memories, Kat. They will have to do."

Had I said goodbye to Ye? Had I given him a kiss, a blessing, a smile? Had I wished him long life and happiness? I couldn't remember.

"Gone. Lost."

A few steps more.

"Just like that—they're gone. Ye, Dillon, Mom. Suddenly, they're gone and you realize you couldn't have prevented it. You couldn't have said goodbye even if you'd tried a thousand times."

I nearly tripped on a break in the concrete.

The sirens came screaming. Two big red trucks with cripple creek volunteer fire dept. in gold lettering on the sides roared by, screaming me awake from my dream state. Residents came out of their homes to gawk in their pajamas and robes and hairdos gone don't.

"I just want to go home," I whispered.

The handcuffs dug into my wrists, my head was back down. I began counting cracks in the sidewalk, careful to step over each one, even if I had to stop. I stepped over a penny, which I normally would have taken, but the thought of doing that did not occur to me.

I started shaking and couldn't stop. My chin began chattering to itself. My jeans were damp from the stream and the coating of mud and minerals from the cave.

I looked up. The street sign said bennet. I'd seen that before.

And I'd seen that car before: Rex's black colt, polished and snorting, went prancing by. I stared after it. The brake lights flared, the car reversed itself, halted, and Rex jumped out.

"Fancy meetin' you here!" he said, as if we had just met at the Digs. But the look he gave me was far from casual.

I hiccupped and stood swaying with the pillowcase swinging behind me.

"What in the blessed blazes—" He circled me once, pulled off his hat, felt around its inside band, and produced a hairpinlike tool. "Have these off in a jiff."

It worked—my hands were free.

"Thanks!" I gasped, and gave him the pillowcase, babbling, "I picked this just for you. Collect your thousand dollars without passing Go, dead or alive . . ."

———)(———

WE SAT ON THE CURB, IN FRONT OF HIS CAR'S grinning grill, as traffic rolled randomly by. Rex had insisted we sit inside the car, but I didn't want to ruin his upholstery. As soon as I'd recovered my senses, I told him Dillon had disappeared and might even be hurt.

"We need to do something," I begged. "Now!"

"He ain't hurt," said Rex. "He's in custody."

"Custody?"

"Trespassin', arson, assault. The ones what's hurt is five men that was rushed to the CO Springs Memorial ER for second and third dee-gree burns."

Oh no, I thought. *Dillon's in jail? What would he have told them? Probably not much, if I knew Dillon.* So I asked, "Did the men say what happened?"

"But now I'm havin' second and third thoughts. On account of your handcuffs." He scowled. "Why not you tell me?"

I had to think that one over. I thought it over and

decided to stall. I said agreeably, "I'll be glad to tell you if their story's true or not."

"You're bein' catty." He lowered his head at me and cleared his throat. "All right. I'll play your dodge for a while. You tell me if their story's true. They said they found two kids—a he and a her—playin' with matches in the woods. The her ran, but they caught the he. The men burned theirselves puttin' out the fire the kids started."

"So they're heroes," I said.

"Just doin' their duty."

"You believe that?"

"Is it true?"

I couldn't stall forever. I said, "Well, obviously the girl escaped and the boy was caught. Right?"

"I'm listenin'."

"There was a fire. Right?"

"I'm listenin'."

"Obviously, there was a fire," I said. Then I shrugged. "It's true."

"The matches, Blondie. I don't think the he and the her is the match-playin' kind." He pulled on his ear. "So you tell me. Why matches?"

It was time to change the subject. "Rex," I said with

concern in my voice—and I *was* concerned. "You haven't told me where Dad is."

"I'll tell you that if you tell me this: Where you been?"

"Please, Rex—"

"If you take a look-see at yourself, Missy Mae, you'd know I'm not askin' out of ignoramus-ness. You have cavern mud written all over you."

"Then why are you asking?"

"I want you to explain the what, when, and wheretofore of the matter."

Maybe I could stall just a *little* bit longer.

"OK, OK," I said. "But please tell me where Dad is."

"Why're you puttin' me off?" he said sharply. He removed his hat to run his hand over his head stubble. He sighed. "All right. Your daddy's finally got the old gray nag to trot, on my recommention. At this momentum, he's drivin' to boot quarters—"

"Boot quarters?"

"Headquarters. Po-lease station." He was getting testy. I was trying his patience. Plus, I think he hated to reduce his lingo to ordinary terms. But most of all I think it was because of the gold he'd missed out on. "We're gonna get your brotherkin off, but he's gonna need my help." He replaced his hat forcefully. "And I see now, due to them handcuffs bein' on you, that Crane did an underhanded thing, pun intentional. That was his doing', wasn't it? And he put 'em on you both, didn't he?"

I nodded.

"Your turn."

So far, I had avoided any explanation, but I knew I had to come up with something about the fire. It might even be the truth. Besides being branded a lunatic, what harm would it do? Ye was gone.

But I wasn't quite there. I felt I had another way out. So I said, "Have you looked in the pillowcase yet?"

"That's question numeral sumteen!" fumed Rex. "To my singular ones!" He was more agitated than I'd ever seen him. "And it's *my* pillowcase, which it used to be laundry-mat clean."

"I think if you take a look in the pillowcase, you'll understand." I said, surprising myself for my challenge.

Rex glared at me sharp-eyed, and I was reminded of our keyhole encounter. Funny how I thought so much differently about him now.

"I'll take a look," he huffed. "If I don't like what I see, you're over and done with."

I nodded. "Agreed."

He took a look. He took a long, attentive look. He said,

"This skull's cracked up to what it ain't used to be," and he continued to look, until it became one slow, now-the-truth-dawns look. His eyes began to widen as if Cotton-Eyed Joe's skull had turned to gold.

Finally, he raised his head. "You just won yourself a silver ribbon around my heart."

"THE CAPTAIN HAS TURNED ON THE FASTEN seat belt sign."

I was now a UM—an unaccompanied minor—on the way to D.C. They had plopped a gray-and-gold Denver Nuggets b-ball cap on my head for easy identification. It even had mining picks stitched on it. How ironic could you get? (Ironic being something that makes your inner pain worse in a funny way, not something made of iron, which is what I once thought.)

I'd been through Denver airport with Dad and an airline attendant, hustling through thousands of travelers—gold rushers—who were arriving. As we raced to the gates, all the news headlines said gold was the rage and Cripple Creek was the place.

I had been through security, which was nearly as bad as a police pat-down. Though my leaded die was in Dad's keeping and my tobacco tin was gone, I triggered the detectors again and again. The security team made a long thorough search of my scant belongings and of me.

Finding nothing, they eventually gave up.

Dad had seen me off. I'd given him the "I love you" sign just before losing his face in the blur of the crowd, where he'd stood like a wax figure, the kind on display in the Mollie Kathleen. After all we'd been through, by the seat of our pants and the skin of our teeth, California or Bust, with Nellie breaking down then getting her second wind, he was not flying to San Francisco.

He was not *driving* to San Francisco.

He was driving home.

There was no way he could do what was necessary to get Dillon released and still make it to SF in time. He had given up on that. Except for the unfinished business, he had given up on everything. At this point, he just put one foot in front of the other and said whatever had to be said.

When I thought of the reasons I was flying, I got lightheaded.

Rex had promised he'd fly me *somewhere*, as a reward for telling him about the back entrance. Now that Ye was gone and his cavern plundered, I didn't see any point in turning Rex down. The mine was now watched night and day, and it was close to impossible he'd get any gold. Dad spoke of gold no more, but Rex raved about it. He had checked the police archives, and the case against Cotton-

Eyed Joe had never been closed. Technically, he *was* entitled to the reward money. That's what I intended, I told him. He said there was hardly a chance he'd see the reward, but the gold bits were "awesomous."

"Gold bits?" I asked.

"Them ones stuck inside the skull."

I gaped at him.

"You didn't know?"

I could only shake my head.

"Stuck in the crevices and teeth. Must be worth a few thousands. Thanks, sister!"

So his delight over the skull had been due to the gold, not in seeing his grandfather's killer. Or maybe both.

What amazed me more was that Crane's gang had failed to notice. I hadn't noticed because gold was the farthest thing from my mind. I suppose *they* hadn't noticed because a skull was the farthest thing from *their* minds.

The second reason I flew was serious: Mom. Dad had lost touch with the Home and feared for her condition. If the staff were neglecting the phones, he said, how were they handling the patients? He wanted someone to see her as soon as possible, and I was that someone.

"When you arrive," he instructed, "go straight to the

Home. Ms. Morro will pick you up at the airport; she has all the information and your number, just in case." Ms. Morro was our old neighbor and the "just in case" meant I had the cell phone in case something went wrong. "You'll stay with her until I figure out what to do."

The third reason I flew was phenomenal.

Two talk show scouts had hunted me down (via Rose Robbins, who found me via Rex), both from separate networks. As they made their proposals, a call-in show rep joined the quest.

Lights, cameras, action. I was looking at celebrity status. It looked godzillion times better than calamity class. I knew it wouldn't be a hotel lounge scene with flying biscuits and jeers.

But more important, I thought there'd be money to be made—legitimately for a change.

While Rex worked on the Dillon defense, Dad drove me to the airport.

Leaving Cripple Creek was easy. Once a magical place, without Ye its magic was just a card trick, as in Fifty-two Pickup. All the traffic was rushing, often creeping, upstream. Every kind of vehicle—luxury, terrain, truck, van, wagon, sport, mini, motor home, motorcycle. A converted school bus chugged by with cripple creek or bust painted on its side in big black letters.

Since Dad was in a slump, I switched on the radio. After flipping through the usual—country, golden oldies, hip-hop and cosmic noise, that weird static you get between AM stations—I got Rocky Mountain news. Due to "growing unrest" from "various interest groups," particularly gold seekers, and an "unauthorized explosion" deep in the Mollie Kathleen, the National Guard was called in. I found a talk show that was all about gold. Among the discussions were the limits of mining claims. An engineer was saying that a lode claim could be only so many feet long and so many feet wide, and I concluded Ye's cavern *was* outside the range. Better, it wasn't a lode, it was loose.

I was right after all. I could have claimed it myself, had I wanted to. Just like Mollie Kathleen.

• • •

So there I sat thirty-five thousand feet up with a guy next to me asking what I thought of the season so far, and I said I liked everything turning red. He said you mean the players, and I said no the trees. He said you mean the tall guys, and I said it didn't matter how tall they were and that I'd never heard trees called guys. He said he'd never heard guys called trees.

After that, he watched his TV and I looked out my window.

Somewhere over Kansas I thought, *We're above the fruited plains, like in the song.* But they looked unfruited to me. I guessed it was the time of year. I got sleepy and pulled my sweatshirt out to ball up for a pillow. It smelled like Ye's lair, but I'd removed most of the muck. I'd hardly had time to wash up. While Dad had been waiting for Chief Huffman to show and Rex was arranging my flight (though the big-name show folks ended up paying for it), I'd gone into a restroom. My cleanup wasn't complete, but at least I had a change of clothes.

I didn't sleep much. I saw images on the TV through my lashes. It was a half sleep, where you're aware of your surroundings while your mind drifts like a cloud. I finally gave up and put my earphones on. I scanned the channels, looking for news of Cripple Creek. I found a Man-on-the-Street program, and the microphone man was saying, "We're here in the heart of gold mining country, with Pikes Peak over my left shoulder. The smoke? That's not from the reluctant dragon holed up in the Mollie Kathleen—it's from the tourist train that circles Cripple Creek. You there, miss, what do you think of the new gold rush?"

"We should give the gold to the Indians," said the woman on the street. "This was once their land."

The microphone man quickly turned to a boy. "You, what's your name?"

"Moth."

"Moss?"

"Moth."

"OK, Moth, what's your opinion of this dragon affair?"

"I think he should go free. He might find another dragon somewhere in the world to marry, then we'd have more dragons."

"Very good! And you, sir?"

"No scaly reptilian's gonna smoke us outta here! I say slay the beast and put an end to this nonsense! Bury him along with his gold! We don't need no more billionaires! The rich are gettin' richer 'cause they can afford to! Where does that leave us plain and simple folks?"

Some moron said they should catch the dragon and put it in a zoo to educate people, to not be stingy, share an original with the rest of the world, that it may even be a long lost dinosaur, for all we know, like in *Jurassic Park*.

A skateboarder said, "Extreme dragon sports. You get a guy or a girl, put 'em on a motorbike, give 'em a lance, and have a go at the dragon—dragon jousting."

On and on it went.

Most people said it was all a crazy rumor. The gold may be real, but the dragon wasn't. It was made up to scare folks away.

I took off the headphones, looked out the window, and dreamed of Ye.

In the middle of my reverie, as the plane turned and the sunlight shifted, something sparkled near my arm. It sparkled faint and fine, like dancing motes. It sparkled on my sweatshirt, near the cuff.

My reverie fell into woe.

I knew what it was.

—⋇⋇—

GOLD DUST.

Despite the sun, despite the metallic magic, my face went cold, my heart became wax.

I slowly unrolled my cuff. I held out my hand. Gold dust flowed out like sand. It was less than a thimble full, but enough to tell me what I did not wish to know.

Ye had bled after he'd washed out his wound.

That some of it ended up on me was not a surprise. I had stayed as close to him as I could in the tunnels and in the woods.

I stared at the glittering patch until it faded. The sunlight had gone. I closed my hand.

The blow Ye had taken when he first rose in flight—had it done him more harm? Could he fly like that, with a hole in his side and a hole in his wing? Would he helplessly fall, to land in some cornfield or on a hilltop or city street?

Had he done so already?

The image that darkened in my mind was strange— both precious and chilling. I saw the wound spilling blood, turning to gold as he flew, like it had done in the mountain stream. The flight trail of a dragon. I saw it falling in slow motion, golden on the wind. Some child playing in her yard would thrust out her hand and say, "It's raining gold!"

I closed my eyes, slamming the scene shut like a book, and opened them again to keep from picturing it. I peered out the window, my mind on the edge of a moan.

The plains below had not changed, a study in agricultural geometry broken by patterns of clouds, and the shadow of the jet explored the cloudy hills and hollows.

· · ·

When the flight attendants passed snacks around, I took the small foil bag of nuts, emptied it out, wiped the inside clean with my napkin, and put the gold dust carefully in. My next-seat neighbor was too occupied watching a sports channel to notice. I rolled the bag up and placed it in my shirt pocket.

That's when it occurred to me. The security check. The gold dust, pure dragon gold, had triggered the detectors.

I took out my journal and opened to a blank page.

As I had done with the word *Mom* long ago, I wrote the word *Ye*, in the center of the sheet, and followed it with a question mark. Then I turned the *Y* into wings, and the *e* into the body and tail of a dragon, and turned the question mark into smoke.

Hope is a risky thing. It might be dashed to pieces on something—like rocks and reality. But I had to have hope. I hoped Ye would heal and live another hundred years or more, curled contentedly in a cave or on some lofty ledge of the world. I made myself think that. Picturing him strong and mysterious, lifting his wings . . .

I looked out the window again and saw something odd.

The jet had *two* shadows, one up close, skimming the clouds, the other far below, smaller, fainter. Now, what would be the cause of that?

Leaning forward, I pressed my face to the glass. A chill of excitement ran through me, the kind I got whenever my horse, Angel, flew on the wind.

Ye!

Shadow to shadow, both pairs of wings spread wide— one riveted and rigid, one willowy and veined—a jet and a dragon soared eastward. A twenty-first-century flying machine and an ancient world wonder, each passing each in a snapshot of time. Ye was no match for the jet, nor did he intend to be—he was following nature's course.

It was incredible.

I glanced around the cabin: Every passenger was involved in gadgets, books, naps, TV. My TV showed a map tracking our location, and I looked back out.

Through a momentary rift in the clouds, Ye flew, in royal living color, across the snaky brown Missouri, and I knew we weren't in Kansas anymore.

—⟩⟨—

MY STORY ENDS NICELY THERE.

But, truth to tell, it's not a fantasy, and I must tell all.

I watched Ye with burning eyes and a burning heart, before he slipped back into the clouds. I did not see him again.

The flight continued without incident, except that my seat neighbor, who'd earlier asked me about "the season," turned and asked, "So . . . have you been to any of their games, or are you just a couch fan?"

We were touching down on the runway. I gave him the kind of look you'd give a baboon and said nothing. There was a serious disconnect going on. It wasn't until the airline attendant who met me at the ramp, said, "There's our Denver Nuggets girl!" that I understood the misunderstanding.

My hat.

Ms. Morro spotted us, showed her ID to the attendant, and we were on our way.

"How's Mom?" was the first thing I said.

"Oh, Katlin! Haven't you heard?"

My soul sank.

"The home's under a malpractice suit due to patient neglect. I don't think your mom's going to make it."

"THIS IS *SAY-SO*, AND I'M MIRANDA BATES.
My guest today is Katlin Graham, a name synonymous
with gold and dragons and the new Wild West. Hello,
Katlin."

"You can call me Kat."

"Kat, you're quite a celebrity now. You've been on two
major talk shows, your story's been told around the world,
we've seen the video clips. The gold rush phenomenon's
upon us—"

"Pandemonium's more like it."

"—gold is at an all-time thirteen hundred an ounce.
Lawsuits and the crime rates have spiked. The economy's
been redesigned. All this because a girl fell down a mining
shaft and appeared with a nugget of gold. Tell us, Kat,
just how much gold did you find?"

"Not much. About this size."

"Kat, the listening audience can't see your hand."

"Sorry. Bigger than my fist."

"That's quite a big nugget."

"I suppose."

"Where is it now?"

"I put it back. Who knows who has it is now."

"You put it back. Don't you wish you'd kept it?"

"Never."

"Is it the greed thing, as we've been told?"

"It's the greed thing."

"Help me understand this. Now that they've found more gold, lots more, estimated to be worth billions, a fist-size amount is nothing."

"Still, I would have put it back."

"You know, with all due respect, that's either excessively moral of you, or crazy."

"So—take your pick."

"Don't most girls have a wish list, things you'd like to buy?"

"Two things are on my wish list. They can't be bought."

"Give us a hint."

"My mom is one."

"And the other?"

"I'd rather not say."

"We've heard you mention a dragon."

"So?"

"Tell us about it."

"Him."

"Tell us about *him*. Is he magical, like Puff?"

"He's not a cartoon. He's not a fairy tale. He's not cute."

"What is he?"

"Gone."

"That's convenient. What *was* he then?"

"Mystifying."

"Anything else?"

"He's the last one."

"Would you describe him for me?"

"I might as well describe daybreak."

"Was he frightening?"

"He was beautiful. Beautiful colors, beautiful eyes, beautiful heart . . ."

"You mean he was a *civilized* dragon?"

"More civil than civilized. More civil than most of us."

"Tell me, Kat, be honest—isn't this just a publicity stunt, like some people have accused?"

"Why did you ask me about him then? Just so you could say that?"

"I thought I'd give you a chance to deny it. I mean, do you really expect us to believe all this?"

"No, I don't. We believe whatever we choose. We believe in things that are not true, and don't believe in things that are."

"Give me an example."

"Fame. Fortune. We believe they bring happiness."

"Well, they help, don't they?"

"You can be poor and unknown and happy. You can be rich and famous and unhappy."

"All right, what brings happiness then?"

"Having an honest heart."

"An honest heart. That's it?"

"Isn't that enough?"

"Let's see what our callers have to say. To the phones. Here's Yusri, from Jersey City."

"Hi, Miranda. Yusri Rab of Rab and Associates. Just wanted to make a few comments about the stock market, if I may, particularly gold."

"We're here to have dialogue with Kat Graham, but since it's related, go ahead."

"I'll be brief. Contrary to public opinion, the reason the gold market's good is not due to all the gold that was found, but the rising popularity of gold jewelry. Now's the time to sell your class ring or teeth or what have you, while gold's going up. It's a seller's market."

"OK, Mr. Rab, you must be a broker, or a jeweler. But it's my understanding that investors diverted their monies into the gold, and virtually all but gold has plunged. Kat, any thoughts?"

"No thanks."

"And to give Kat due credit, I believe it *was* her discovery that started the gold trend in the first place. Now we go to Lee, in Sacramento."

"Hi . . ."

"Go ahead, please."

"Hi . . . Kat? I've followed your story since those two witnesses said they saw some fantastic creature flying above Pikes Peak—"

"Really?"

"They shot a picture with their cell phone. It's on the Web. It's kind of blurry—"

"So, Lee, what's your question?"

"What I'd like to know is, what direction was he headed?"

"Um . . . far, far away."

"All right, Lee?"

"Hey, wait—"

"Next caller. Thomas, here in Washington, D.C."

"Yeah. What the"—*beep*—"so special about dragons? Dragon movies, dragon games, dragon books! All this dragon"—*beep*—"it's all about the mighty buck! People are makin' tons of money off any idiot who'll dig in his pocket—"

"Care to respond, Kat?"

"I agree. If you're talking about the fantasy media-greedia."

"Yeah, but that's just what you're—"

"All right, Thomas, you've had your say. We go now to Boston. Rebecca?"

"Hi. How are you?"

"I'm good. Go ahead."

"Hi, Calamity? You are my hero. Even if your story's made-up, the gift of make-believe we lose too early in life, if we ever had it at all. I think girls should dream big, and you've captured the yearnings a lot of us have. Imagine! A dragon at the bottom of a gold mine! That's genius!"

"Your question, Rebecca?"

"I don't have one. I just wanted to say—"

"Thank you. We'll take the next call. April, from New York."

"No, Manhattan—in Kansas."

"There's a Manhattan in Kansas?"

"Sure is. Right off the main drag to the Rockies. You should see all the traffic going west."

"What's your question?"

"Since you hung up on the last caller who didn't have a question, I'll put it this way. Kat, do you realize you've championed honesty by returning the gold?"

"I hadn't thought of it that way."

"That was an act of anti-greed. We need more people like you. Hats off to you, girl."

"OK, April. On to a caller who's even closer to the action: Colorado Springs. Your name, please?"

"Hello, Kathleen, remember me?"

"Katlin."

"Of course. Genius is doubtful, but you are pretty clever. I understand you denied starting the fire."

"That's true."

"You deny it?"

"Yes."

"Five witnesses say otherwise."

"Caller, your name please?"

"So, you lied about that."

"Caller, your name."

"I know her name. She calls herself a journalist,

but she doesn't know Yeats from yodeling, snip from sesquipedality."

"I know true from false, Katlin Graham. If you lied about that, you could lie about other things."

"What about the fire, Kat?"

"I—"

"It occurred the morning that Kat's family skipped town."

"Is that so. How does that relate?"

"It fits, doesn't it? You cause trouble, people get hurt, you leave before anyone can catch you."

"Caller, you'd have more credibility if you gave us your name."

"Rose Robbins, KOLT-TV."

"OK, that certainly helps. What do you say to that, Kat?"

"She can think what she likes. That doesn't make it—"

"I do think what I like. Here's what I think. Somehow you knew about the mine's back entrance. You and Havick were in this together—he's notorious for shadow work. You paid him in gold nuggets, a paltry amount compared to what you have hidden somewhere. Yes, I know about the nuggets—I can dig, too. When things didn't go right, you had to fabricate something to cover your tracks. So you made other tracks. Dragon tracks. Anyone can do that kind of thing—I did when I was a kid, in the mud. You started a fire because, duh, dragons breathe fire."

"Those are some valid points, Rose. Anything else?"

"As to the gold, I'll bet her family's got a new life—new car, new clothes—"

"Yeah, we're filthy rich."

"Really, Kat?"

"Not."

"—new rock for Mom's hand—"

"OK, Rose, we get it."

"—or maybe an all-new mom."

"How dare you!"

"Kat, the headsets."

"Mom's on her wish list, right?"

"Kat . . . Kat . . . it's OK. We'll take our next caller. Judd, from Austin."

"I don't understand why this girl's getting so much attention for being irresponsible. She doesn't belong on your show. She's a poor example to other kids. She's a common thief. She's—"

"Let her respond."

"No, he's right. I shouldn't have let my curiosity

get the better of me. I broke through a barrier. Life is like that: You break through barriers, you suffer the consequences."

"Satisfied, Judd?"

"Suffer? What kind of suffering has she done? She gets all this glory—"

"We have time for one more call. Robin, in Rockbridge, Virginia, you're on."

"Thank you. I love your show."

"Thanks. Where's Rockbridge?"

"Near Lexington."

"Go ahead."

"I wanted to ask your guest about the footprint on the Appalachian Trail."

"Footprint!"

"Here in the Blue Ridge Mountains. A hiker found it, you know, identical to the kind they found in Cripple Creek."

"Kat?"

"I mean, why would you go to the trouble of planting another track?"

"Kat?"

"It's fresh. Either it's a hoax, or there really is some kind of beast."

"Kat? Katlin? Katlin Graham. People, you've been listening to *Say-So*. I'm Miranda Bates."

———⟫⟪———

I WAS OUT OF MY CHAIR, HEADPHONES flying—I'd forgot I had them on—and out the studio door. Behind me the producer was puffing, "Miss Graham! You can't *do* that, Miss Graham! Are you *crazy?*" And behind her, my interviewer, Miranda Bates, was pitching fits in a shockingly un-audiogenic voice, and behind *her* the recording crew were cursing me up and down. Somewhere in the mix, weaving and worrying, was Dad.

I made it out to the street and to the limousine. Yes, limousine—the kind of white sleekness that slides in and out of traffic for people with slinky limbs and smooth skin and sunglasses, whose lives are like a dream.

Only I wasn't that kind of person.

And my life was not a dream.

Despite the fame, there had been no fortune.

After Rex had got Dillon off, Dillon and Dad had driven home, and now they lived by turns out of the workhorse or the storage unit where our belongings were kept. They washed at the local Y. It wasn't as bad as it sounds. In the unit, they had the sleeper sofa, a card table and chairs, a camp stove, an ice chest, and other small comforts. They hardly spent time in there anyway. Dad had got a job selling mattresses, though it barely covered the storage rental. Dillon was back in school.

So was I, but I stayed in the Home where Mom lay, which was under better management. I was allowed some space in an unoccupied room until a new patient would be admitted.

Mom had taken a turn for worse. Actually, she was worse because she had not been turned. Since the Home was short-staffed, her support had not been constant, which meant she'd been turned too seldom. When someone's in bed for long periods of time, their bony points—heels, elbows, shoulders, hips—push into their skin. When these pressure sores show up, it's almost too late, because the bruising comes from the inside.

At least I was close to Mom. In exchange for my temporary lodging, I helped out with the new nurse assigned to her.

. . .

I hopped into the limousine and left the door open for Dad, who was ahead of the others. The others had either dropped out or quit. The producer stood at the top of the steps, gazing at me as if I was a world away, and I suppose

I was. My world still revolved around Ye, and no one else was in it.

"Driver!" I said. "Take me to the Blue Ridge Mountains!"

——><——

IT DIDN'T WORK.

Between Dad saying no and the producer calling the chauffeur to say go straight to the Hotel Dupont, I didn't have a chance. The limo was hired to get me from the hotel to the interview and back—that was it. Interview over, so were the amenities. We packed our bags, which were the same ol' same ol', and left D.C. behind.

I begged and begged Dad to take a small detour along the Blue Ridge Parkway, which was *kind of* on the way back to Richmond, but he would not.

"A hoax, Kat," he said curtly. "The whole thing's been a hoax."

"Dad, how can you say that?"

"You made a few suggestions and the madhouse world ran with it."

"But you heard the caller! A footprint! That's a real piece of evidence!"

"It's a real piece of you know what."

"Dad, please! Just a small detour? It wouldn't hurt a thing!"

He gave me the kind of look lots of people were giving me those days. "Remember the last time you asked me to do that?"

"Do what?"

"Take a detour."

That ended the discussion.

⟺⊱⊰⟺

A month since I told Ye goodbye.

Hung one of Mom's wind chimes out the window, where I could see it from my cot.

I'll watch the sky the rest of my life, no matter where I go or how many situations or people I run into. It's hopeless, but still I hope.

My bio of Wash Irving for Eng is not 1/2 done.

All I think of is Ye.

Tried talking D to talk Dad into driving to the Blue Ridge, only 90 min. away, but he said just leave it alone. Checked the news & chats to find out about the footprint. Got the guy's name—Jay Zohn. He started hiking the Appalachian Trail somewhere in Maine. I checked for phone # or address—nothing. Keep trying!

Really miss Orr Academy. Wish we could afford a dentist. All the kids in school call me Goldie, Dragon Girl, Calamity Cat. Old Mrs. Hamilton subbed last week. When she saw me she blabbed about that time on the museum trip when I accidentally drooled on a display glass w/ gold doubloons. Told the whole class! When they're not mocking me, they avoid me. Bus rides are the worst. I don't get tired of walking.

Weather's gone cold. Fierce front coming down from Canada. I'm wearing my sweats tonight.

I love early-season cold—while autumn lingers inside you & winter chills your skin.

It's snowing!

. . .

When the first flakes fell, I opened the window and leaned on the sill. I listened to the silence. Flake after flake touched my skin, my hands, only to vanish.

Whenever I see my hands, I'm reminded of the ring. Whenever I sit with Mom, I keep my right hand out of sight, in case she has an intuition, a feeling that the ring is gone.

The snowflakes fell.

I thought of Ye. I imagined him lying under some rocky outcrop, curled and warm within himself. Maybe the flight had done him good. Maybe his wound had healed.

Maybe he had swallowed the pearl. He must have, surely. After finding it still on his claw, why would he not?

It was late. The staff had made their bedtime rounds, and I'd seen that Mom was OK. Her breathing was uneven, her sores were slow to heal, but her color looked good. I can always tell when she's good or not by her color.

I turned off my light and lay gazing at the phantom-blue night. I thought of Dillon and Dad bedding down in the car. They did that now and then to avoid suspicion by the storage management, because the terms of agreement prohibited occupancy.

During the first few weeks after our return, I'd kept a scrapbook with clippings and interviews I'd had, until I got tired of reading about "Calamity Cat." I didn't mind the name so much, but I was trying my hardest to be uncalamitous, and I think I was making progress. I got tired of the gold-rushing mania. I saw it all as a massive game—a jumble of tug-of-war and Wheel of Fortune, pickup sticks and Snakes and Ladders. The few who won lost something in the process, and those who lost numbered in the millions. Even Sterling Blair, the lawyer who'd hounded us at Rex's—he'd been charged with fraud. The Mollie Kathleen is a family-owned business, all good people, and had not been out to sue us. Blair had once represented the mine, but not this time—he'd used them to cover his own scheme in trying to get the gold.

If I'd been selling something, like a book, I would have made a killing off my interviews. As it turned out, they were only slices of the high life when I was queen for a day. They were momentary thrills. I knew that money didn't bring happiness, but the low life was getting old.

Would things ever change?

. . .

Sometime in the predawn, I awoke. I'd heard a sound through my sleep. I could sleep through the care home sounds, the hiss of humidifiers, the creaking of a bed, a toilet flush, but this sound was unusual enough to wake me.

It was familiar enough to hold me.

I sat upright, listening.

Mom's wind chimes shivered in a sudden brisk wind.

I heard the sound again.

It was not a car or truck. It had a sky-high echo, but it was not a plane. My heart skipped a beat. I could not breathe. Deep in the tunnels of the Mollie Kathleen, when I hadn't known which way to go, I had heard such a sound.

I bounded from my cot.

The night was swirling like a Christmas paperweight. The snow was sticking. On a building across the yard the bare twigs of a bush scribbled secrets on a wall.

I clambered out the window and stepped into the snow.

White bees stung my face as I peered up. They spiraled and spun, gathered in the hollow of my throat, shimmered along my lashes, swaddled my socks. I stood crystallized, listening, looking.

I dared not tremble, but trembled.

I dared not speak his name, but spoke his name.

The sound did not come again.

There was nothing.

There was only the ghost of Ye, falling all around me.

—⟩ ⟨—

HOW LONG DID I STAND THERE?

At some point, I crawled inside to get my quilt, the only one Grandma Chance had ever made. It was her own design, with a golden sunburst on a midnight sky and midnight stars along a golden border. I shoved my frozen feet into my shoes and scrambled back outside.

I wrapped up in the quilt and shuffled to the flat stone on the lawn where a birdbath used to be. A reporter who had staked out the Home had broken it while roosting there, as he spied my coming and going. There I stood, swaying and napping from time to time, snapping awake, my thoughts spinning like the snow, napping again.

For a false sleepy moment, I stood on my path. My unfinished stone path. The path that had led us down this strange, fantastic journey, so long ago.

. . .

"Kat?"

I opened my eyes. Morning. The world was under a white-magic trance. The snow was damp and clingy, bending branches low and conjuring up shapes where shapes hadn't been.

I was still standing.

"Kat!" One of the care assistants was walking up the sidewalk, arriving for her work shift. "What're you doing? You'll be sick!"

Despite my numbness, I managed a smile. I managed to move my feet.

"You dropped something."

"Huh?"

"There." She nodded toward the ground.

I looked down. Where I had stood, where the quilt had stamped dreams in the snow, lay a small brown object. It glinted once as I picked it up.

My lost tobacco tin.

———⟩ ⟨———

YE WAS HERE, I SAID TO MYSELF OVER AND over again. I don't know how many times I said it. *He was here. He flew by. He dropped the tin at my feet!*

Turning around and around and wandering across the lawn, I looked for any tracks in the snow, any signs in the sky.

"He's alive."

Nothing else mattered. Catching the school bus wasn't even a thought.

I held the tin as close as a promise. I had lost it way back in Cripple Creek, and Ye had picked it up. Had it been his keepsake? Owned by one of his Chinese friends?

What was inside?

I tried to pry it open and had trouble as before. I stopped trying. I could be looking for Ye instead. Wrapping the quilt tighter around me, I clutched the tin as I went.

I had to go somewhere, start searching, start calling. The Home was in the suburbs. Not wanting to be seen or questioned, I headed for the outskirts.

I wandered with my head down, watching for his tracks. When that brought only blankness, I wandered with my head up, watching the falling flakes. My glasses kept fogging.

Houses were in a stupor. Smoke rose from chimneys into the fluttering dove-gray sky. I walked into a cul-de-sac and out again. Little kids were laughing and making snow angels while their mom sat smoking on the steps.

I passed some wooded acreage that a sign said would soon be stripped for lots. Perched on the sign was a blue jay with a beetle in its beak. Squirrels played hello good-bye with me. Cardinals spattered the snowscape with bright red surprises.

The tin was in my quilt-bound hand, a desperate mystery.

Walking down the middle of the street—so far untouched by tire treads—I heard a snowplow coming. I ran from its path, slid into the snow-slick curb and sprawled, belly down, embarrassed.

The plow went by.

I no longer held the tin.

It lay open in the snow, and lead-gray rocks spilled out.

To my shame, I was disappointed. I had expected gold. I couldn't tell what type of rocks they were. They seemed heavier than gold and felt flaky. I wished I had one of those little 10x glasses they used in science. Not that I knew rocks. First chance I'd get, I'd find a field guide on minerals.

They must have been tightly packed, fitting like a puzzle, for as I tried to replace them, there was not enough room.

But more puzzling, was why. Why had Ye dropped the tin? I had wanted it back, but how would he have known that? He hadn't known I had it in the first place. That is, I didn't think he had known.

And if he was going to do that—return an old tobacco tin—why hadn't he stopped to see me?

Why gray rocks?

As I sat staring at the words *Lucky Strike*, trying to make sense of it all, a car came sliding against the curb, just as I had done. Two doors opened, and instead of gray rocks, two men spilled out.

Dillon and Dad.

"What are you way out here for?" yelled Dad.

"What's that in your hand?" asked Dillon.

"This," I said proudly, holding up the answer to both their questions.

⟶⊶⊷⟵

"WHEN MOST PEOPLE GO FOR A WALK," Dillon said, after I'd asked how he and Dad had found me, "they usually don't wear quilts." They had made inquiries along the way, he explained, and people said some girl in a blanket went *that* direction. School had been canceled, and Dad had called the Home to be sure I'd heard.

"They said they last saw you on the lawn, wrapped in the quilt," said Dad.

"So we knew it'd be easy to spot you," said Dillon, and flipped his thumb at me. "Your turn."

I was kneeling behind the front seats; the backseats were down and their bedding was wall-to-wall. Dad had the engine running and the heater on high, so I could thaw out.

I fitted the last rock in place and held out the tin. "Ye was here."

"Let me see," said Dillon, and I gave it to him.

Dad fired off the usual protests and ridicule while Dillon went through the same series of motions as I had.

He gave the tin back. "Let's look around in the snow. There must be some kind of message."

"Let's not," said Dad, in his speakerphone voice. "Time for me to work."

"You told me they were closed for the day," Dillon said.

"I can still go in," Dad piped. "I've got to do something! Better than sitting here listening to the finest children a man could ever want go completely out of their wits! Enough is enough!" He turned the heater fan off, then turned it full blast again. "*Somebody's* got to stay sane!"

Dillon was out the door and in the snow, searching on hands and knees.

Dad whipped around and stuck out his hand. "Let me see that!"

My eyes went wide. My knee decided to hurt. Dad's face had gone hard, and I knew his rage was reaching the danger zone.

I had just got the tin back—how could I let it go now? Would he pitch it out into the snow? Call Dillon inside and speed away?

Delicately, I asked, "Why?"

"Give it."

I looked out at Dillon. He was pawing the snow like a puppy after a bone. I looked back at Dad. His face was made of iron.

But then the iron spoke. It spoke the softest words. "For your mother's sake."

My hand went limp. I bowed my head. I gave him the tin.

With a rush of winter, Dillon was back in the car. "Not a thing!" he said.

I kept my head bowed, expecting some kind of explosion, some horrible calamity.

Everything was quiet.

I raised my head.

Dad seemed oblivious to Dillon and me. He had the rocks in one hand, the rocks I'd so tediously arranged, and the tin in the other.

The sprint of a smile appeared on the left side of Dillon's face, which meant something smart was going on. "Kat—that's it. The rocks give it weight."

I frowned.

"Picture it. The tin needed weight so it would land where he wanted it to."

Dad was sniffing the rocks. He tasted them.

I closed my eyes and pictured Ye swooping from high above, releasing the tin from his grasp, the tin turning through the falling snow. I pictured him veering away, back into the heights.

"How did he know where to find me?"

"Well, for one, I told him"—Dillon's voice cracked—
"when I met him in the tunnel."

"You gave him our *street address*?"

"Just the general neighborhood."

"What else did you tell him?"

He looked a little guilty. "I mentioned, you know . . .
what happened at the quarry . . . our troubles"—he
shrugged—"it was part of the picture."

Dad ran his finger inside the tin.

All I could think of was why. *Why* had Ye dropped it?
Was it his way of saying he was alive?

Or just the opposite—that he was dying?

Dad blew out the gritty dust.

Then he held up the tin and asked, "Did you do this?"

—⟫⟨—

"ONE REASON I'M GOING THERE IS TO PROVE
you wrong. You need help. Ever since you fell down that
mine, you haven't been right. You've been obsessed.
Possessed! Some weird notion has taken hold of your
thoughts and yanked you around like a dog with a rag.
You've seen a dog with a rag, haven't you? Or with a doll?"

Dillon said, "Turn right at the next road."

I said nothing. I saw snow fall heavily from a branch and the branch spring into the sky.

"They tear it to pieces. Then they leave it lying under the couch or a bush and forget about it." Dad shuddered to himself as he gripped the steering wheel. "I should have done something a long time ago." He made a sizzling sound. "You and your make-believe dragon. Dragon this and dragon that. Ye, Ye, Ye!"

He went a little too fast around the curve and fought the wheel to pull us out of a slide.

It didn't stop his tongue. "I should have taken you to a doctor! Put you on therapy! They have all kinds of medications now to treat your emotions."

"Yeah," said Dillon. "Like eradicate them."

"Stay out of this, son! I know what I'm talking about!"

Leaning forward, I whispered to Dillon, "What's eradicate?"

He whispered back, "Erase."

I lay on the bedding with the tin in my hands. The rocks no longer mattered. They were probably being ground underneath Dad's brake pedal foot.

When he had first held up the tin, my glasses were too

blurred to see. I had wiped them clean while he waited. As I put them back on, Dillon's face was lit up as if the sun had come through. Dad's face was deadpan.

"*Did you do this,*" he asked me again, stressing every word.

"I—" I could hardly comprehend the sight.

Scratched bright into the metal at the bottom of the tin, where the rocks had lain, was an unmistakable design: a heart with a circle around it.

"Do you know what this is?" asked Dad, his face on the verge of despair. "Do you?"

I did know. I remembered seeing it on the door of a truck, on a paint-chipped sign, and stitched on a foreman's shirt. I knew Dad knew, too. And Dillon.

For all three of us, the design was unforgettable.

With the words like pebbles in my throat, I said, "The quarry symbol. True Stone. Where . . . where . . ."

Dillon finished it. "Mom fell."

—➤ ⊱—

THE GATES WERE WIDE OPEN AT THE QUARRY, as if to invite us in. Dad stopped and studied the entrance for a while. I could tell his curiosity was up—the logo scratched in the tin had obviously shaken him. He might have been picturing Mom driving in. He hadn't been here since that dreadful day.

Or he might have been reading the new sign, which stood where the old sign had been.

It had the builder's name and an artist's version of the architect's flashy dream.

But, still, Dad resisted. "Kat," he declared, "I'm doing this to prove you wrong."

He drove inside. He found a level place to park that was out of view of the highway, and we got out.

Looking across the vast, snow-covered rock scape, he said, "This is a big area. There's no way you could cover a tenth of it."

Dillon said matter-of-factly, "We'll look for tracks."

"Tracks! Dragon tracks? You're talking like Kat!"

"Dad," said Dillon patiently, "I saw him, too. With these eyes."

"You've got blinders on then."

We walked in silence. We passed the old office, which had three stories of block walls and broken windows.

Dad suddenly stopped and turned to me with a pitying look. He reached out and clumsily took my hand. "When you were a little girl . . ." He looked for a moment at my hand in his—my left hand, fortunately—as if wondering at its firmness or coolness or unfamiliarity. "One summer night, you were at the living room window and you kept pointing and saying something about a face outside. I ignored you as long as I could, thinking you would give it up. But you were persistent. Finally, I went to the window to look. I saw nothing but our reflections. But I took you by the hand and together we went outside. The face you saw was a balloon caught in the dogwood tree. Not a face at all. A child must have lost it."

Dillon was frowning hard at Dad, and my hand began to tingle. I couldn't remember that Dad had ever taken my hand.

"Dad!" Dillon said sharply. "There *was* something out there. It wasn't her imagination. Her little girl eyes were better than yours."

Dad's hand twitched in mine. "I knew you'd say something like that. But there was no face, Dillon. There was *something*, there may *be* something, but it's got to be explainable. Something in the real world. You know what the real world is? See these rocks? You hit your head on a rock—" His face went dead as if his own echo had struck him. He let go of my hand.

He said quietly, "I'm bringing you out here to show you it's your imagination. There are . . . no . . . dragons."

—⟩⟨—

WE SEARCHED FOR ABOUT HALF AN HOUR. We each went our own ways: Dad along the main quarry road, not searching at all, unless it was inside himself, the cracks and cliffs of his life without Mom and money; Dillon in the direction of Mom's accident, where we had collected the stones; and I toward the excavation pit.

If I were a dragon, that's where I'd go.

• • •

How do you call a dragon? What kind of words do you use? Big words? Impressive words? *Long* words? But this wasn't *a* dragon. This was Ye.

Standing on the edge at one end of the pit, which ran like a huge deep gash as far as my eyes could see, I surveyed each hollow in the whiteness, each exposed rock, looking for any movement, even a wisp of smoke. I listened for a cough.

"Ye!" I called. "It's me! Kat!" My calls disappeared in the falling snow. After fixing my gaze on one big flake and following it to the ground, I realized that if Ye had left tracks they'd be covered by now.

"Ye!" I called again as loudly as I could, and heard a responding cry.

Dillon's.

It didn't sound like a cry for help, so I lingered a long moment, feeling I should not leave. The same feeling you get when someone smiles at you and you walk on by and then wished you hadn't.

Ye was somewhere here. I just knew.

Wondering what lay beneath the overhang at my feet, below the rim of the pit, I scurried away to find Dillon.

• • •

Dad had got there before me. They stooped in the lee of a high rock pile that ran along the quarry road, where the snow was not as thick. They were in disagreement.

"It's a play of light," Dad was saying. "A leaf could have made it."

"A leaf?" Dillon argued. "In November?"

"There are leaves in November."

Something sounded familiar about this conversation,

like the one Dillon and I'd had down in Ye's cavern, about fossilized starfish.

I knelt to inspect the track, and a thrill jumped through me.

"This is Ye's," I said. When I placed my hand in the impression without disturbing it, my hand shrank in comparison. "It's the right size, the right shape."

"I looked for more," said Dillon. "This was all I found." He pointed the way I had come. "It's going that direction."

Dad said bluntly, "I'm going *that* direction—to the car. I'll give you fifteen minutes. That's it. We're not coming back. It's cold."

"Fifteen minutes?" muttered Dillon. "In all this wildness?"

"Fifteen minutes. Then we—"

We heard the growl of machinery, and two earthmovers rumbled in. They were headed our way, bladed and armed to the teeth. One had a huge metal spike coming out its back like a scorpion's sting.

Dillon and I retreated, but Dad stood where he was as if to block them.

"Dillon!" I said breathlessly. "This is our only chance! I want to check out something, and I need your help!"

"Wait," he said, staring. "Do you think they will stop?"

"They'll either stop or Dad will move. They wouldn't run over Dad."

"I hope you're right."

As I led Dillon toward the pit, we both looked back. Dad still stood there, like the lone man who faced down a tank in Tiananmen Square in that famous photograph.

—>)(—

"I CAN'T QUITE—" THE BLOOD WAS RUSHING to my head.

Holding tight to my ankles, Dillon grunted and moved me forward.

"I can see a ledge below," I said, stretching. "But I can't see beyond it."

"Kat, I'm losing grip."

I arched my back and squinted to my left. "Wait. I think there's a path . . . or a road . . . it's hard to tell."

Dillon pulled me back, I got up, wrapped the quilt around me, and together we slid, scuttled, and slogged our way to a gap in some snowy rocks. The ledge I'd seen was an access road angling down the side of the pit.

Partway down was a nook, a cavity in the wall.

"How deep is it, I wonder?" said Dillon, as we made our way there.

"I don't know. But it looks dragon-size."

We reached the cave, and I slumped in disappointment. The cave was shallow, yet roomy enough for a dragon to lie in.

There was no dragon.

"We just wasted our time," said Dillon, digging snow out of his collar.

Facing the pit and cupping my hands to my mouth, I shouted, "Ye! Where are you?"

"Shhh, Kat! They might hear."

"So?"

"They might come looking."

"So, what do you suggest?"

"Well . . . why don't you whistle?"

"Whistle?"

"Yeah. His hearing might be, you know, on another pitch."

"Dillon, he's not a dog."

"Then *I'll* whistle." And he whistled a wobbly wretched something—something that, if anything, would have wilted Ye's ears. But it gave me an idea.

"Shush, Dillon! Let me try."

I'm not much of a singer, but I can carry a tune in a cup. I took a big breath, hummed a first note, and began to sing.

O beautiful for spacious skies,

"What!" blurted Dillon.

For amber waves of grain,
For purple mountain majesties
Above the fruited plain!

I sang the lines through into the dizzying, downward flight of white. I forgot myself as I sang, spinning the song into a wish that would bring Ye back. And a scene flashed by, like a single frame in a film, where a girl sat singing for her mother to wake up.

When I got to the part *From sea to shining sea,* I heard him, like a current of air that melts into your mouth when you're running. Ye sang along, some octaves lower, or rather, mine being some octaves too high. From the far end of the pit he came, gliding between the two slopes, up its length, bringing snow flurries in his wake.

We scooted aside for him. The sky grew dim as he landed on the ledge. Before he tucked in his wings, I saw it.

His tattered hole.

"Dragons can be chameleons when we choose," Ye said casually, draping his tail across the entrance.

The hole in his wing was bigger than before. I'd seen a butterfly with a hole like that, after escaping from a spider's web, only to stumble and die.

Ye saw that I had seen it. "The ice did not help," he said, answering my worried look. "Crystals form at high altitudes."

"Oh, Ye!" I breathed, and hugged his foreleg. I wanted to say so many things, like, *I'll stay with you forever, Will you ever be well again,* but I said instead, "You never told me."

"Never told you what?"

"Who wrote 'America the Beautiful.'"

"Katharine Lee Bates," he said studiously. "After seeing the land from Pikes Peak, during the great gold rush."

"There's another one, you know," said Dillon.

"Another what?"

"Gold rush."

"I am not surprised," said Ye, his teeth gleaming in

a grimace. "There is always a rush for something." He coughed, then he scoffed, "*May God thy gold refine,* indeed!"

I was confused. "If you don't like the song," I said, "why do you sing it?"

His eyes softened. "Memories. My visits with Hou and So." He gazed at a faraway place. "And you must admit, *From sea to shining sea* is poetic. Especially if you have flown it with the wind in your face and in your feet and wings."

I said, "But Ye, the hole—"

"—is not a problem," he said quickly. He stretched a wing to prove it—the one without the hole.

"You weren't flying just then," said Dillon. "You were gliding."

Ye looked at him respectfully, and with some small surprise. "I love to glide." He said it with finality, as if to end the talk, but he added, "Time will heal it."

I laid my hand on his folded wing, which trembled beneath my touch. "It hasn't yet."

He looked at me with sad amusement. "Is this why you have come? To scold me like a child?"

"Oh no, Ye. I—" I wanted to say "I love you!" but that

would have embarrassed us both. So I said, "Thank you for the tin."

He accepted this with a gentle wink.

"How did you find me?" I asked.

"Ah," he said secretively. "Let us say that with the will there comes a way." He cleared his throat. "Speaking of wills and ways—"

"Do you hear that?" Dillon interrupted.

"I have been hearing it," Ye said calmly. "I have been feeling it."

"What?" I asked. "What?"

Dillon turned to me. "Stay here. I'll go distract them." He climbed out of the cave and out of sight.

—⦿⦿—

"KATLIN, DO NOT BE AFRAID," YE SAID soothingly.

"OK," I said, though I was not OK.

"Before I was interrupted—" he said. "Twice now have I been interrupted. The first time was below Sun Mountain, when you and I last talked."

I knew what it was he meant, but I wanted to keep that thought buried—the thought of saying goodbye.

"I forgot how time rushes you, Kat. Or I would have returned that day." Ye looked at the snow collecting on his tail. He looked at me. He extended his claw as he had before.

"Here. I have loosened it for you this time."

The ring.

I didn't want to see it.

I didn't want to take it.

I didn't want to have it.

"Ye," I said, my voice quivering, "I'm so happy you're alive."

"The ring is yours, Kat," he said. "And your mother's, and her mother's. It is *nianzu*."

"*Ni*—" I began to repeat, but stopped. He was drawing me in and I didn't want to go.

"*Nianzu*—something that honors your ancestors."

He was making this hard. I tried thinking of all the things a damsel could do for a dragon in distress, and could hardly think at all. I laid my hand on his chest. "How is your cough?"

"The flight did it good."

"Really? You feel better?"

"Good as any old dragon could feel."

"Are you in pain?"

"What is pain but the anguish of truth?"

"Oh, Ye! I don't know what to do!"

Gently turning his head until his eye looked into mine, until I saw my face peering into it, he spoke a word that went straight to my heart.

"Promise."

I saw my eyes go wide, my face go slack. In a stunned whisper, I said, "Promise?"

"Promise me, should you find more gold someday, you will take it and use it well."

"Ye!" I moaned. "I couldn't! I can't!"

"Your world, the human race, spins on a golden axis."

"But, Ye—"

"Promise."

"I promise! I'll do anything—"

"Open your hand."

I opened my hand. He touched his claw into my palm so lightly, it could have been a snowflake.

The ring was on its tip.

"Listen to me. There comes a time when nothing can be done. Some things cannot be controlled, no matter how strong the desire to overcome them. But fear, Kat, you can control."

"Do . . . do you know what I'm afraid of?"

He nudged my chin with his mighty snout, and said simply, "Yes."

The heat trickling down my cheeks turned cold.

"Everything dies in its time, Kat."

"But I don't want you to!" I gasped. "You don't have to!"

"You have taught me to think of now, and now is sweet."

His face was a beautiful blur.

"Take it, Kat. Close your hand."

"No, Ye!"

"I must go. So must you. The pearl will not go with me."

I tried blinking my vision clear. "Where are you going? Someplace warm?"

"Someplace warm."

"Tell me where! So I can—"

"It is too far away, dear one. Be still. Take the ring and leave."

I began crying again. "Can't I watch you go?"

"I dislike goodbyes," he said tenderly. "I will say good day, fare ye well."

"Ye!" I laughed through my tears. "The 'ye' should be *you*."

The smile that shimmered in his eyes I will never forget.

I closed my hand.

—⟶⟨⟵—

THE FOUR OF THEM WERE ON THEIR KNEES inside the abandoned building. It was Dillon and Dad against the earthmover men. They were throwing my dice. Dad had figured it out—a pile of dollar bills lay by his side.

I stood in the broken doorway. Snow spattered the windows; snow drifted through the missing panes.

I could have turned around and gone back to Ye. But I respected him too much for that. I respected his wish to fly away unseen. It could be he wanted to spare me from seeing his damaged wing again.

We needed to go. I was too sad to think, too dumb to speak. I turned Mom's ring.

I'd have to say something . . .

I didn't have to. The earthmover men were suddenly up and out the front door.

A vehicle was entering the quarry. Two vehicles. The first was a big, gold, luxury all-terrain, the kind a commander in chief would drive. The next was a white work truck.

The driver of the gold tank got out. It was a woman. She shouted, and the earth machines began growling.

Dad was counting his money.

Dillon stood gazing at me. He said, "He's gone, isn't he?"

"No, he's not. He's waiting for us to go."

"Twenty-two dollars," said Dad, his hand in his pocket and a grin on his face. "Not bad."

I was watching the earthmovers.

They were moving in the wrong direction.

—➤ ⟨—

THEY WERE MOVING THE WAY I HAD COME, rumbling toward the road.

The road that went into the pit.

"No," I said. "They can't."

Dillon understood. He looked urgently around, as if a solution would appear out of snowy air, as if he could save the day.

Dad said, "Dillon, Kat, let's go. We're trespassing." Brushing past us he headed for the car.

"Dad. Wait. Stop," I said.

"Dad," said Dillon. "We left something over there."

Dad stopped and frowned. "Over where?"

"Over there. Where the dozers are going."

Dad studied our faces. "What did you leave? If it's that stupid tobacco tin—"

"No," I said, pulling it out of my pocket. "See?"

"What, then? It can't be so important that—"

"But it is!" I yelled. "I've got to go find it!" I turned and ran.

I scrambled, stumbled, tripped, recovered myself, cast off my quilt, and kept running. There were shouts behind me. I did not look back.

The earth machines flung mud and snow without a care in the world, and nothing could keep them from it. In this terrain, they made better sense than a girl of twelve wearing snow-packed shoes.

They made better time.

I expected Ye to take flight, to shake off this nightmarish mess. I expected to see him rise up on wings. Any minute now. No way could he fend them off. His fire would not stop them. He might not even try.

He might even be too weak.

The machines dropped out of sight.

More shouts behind me, more distant.

I rounded the crags that led to the road. The machines were there, rolling downward on armored treads. I eyed

the operator's head inside the glass cab. A stone's throw
away.

I plunged my hand into snow. I felt for a rock—groping,
grabbing nothing but mud. I pulled my hand out.

The ring was gone.

The earthmovers slowed on the slope. They neared the
place where Ye lay.

I moaned, grubbed in the snow, wailed. "The ring or a
rock? The ring or a rock?"

I found neither one.

I got up again.

The first machine jerked forward. It crunched along
near the cave's mouth. Its blade hit a boulder that burst.
It jolted on a bump. The operator turned his head as if to
say, *What was that?*

I raced ahead, ready to pounce on the huge metal sting
that drew a line in the snow.

The first machine revved and continued down the road.
The second one advanced, jumped, stopped, and raised its
sting. The sting went up, loomed over me, pointed down.

I was close. I reached out my arms.

The machine jumped forward and rolled on.

Into the pit they went.

THE SNOWFALL HAD CEASED.

"He's gone," said Dillon, who had caught up with me. I was gazing at the sky, at a warm spot in the clouds. I said nothing.

"Only snowdrifts inside."

I said nothing.

"So he wasn't harmed," said Dillon.

I shook my head once.

The warm spot in the clouds flared like a beam far out at sea, and the dream I'd had, back in Cripple Creek, after Ye had flown away, came to me again. I saw him in flight, pointing to a distant shore, flying toward the light, and the wind was in his wings.

"These are big drifts," said Dillon.

Then the beam blazed crisp and became the sun. The sun bathed the scene all around me, a diamond-drenched Wonderland.

It bathed my face.

I turned to see it bathe the hollow behind me, and bathe the high drifts, and bathe Dillon, who knelt beside them.

It bathed the gold nugget he held.

—≫ ⊱←—

HE KNELT UNASHAMED AND UNMOVING, but for his trembling, gold-heavy hand, tears streaming down his face.

"Oh, Kat!" he cried.

"I know," I said.

Someplace warm, Ye had told me. *Too far away.* Why hadn't I known what he'd meant?

Circling the snow-covered mounds, I traced the outline of a dragon. The mounds were crumbled along the edges, the highest ones rising in the center. I followed the line of his tail, curled tight like a seahorse. I followed the shapes of his legs, which he had gathered up beneath him.

I came around to his head. I got down on my knees. I brushed away the snow, as I once had brushed away his soot.

There was his golden snout, broken in places.

I kissed him as I'd once hoped to do.

And for a moment, I could not lift my head from his. A sob shook me hard, and I let it return, slowly, slowly, like a wave. More sobs came, more waves.

I took a steady breath and brushed away more snow.

There was his eye, shining pure gold.

I got up and faced the light. The spot in the clouds was closing, an amber slit in the sky.

A dragon's gaze.

I gazed back through my tears.

Snow was falling again.

⟶⟩⟨⟵

THE WHITE TRUCK WAS COMING. BEHIND that, the all-terrain.

We were standing in front of the cave, and I had tossed snow back on the exposed gold patches.

The truck went on by, heading into the gulf, but the all-terrain stopped. The woman and Dad got out.

"OK, kids," said the woman, who had a combative face. "Time to go."

Dad's face was confusion and fury, held hostage by the need of self-control. "Did you find it?" he asked in his public-announcement voice.

"Find—" said Dillon, still in shock from discovering Ye.

"Mom's ring," I said quickly, just as Dillon said, "What?"

Dad gaped at me loose-jawed, then at the woman, who was nodding her head in approval and looking less combative. This had to have been a sequel, and I'd missed out on Part One. But that was just fine—I must have said the right thing, because Dad's fury was gone.

"See, it *was* important," he said to the woman, though he seemed more surprised than she.

"It wouldn't have been a problem, Mr. Graham, if you'd have *told* me."

Dillon was still adrift, while my mind was hard at work.

"Dad," I said. "It could be anywhere starting from up there"—I pointed to the top of the road—"to somewhere here." I motioned down the road from where we stood. "My hands were so cold, the ring slipped right off."

"That happened to me once," said the woman, who looked even less combative, "when I helped my son build a snowman. It was my wedding ring."

"Did you find it?" asked Dad.

"Yes," she said.

Dad looked a little embarrassed.

"Oh . . . oh," said Dillon, as if he'd just got the punch line of a joke.

"OK, Mr. Graham, I'll give you a little more time." She scanned the stretch of road. "Good luck."

—→)(←—

THAT WAS A FRIDAY. ANY OTHER DAY OF the week and it would not have worked. There would have been laborers on the grounds, and another raging gold rush. It would have been quarry turned corporate site turned chaos turned crime scene.

We'd still be beggars.

And Ye would not have liked it.

But the next day was Saturday, then Sunday. Two days to collect the gold, with no one in the way.

It was hard, but the hardest was the sadness. With every step, every sack slung on my back, I pictured my glorious, greathearted friend.

It took eighteen carloads with the backseat down, sixteen to eighteen sacks per load, thirty to forty pounds per sack. Dad had got thirty-four gunnysacks from several feed stores, and while one of us filled them one by one, two of us hauled them to the car. The workhorse wasn't an *Oreamnos americanus*—a mountain goat—so we had to park at the top. Dad and Dillon then drove to the storage unit, unloaded the sacks, and returned. To make room for the gold, they had to clear the unit out, and ended up putting our furnishings along the highway, for people to take if they wanted.

By Sunday afternoon, our furnishings were gone.

. . .

As I filled the sacks, I had time to think and argue with myself. I played back the previous day.

After the heavy machinery had been parked inside the pit, after the white truck had picked up the drivers who rode back with hardly a glance at us standing in front of Ye's nook, after Dad had found the ring—

Yes, it was Dad who had found it. I was grateful that he had. For his sake more than mine.

Dillon and I dared not leave the cave area, for fear the gold would be uncovered, so we pretended to look there for the ring. But first, I had directed Dad to the spot where I'd lost it, scored an X in the muddy snow, and said, "Start here." As he searched and searched, explaining to the woman that it had been his wife's ring, and her mother's before her, and in this very place his wife had last worn it, before giving it to her daughter, *his* daughter, Kat Graham, right over there, who started the new gold rush.

"He needs a sacred burial," I whispered to Dillon.

"We can't cremate him," said Dillon. "He wouldn't burn—he's solid pure gold."

I said nothing, out of a reluctance to talk grim details.

"We can't bury him. Between the two of us, we'd end up with broken backs and bent shovels, or bent backs and broken shovels."

"Same thing," I said.

"We could use one of those dozers down there," he said. "Dig a deep enough hole that no one could find him."

A lone, belated cricket cried from a nearby rock, agonizingly slow. "Hey, cricket," I called. "It's too cold for you to be out."

"But then, eventually he'd be discovered, with all these building plans."

I sighed. "Dillon—"

"I wonder what Ye would have wanted."

"Dillon, I know what he wanted."

Dillon, kneeling in the snow, paused.

"He made me promise."

Dillon said slowly, "OK."

"Promise to take any gold I might find."

Again, "OK."

"He said to use it well."

The snow suddenly went black. I clutched at Dillon for support. Whats and hows and whys buzzed around in my head. *Ye had done this all for me! He knew he was going to die! He had planned the whole thing out, including the message in the tin!*

He had given me himself. What greater gift could there be?

"Kat, are you all right?" Dillon had me by the shoulder.

I breathed in deep and nodded. The snow became bright again.

"That settles it," he said. "A promise is a promise. You're bound to him for life."

In more ways than you know, I thought.

• • •

At the end of that backbreaking day, as we slumped on the tail end of the workhorse, we went from small talk, like, was the snow safe to eat, to big talk, like, how much gold do you think it is.

By default, Dad became a believer. At first, he refused. He considered the overall form of the gold to be unremarkable and saw no dragon there. The gold must be either some century-old pirate's cache or a quirk of nature, he said. After all, there it was, in a cave in a quarry.

"A *marvel* of nature, you mean," said Dillon.

But Dad had to justify taking it from this place. When I contended that the gold wasn't part of the land no more than a bird was part of a tree, that settled it.

Still, he was astonished. He walked with a foolish grin, up and down the rutted path. Once, his face rumpled like a child who doubts his own existence. Once, his face filled with expectancy, as if every myth in the world would come true.

But he astonished us both on Sunday.

He had picked me up at the Home. In the light of an emerald-green dawn and the orange glow from the instrument panel, I saw something I'd not seen in eons. I saw my long-ago Dad. His eyes were alive, as if he had a purpose now that sadness couldn't stain.

Dillon raised his eyebrows as I climbed into the car, which meant, *Now hear this.*

"I've been thinking," Dad said. "But it all depends on you, Kat."

"Me?" I said, still unwilling to let my sleepiness go.

"It's your gold—you found it."

"Well, it's yours, too, you know. You're my father."

He looked pleased. "We can afford this place."

That jerked me awake.

Dad's face got dreamy. "I can picture it as a park. The pit would be a lake. We'll plant weeping willows."

"You're *buying* it?" I said.

"Corey—the woman who owns the place—wants to wash her hands clean of it. She's had trouble from the start. The contractor's not coming through, the investors are waffling, she has better properties to manage."

I looked over at Dillon, whose eyebrows remained upright.

"Yes," said Dad, meditatively. "A place where people can come, where they can be at peace."

I didn't know what to say, so I nestled into the warmth of the dream.

"I'll bring your mother there."

—⟶⟨⟵—

"THAT'S ALL," I SAID, AND TIED THE GUNNY-sack closed.

Dillon held the light. He flashed it around the shallow cave, to be sure there was no gold left. "What about that?" he asked, spotlighting the gold by my side.

I eased myself up, massaging my old knee injury. "I'm keeping that one."

"Why is that one special?"

I didn't answer at first. I picked the gold up and weighed it in my hands. It was larger than a human heart, yet similar in shape. Something about it agreed with me.

"It just is," I said.

But I knew—it was how a dragon heart would look.

. . .

Before carrying the last sack to the car, we stood in the cave's mouth.

There was one smudge of rust in the western sky, from either downtown Richmond or an industrial plant. But high overhead the stars shone bright.

I didn't know how to feel, I didn't know what to think. But I knew a wonder was still a wonder, though you've seen it in lamplight and flashlight and daylight and starlight, you've touched it and walked with it and pressed it to your ear and felt it in your soul—and lived it in your dreams. I hurt in some place that I couldn't touch, a hurt that would never heal, no matter how many pools of tears I cried.

I gazed up, awed by the spangled skies, the rush of the Milky Way.

"Dillon?"

"Hmm."

"Point it out to me."

He looked up, covered the light with his hand, orange and skeletal, and studied the stars. "OK," he said. "Find the North Star, the Little Dipper. See?" He uncovered his hand and waved the beam across the constellation. "Now look." He shut the light off and pointed. "There—just below it."

"That's Draco?"

"That's Draco."

Later, I would write in my journal: *I am but a spark in time to Ye.*

. . .

When we reached the car, Dad had it running to keep it warm. As we loaded the bag, a figure passed by. Dillon shone the light—it was a man, homeless by the look of his scarecrow limbs. He stopped and turned, blocking the glare with his arm. Dillon lowered the light.

"Any spare change?" he asked. "Spare change?"

I peered at him, while Dillon dug in his pockets. "Nope," he said. "Sorry."

The man turned to go.

"Wait!" I called. I reached into the car and pulled the nugget out, the one like a heart, the one I had set aside. I did not hesitate. I went to the man and said, "Here."

He gazed at the gold in my hands, his face fidgeting

between a sneeze and disappointment. "No," he said. "I
mean money, spare change."

"Sir," I said. "There is more money here than you
could ever wish for, and more secrets, too."

He touched it then, with a slim brown finger.

"Take it," I said.

He took it in both his hands. He gazed into as you would
a crystal ball. He gazed and gazed, until understanding
awoke in his eyes. He began to tremble and weep.

"Oh, Lord!" he said. "Oh, Lord! Oh, Lord!"

"Take it to a banker or coin dealer," instructed Dillon.
"Make sure they treat you right."

As we drove away, the headlights caught the man. He
stood unmoving, holding the gold high as if he knew the
terrible wonder that it was.

—❧ ❧—

I can't believe where I'm sitting. I'm sitting—literally—
on a golden nest egg, my future, our future, piled up in
some flimsy storage rental. It must be the purest gold
on the planet. Using a scale I found at the Home—the
kind you weigh babies on—we figured the total amt to
be about 13,000 lbs. It took forever! What we couldn't
have figured, not in a riotous dream, was how much

the gold was worth. Godzillion doesn't do it. Dad made a call to a gold broker in NY, & he's never been more zoned, tiptoeing around with this mind-staggering fact. None of us can comprehend it. Gold—heavier than most rocks & weighed in troy oz. (12 oz. per lb., not the usual 16) & using rough est. of troy oz. weight—which would be approx. 190,000 oz. (Dillon plus a conversion chart & calculator had to help me on this) & X-ing that by current price, approx. $1,700. per oz. the gold is worth $322,000,000! I'll spell it: three hundred twenty-two million dollars.

That blank page is not an overturn. I left it that way on purpose. It's how I feel when I think of it—draw a complete blank, a blazing white nothing. Like flying into the sun.

We try not to dream too big. Besides the park, Dad's biggest plans are to fund advanced research into brain trauma & injury. He's practically an expert already. Hopes to become a director.

The Home will get a new facility on the grounds. Bet that'll be nice.

We had Chinese takeout for dinner, bought w/the money Dad won off the b/dozer men. I'll always laugh at that.

Oh! Dillon just looked over my shoulder and said, "You'll make a great journalist." "Thanks," I said, "but I'm not going to be a journalist." "Why not?" "Cause every day the news tells you stuff that happens to people—tragedies—but not <u>about</u> those people, how they <u>deal</u> w/tragedies."

"A writer then?" "I think storytelling gives greater truths than news reporting does"—me, pontificating (Ye would know that word)—"but no. Geology, brother. Fascinates me. I want to study precious metals, explore the lost worlds of dragons."

I asked Dad what it meant to keep riches to your own hurt. He asked where I'd heard that & I told him Gideon Bible, Cripple Creek. After self-conscious throat-clearing, said he wasn't a Bible scholar—that was Mom's dept—but it sounded like it meant being careless with your riches. "Why have them if you don't use them for good?" he said. D asked if we remembered Mom saying "Use it wisely or not at all" which is so much like Ye's "use it well" it's uncanny.

We drove by our house tonight. Couldn't stop turning Mom's ring, which Dad gave back to me once we'd finished w/the gold. House was lit up for people other than us, who sit on furniture other than ours, who walk the floors that we once walked. Dad said he'd make them an offer & see what happens. "Give them an offer they can't refute," I said. Hope they'll give in. Though we're impossibly rich, none of us want more than what we had before.

—➤ ❳❲ ◄—

IT WAS EARLY. THE WIND CHIMES OUT THE window hung silent in the dawn.

I had opened my eyes realizing I was turning Mom's

ring. Ye had flown with this ring. This ring of pearl, of wind and ice and fire and mud. He had preserved it for me, for Mom, for us.

I got up.

The hall was quiet and the floor was cool. Room 4 was gray and moist. I entered and pulled the window curtain aside. A small pink moth flew out, circled, and flew back against the glass.

I pulled the chair close and sat down.

Her hair strayed halo-like around her face; her skin was like skim milk. I took her right hand and removed the rolled-up cloth that helped her fingers from curling. I slid the ring to the tip of my finger and touched my finger to her palm.

I gazed at the pearl.

There are things in life that are hard to define, things you feel rather than know. Things you don't see at all, yet they're anchored deep inside you—a cherished ache or a spot of light.

Like a moon in a far-off galaxy, a pearl is shaped in secret, in a private womb in the sea. It is accidental beauty. It happens when a speck of harm invades the creature's calm world. That world reacts, and a pearl is made.

I gazed at the pearl and I saw no one's face. I saw

beauty. And somewhere inside, unseen, lodged a speck of harm. If not for the beauty, the harm would have spread. The creature would have suffered and died.

So, the pearl is a promise.

A promise to protect.

I pressed my finger into her milky palm. I studied her face until I saw what I was looking for: my long-ago mom. The mom I'd always kept in my heart.

"Mom," I said. "I'm giving this back to you." I closed her fingers around the ring. "I believe you're still here. You're still here with me."

I drew my hand away.

In that moment, the one I had longed for with all of my might but had found so hard to imagine, her eyelids quivered like the moth against the window.

Or a dragon in the wind.

AUTHOR'S NOTE

For any who might care to do a little mining within this book, you can take a Magical Mystery Tour and explore Wonderland—nuggets from both are scattered throughout, besides dream references from literary works. I've shuffled the actual mountain community of Cripple Creek to suit my story. All good fortune to the Mollie Kathleen—I've taken the thousand-feet plunge twice, and it still fascinates me. Contrary to Kat's experience, it's safe.

ACKNOWLEDGMENTS

Many thanks to those who cared about this endeavor of mine: my daughter, Ava, who patiently attended my first gold discovery; Dan Elasky, who helped remove the story's tarnish over cups of Hyperion espresso; retired sergeant Dan Mayer, whose police experience made Chief Huffman's day; my agent, Sara Crowe; and my editor, Howard Reeves, who believed in me and Kat and Ye. And to Emma, who posed.

ABOUT THE AUTHOR

TROY HOWELL is the cover illustrator for the best-selling Redwall series by Brian Jacques, as well as the illustrator of a number of children's books. His work has been awarded the Educational Press Association of America Distinguished Achievement Award, New York and Los Angeles Society of Illustrators merit awards, and has also been named a *Redbook* Best Children's Book of the Year. This is his first novel. He lives in Falmouth, Virginia.